'BOOK ONE IN THE FOREVER EVERWOOD SERIES'

INTO THE EVERWOOD

ELSA KURT

INTO THE EVERWOOD

INTO THE EVERWOOD

authorelsakurt@gmail.com
www.elsakurt.com

Ordering Information:
Quantity sales. Special discounts are available on quantity purchases by corporations, associations, and others. For details, contact the publisher at the address above.
Orders by U.S. trade bookstores and wholesalers. Please contact authorelsakurt@gmail.com or visit www.elsakurt.com.

Printed in the United States of America

INTO THE EVERWOOD

DEDICATION

As always, for my three loves Paul, Kayla & Carey

&

For every girl who's just a little bit different.
Remember: Different is Good

INTO THE EVERWOOD

Contents

1 THE VAGUE

"More."

One thousand years, one hundred, or one day. It is no matter to the Vague. What is time, but an irrelevance? It waits, indifferent to all. Until... until the girl. Now, it has a *want*.

"Girl. It. Her. Human."

These words that had no place, no meaning before, now mean something.

The Vague doesn't know what is happening, why it is changing. But it is collecting, absorbing, *feeding* from everything in its path. And in doing so, it evolves. It learns. It thinks.

And what it thinks repeatedly is, "More."

2 MALA

"What the… hey."

The moment Mala stepped through the door, leaving Jaime on the other side, the adventure began. This place… this land is not the same as where she'd just been. Even the air smells different. Subtle hints of mint and chamomile drift on the warm breeze.

"Okay, Mal, okay. Let's be logical, here."

She blinks at her impossible surroundings. "Nope, that won't work. It's broad daylight here, and there's a midnight sky on the other side of that door. Screw logic and go with… with whatever is happening here."

She exhales, shakes out her arms, and stretches her neck to the right and the left. Next, Mala squeezes her eyes shut and opens them again. Everything still looks the same.

"Okay, logic is out. Acceptance is in. Talking to yourself, cool. Think. Think, damn it. I haven't hit my head. Pretty sure I'm not dead. Although, this is my idea of heaven… no. Stop it. Get a grip."

Mala shifts her weight onto one side and bites her thumb nail. She takes another sweeping glance. "It's fricking beautiful here. And Jaime has been a jerk…."

She sighs, realizing she should go back and get Jaime. But instead of turning back to the weather-beaten, scarred wooden door, Mala steps further in… or out. Or is it in? It's all kind of confusing… and absurd.

Over her shoulder, she calls out, "Think you're so smart, don't you?"

No muffled reply answers her; Jaime is still somewhere on the other side of the door. He would never just leave her. Still…

"Big, funny joke, huh? See what's on the other side, huh? Well, I did. And guess what? It's a—it's a freaking parallel universe." She mutters, "Or something."

Raising her voice again, she says, "So what if I can't pass up a dare? Well, joke is on you, smart guy. While you're stuck in the cold, dark Everwood, I'm here in sunny, warm," she looks around, "wherever I am. So, ha."

In the moments before she stepped into the darkness, Mala knew she'd go through the weird old door even before his taunts left his lips. Worse? He knew it. Just picturing Jaime's expression—one dark eyebrow raised in mocking doubt, paired with that grin. The one that made the crescent scar at the corner of his mouth look like a misplaced dimple, and the laughter in his black coffee eyes… it infuriates her. So much so she stomps her foot.

3

Only Jaime has the power to provoke her that way. Yet he also makes her laugh until tears flood her eyes. And he can de-escalate her too-easily flared temper with a word. And he makes her forget her troubles in an instant. That's Jaime, though.

He is her best friend, her confidant. Her Jaime. They've been inseparable since elementary school, through middle school, and even still now, in their last year of high school, despite the gradual changes between them over the years.

The first perceptible shift came in junior high. Out of nowhere, other girls noticed Jaime. Giggling behind their hands and blushing as he passed by their lockers, tossing notes at the back of his head in class. Even the scar they'd teased him about in elementary school is now is mystifying and cool; even though most everyone knew that when he was four, he fell from a second-story window. It resulted in a concussion, broken arm, and a gash at the corner of his mouth. The gash was non-grata the sharp aluminum edge of the window screen which had fallen along with him. It had required twelve stitches and would later become the infamous scar.

Those same, annoying girls who now moon over Jaime also sidle up to her—the misfit, non-conformist girl—not to befriend, but to get closer to him. Their lame conversation openers were always things like, *Yeah, hi. So, like, um, you and Jaime? Are you guys, like, together or something?*

Each time, Mala rebuffs them with a scoff, irritated they would even ask. Truth is, she doesn't know the answer. *Are* she and Jaime together?

Sure, they're always together... but *together* together? It is too much to think about. Too awkward an idea. So, she does what she always does; bury the uncomfortable stuff under jokes and distractions and wait for Jaime to say something. Only Jaime isn't saying anything now—nothing she hears—because they are on opposite sides of a weird old door. Mala takes another look around and whispers, "No, a magic door."

3 JAIME

Jaime Cromwell sits arms folded over his chest on the moonlit side of the door, waiting for Mala to finish with her pig-headed-pouting fest.

He calls out, "Hope you're having fun in there with the spiders." After a pause, he adds, "If you wanna to hide in a creepy dark closet thing in the woods to prove whatever it is you're trying to prove, knock yourself out. I can wait all night."

Like Mala, he is having twinges of guilt he's too stubborn to fess up to. Also like her, he thinks about those not-so-subtle shifts changing their relationship in ways neither know how to handle.

He remembers the same time—when they'd gone from elementary to junior high school—and how over one brief summer, everything had changed between the boys and girls. The same boys who mere months ago had thrown pebbles at Mala and tried to snip the end of her long blonde ponytail with those stupid, dull safety scissors, are now nudging each other and staring at her ass as she passes them by in the hall. He'd even caught Nico DiAntonio pretending to grab her bottom as she bent down to collect a book from her locker. An instant rage made Jaime see red and without a moment's hesitation, he shoved Nico right as he turned to guffaw with his gang of losers, who'd dared him to do it. Nico caught himself before falling flat, and when he saw who his assailant was, his expression changed from surprise to a forced, superficial cool.

He was about to start a fight, a taunt ready on his lips, when Mala, oblivious to everything but Nico's stumble, said with a smirk, "Nico, tie your shoes." Still smiling, she said, "Jaime, I'm starving. Hurry up and get in the lunch line before it's out the caf door." The bell for class rang, Mala tugged Jaime along, and Nico stood slack-jawed, staring after them.

Yes, things have changed. Other boys notice Mala. This bothers him. Fine, that's an understatement. It pisses him off, big time. And that anger confuses and disturbs him. It disgusts Jaime to think these boys see only the surface of who she is— her long hair, her hazel-green eyes, her developing figure, slight as it still is. He blushes thinking of her like that, but the thought is there. They have no idea how much more there is to her. It isn't only superficial beauty. She's quirky, with a mind out of time for her age. Her sense of humor borders on wicked, yet she's gentle and kind... when it suits her.

For as much as he bristles at their disregard or ignorance of her many qualities, he also doesn't *want* them to know. Were they to see all he does... no, the possibility of what

7

could happen makes him shudder. For the first time, he considers what a world without Mala would feel like, and he doesn't like what he imagines.

Jaime comforts himself with one truth. She never seems to notice the other boys. That could change, though. And the idea of someone stealing her away from him sends a cold dagger through his heart.

They share so many qualities. Introverts who prefer nature and books to people, wild imaginations, a wariness of their peers. All of which made for a quick and easy bond between them, one which began on the first day of kindergarten.

He smiles as he remembers the scene. As chaos swirled around the classroom—some children crying, others running about with maniacal glee, nervous mothers and irritated fathers vied for the frazzled teacher's attention—Jaime and Mala stepped backward, away from the madness, mutual looks of dismay on their faces. Meanwhile, their mothers—having discovered they were neighbors—chatted and laughed with each other.

The tall boy took one look at the small girl, put his hand out to her, and they held on for dear life. From then on, they were inseparable. The adults thought they were adorable and teased that they were like a little old married couple.

"Oh, now aren't your two just the cutest? Our little mini-married couple." They gushed.

The teasing never ended, and they paid no attention to it. It became like wallpaper to them, always there, always in the background. Not to say their friendship is without drama. There were many, many arguments and disputes. Most of which resulted in Mala punching Jaime in the arm, or calling him names, or stomping off in anger, all while Jaime shrugged and waited for her to return to him—without apology—and resume their activities.

To be fair, though, Mala *did* apologize… just not in the conventional *I'm sorry* kind of way. It often involved a peace offering. Cookies her mom had made fresh from the oven, or something she'd made during her self-imposed solitary confinement. Rarely did Jaime get ruffled, let alone mad at her, although he isn't above prolonging her discomfort by acting wounded.

Sometimes, he pushes too far, and tears well in her eyes before she can turn away. It makes him feel guilty... and pleased. Such reaction from her—a girl determined to hold all emotions in check—it proves she cares. However, for as tough as she tries to act, she is extra sensitive, and no one knows it better than Jaime.

Mala has had that confounding effect on Jaime forever. He half wants to protect her, half wants to antagonize her, and never understands why. Even that first day in kindergarten, when he took one look into her hazel eyes, noting the small crescent scar on her left eyelid—like a tiny twin to the scar on side of his mouth—and took her nail-bitten hand into his, he knew she was close to tears, and for as much as he felt protective, he kind of wished she'd cry then, too.

Regardless of their back-and-forth, they've always made up. Even now, twelve years later, he knows when she comes back—*any moment now, Mal*—through the strange door, she'll be fighting mad for about an hour, and then he'll do something silly to make her laugh, and all will be forgiven again.

The trip down memory lane has distracted him from acknowledging *any moment* has already passed. It's been more than a moment, by far. Over ten minutes. Has she gone some—no, there is nothing on the other side. It is a pointless door which opens to a space comparable to the depth of a bookshelf. He knows, because he came out earlier in the day to the wooded land preserve behind their apartment complex…

4 The Door

A reclusive old farmer owns the land, which includes both the meadow and their apartment complex. His chief crop is potatoes. The local children gave a not-very-imaginative nickname to the farmer—Tony Potato—and it stuck.

Despite frequent pleas and orders, he refuses to sell, or even maintain the property. He is stubborn, isolated, and cares not one bit what the town officials have to say (at every town meeting) about his disgraceful waste of real estate and disregard for town development.

The farmer has a daughter named Lavinia. She has long, dull red hair woven with gray, a thin pointy face from which suspicious, dark eyes watch everyone. She slinks into town like a mangy cat. No one speaks to her, and she speaks to no one. Rumors of her being a witch have circulated for as long as anyone can remember and even though they all laugh about it, no one dares tease or cross the woman.

Yet, despite this—or maybe because of it—Tony Potato sends his daughter to listen in and report back to him, with orders to give the town board the middle finger at the closing of each session, which she does without expression and an unwavering predictability.

It is a routine which always receives twittering and chuckles from the handful of locals who show up to either petition, complain, or be entertained by town politics. It also never fails to get a rise out of Town First Selectman Griffin. He is a puffy, self-satisfied, dinosaur of a man unaccustomed to being mocked or insulted. At least not to his face. He also owns half the town, including their apartment complex.

First Selectman Griffin is only accustomed to getting what he wants, and what he wants is the woodland, all two hundred and twenty-eight acres, to be cleared, sold, and developed. It so happens he had just the company to do the work. His.

He believes he can wait Tony Potato out, if need be, and perhaps he's right. Rumor has it, Tony's health is failing, and his daughter—his only known surviving family—is showing signs of interest in a sale, despite the ever recurring raising of the infamous middle finger. But for now, the woodland stands as it had when Tony Potato's grandfather bought it—along with two-hundred acres of farmland in the 1800s—for some minuscule amount. The land passed on to his son, who passed it on to his son. Whether spoken or unspoken, the land use stayed the same; a quarter for living and farming, and three-quarters for wilderness, marked by posted signs.

Those weathered wooden posts bordering the tree line are not what one would expect, however. Especially from someone with a reputation like Tony Potato's. Instead of "NO TRESSPASSING!" and "STAY OUT!" warnings and admonishments, there are instead these…

WELCOME!

TAKE NOTHIN',

LEAVE NOTHIN'!

MIND

THE ANIMALS!

IF YA WANNA COME IN,

IT'S YER CHOICE!

There are more, some illegible and others covered by overgrowth, but the gist is anyone could go exploring in the woods, but don't mess it up. Amazingly—and contrary to human nature—most who use the woods for hikes, walks, adventures, and even camp outs, respect the rules.

It remains as imposing and wild as ever thanks to Tony Potato and his predecessor's refusal to tame that portion of their land.

Perhaps no one has more gratitude for that than Jaime and Mala, who've explored the place they named Everwood since they were eight years old. It was Everwood they headed straight to, with promises to stay meadow side, and not go into the woods. Promises made but never kept; broken before the words were off their lips and into the wind left in their wake. Panting alongside them—and the only reason they could go off alone—ran Mala's faithful old shepherd, Max. The three figures—Jaime with his coal black-hair, so tall and lean for his age, Mala, a skinny little girl, all knees and elbows, with wild blonde hair flying behind her as she ran, and her jolly old black and tan dog—made quite a photo, one Jaime's mother had thought to capture.

That photo is both Mala's and Jaime's favorite. She wedged her copy in her bedroom mirror, he folded his into a wallet that had belonged to his grandfather, who'd passed away some years ago.

Jaime has carried the wallet since he turned seven—despite his mother's misgivings—and carries it still at seventeen, the old creased photo still in its rightful place, but now fragile with age and many careful viewings.

It's Everwood that calls them back, repeatedly, through the changing seasons and over the course of many of Jaime and Mala's life changes. And it is in Everwood they discover the strange old door.

The jolly old shepherd is no more; gone many years back, many adventures ago. The old pup had wandered to the Everwood alone at the end of his days, entering and never returning to them. After their searches and drawn out calls of *Max* and *Here, boy* went unanswered for a third day straight, their parents consoled them as best as possible, but between the two children they decided old Max had found himself a cozy bed of leaves and moss beneath a tall pine to rest his head. He'd loved it so much there, he stayed.

Even after all the years since, Jaime and Mala still like to imagine Max out there somewhere in the wild woods, running free and happy, regardless of how unlikely or impossible it is. There have even been a few times over those years when they've thought they heard a distant bark, one that sounds so much like his. The mirrored expression of hopeful surprise passed across both their faces, and one of disappointed acceptance and a tinge of embarrassment replaced it. It was any of the many dogs from town.

For as much as they pretend the Everwood is theirs alone, they realize others have ventured there for hikes, walks, and mischief. They never run into anyone else, and there are never any beaten paths or trails to speak of. It's like each time is the first time in those woods, and no one can explain it. The strange wooden door is the perfect example. How many times have Jaime and Mala been exploring in Everwood? One hundred? More, even? Regardless, it's been nine years, through every season—even winter, where the heavy canopy of evergreens make it still possible to navigate the ever-changing terrain—and this is the first time seeing it. It can't be a recent cast off. It's too far into the woods to be someone's lazy discard. To carry and drag it over and through brush, rocks and exposed roots, and even fallen logs is too impractical.

The door stands upright with an old willow tree grown up around it, making it look as if it leads to a room or house in a fairy tale. This thick, ancient looking door has been in the forest for quite some time, judging by the emerald moss adorning the cracks and crevices, the shrubbery grown over and around it, and the vines coiling through its most unusual door handle. Jaime has never seen one like it. A brass-like hand cupped over an ornate ball or sphere.

Time and weather haven't tarnished the handle, though. No, this orb is almost luminous in its rose gold sheen. To open the door, one would have to hold the metallic hand and pull, an act Jaime hesitated to perform. To slip his own hand into the eerie life-sized appendage seemed so creepy. Yet a door amidst a forest was much too compelling to ignore, let alone a door resembling something out of a fairy tale.

If Jaime could admit it—which, at seventeen, he could not—a sense of hopeful excitement surged through him. Could this be a door to another world? A magical land with mythical beings? It's like every fantasy story Mala had ever read and forced him to hear all about, and their own version of the infamous C. S. Lewis wardrobe through which four children ventured into their own magical world.

Jaime had chuckled to himself at the thought. Even when Mala wasn't with him, she was there in his thoughts. He'd already imagined her with him for this fascinating finding and felt a pang of guilt as he reached for the odd door handle.

The early October sun forced its still strong rays through the swaying branches, illuminating the parts of the orb not blocked by the eerie hand. A blinding prism of odd rose-golden light burst across the forest and made Jaime squint and shield his eyes. As fast as the light exploded, restless clouds cut it off again.

The sudden shift in lighting had put spots in front of his eyes, blinding Jaime. He blinked hard to clear his vision, half expecting someone to be standing before him when his eyesight returned. Alas, there was just a door, just a hand, just an orb, in just a forest.

"Totally normal, right?" Jaime laughed aloud, startling both himself and some nearby critters, judging by the crackle of twigs and flutter of wings.

Ridiculous.

Again, he reached his arm out, grasping the grotesque hand as if he were a prince and it a fair maiden. Once the image was in his head, it wouldn't vanish.

"Gross." He shuddered.

When he pulled it—*not kiss it, don't picture that*—nothing happened. Of course, it would be stuck. Locked even, perhaps. But there seemed to be no place for a key, only an ugly hand and an orb.

"Duh, the orb." Jaime shook his head at his own stupidity.

Jaime grabbed the orb, still warm from the blast of sun—*sure, that's why it's warm, dude*—and turned it. Despite a gritty sounding scrape, the orb turned with ease, and the door gave a gentle but heavy pop as the latch gave.

"Ha, yes."

Jaime released the orb and punched the air in triumph. After wiping his sweating hand on the back of his jeans, he grasped the doors' edge and pulled it open further. The door—hindered by long disuse, uneven flooring and excessive vegetative growth surrounding it—was reluctant. Jaime had moved it enough to wedge his lean frame between it and the door, and no more. He wasn't about to give up, though. Instead, Jaime braced his right booted foot against the tree bark which served as the door's frame, and dug his left heel hard into the ground, bent his head and held his breath as he pushed with all his effort.

At first, nothing happened. No give, no movement, save the dirt beneath his foot as he lost traction. Without warning, the door gave with an audible *swoosh* and Jaime found himself ass down in the dirt, staring up into a black hole. Or at least what looked like a black hole, since the passing clouds had taken a long-term residency overhead, casting the forest in shadows. They were no help for exploring a strange doorway in the of heart of the woods.

As his eyes adjusted to the change in lighting, he made out a bark wall, and nothing more. Jaime fumbled for his cell phone, cursing himself for forgetting his small but powerful flashlight on his beloved Indian motorcycle. The relic was a remnant of his grandfather just like the battered wallet. It was one of the few arguments he'd won against his mother—not only to fix up, but to ride—making him the only teenage boy in the quaint town of Rocky Knoll to do so.

Much to Jaime's consternation and Mala's amusement, it furthered his reputation as a reclusive rebel, the proverbial bad boy, and the most crush worthy boy in town. The irony always being he wasn't a bad boy at all, and in fact was an A student, never served a detention, and in ninth grade got into his first and only almost-not-quite-a-fight ever with the same Nico he'd pushed in seventh grade.

The three teens—Jaime and Mala walking together down the hall and Nico, leaning against his locker watching their approach with hawk-like intensity all while talking behind his hand to one of his tag-a-long buddies—intersected at the corridor's center. Nico sauntered towards the pair, then blatted, "Oops, whoa, sorry."

He'd walked right into Mala, propelling her backward until the lockers stopped them. He had her pinned against the cold metal, his hands on her chest. Jaime saw it as a deliberate, orchestrated move. Nico achieved his goal; he'd gotten his paws on Mala. Literally.

Jaime saw red, then black. He felt an instant rush of heat as his blood boiled, and Nico—after being shoved off by Mala—came at him with a smirk, taunting him with the classic, *what, c'mon, man* gesture.

So that only Jaime could hear above the noisy hallway, he said, "I've been waiting for this since seventh grade, asshole."

Nico threw a hard punch, or what would've been, had it connected. But Jaime had pivoted like a ninja—as the freshmen boys would later declare with awed voices—and the rest became history. Even the teacher who'd broken up the fight knew Nico had instigated the clash by throwing the first—missed—punch. Jaime's quick dodge away, the grab of Nico's wrist as it passed by his face, then the hard twist up against his back played like a classic action movie-hero move. Jaime didn't even know he possessed the skill to execute such a move. However, he knew that, if Mr. McCann had not come over, he'd have kept twisting Nico's arm until he heard it snap.

Though Mr. McCann got credit for stopping the fight, *Mala* had stopped a chain of events that would've led to an expulsion for Jaime and maybe even legal charges. For through his t-shirt, and even through his rage, he felt her hand on the small of his back and felt her breath against his ear as she whispered, "Don't Jaime, don't."

As fast as she'd stepped up and then away again, Jaime released his hold on Nico, who fell forward, his cheek mashed against the locker. Mr. McCann bellowed, "Party's over, folks. Everyone to class."

The teacher knew both boys well and had seen the entire thing, so with nothing more than a raised eyebrow at both, sent them on their separate ways. As for Mala, he gave a grand sweeping bow and ushered her into his classroom. Before she bounced into class with her typical devil-may-care attitude, she motioned for Jaime to come to her. Like a reluctant sheepdog about to be scolded, he shuffled his six-foot-tall frame to where she stood, hands on small hips, and waited. Once before her, she motioned for him to bend down to her level, and when he did, she grabbed his earlobe and whispered.

"I could've taken him, silly. Next time, let me handle it, tough guy."

His sudden, violent rage disconcerted him. Was it his long-gone father's temper rearing its ugly head in Jaime's body and mind? A temper his mother had not-so-secretly prayed he wouldn't inherit, but perhaps did. It shamed Jaime to know such an unpleasant truth about himself, but worse? Mala saw it.

They never spoke of it again, save Mala's plotting all the ways she would torture Nico if ever the opportunity arose. And if he thought he had a tendency for violence, it was nothing compared to her. He assumed, or at least hoped she was all talk and no action, but man she had a violent mind.

As he sat on the cold, hard ground, staring at the space before him, he marveled at all the contradictions of that girl, like he's done so many times before. She is feisty and funny, irrational, and logical, calm and wild. She can be peaceful and almost Zen-like in her nature loving ways and shrugs off insult or disappointment like an itchy sweater. But then, other times, her behavior turns sullen and moody, and everything bothers her. Even Jaime.

When she acts like that, Jaime steers clear and gives her space, knowing she'll find him when she's ready to engage with the world once again. True to form, she always reappears like a ray of sunshine… or a tornado, or even a little of both, and he never knows which it will be.

From the time they were six-year-old scared children in kindergarten class to the present, it doesn't matter whether she is leading him on some adventure, or they curl up with thick leather-bound books in the cavernous town library, Jaime follows her whims wherever they lead. It all comes down to simple facts in Jaime's mind. She is the only one like her. He loves all her contradictions, and well, he loves *her*, plain and simple.

Not to say Jaime doesn't mind his solitary time, though. He can be on his own and never without things to occupy his time or thoughts to fill his mind, be it working on the motorcycle, reading, or out exploring the Everwood, like he had that day. If not for Mala, he'd be the quintessential loner. She keeps him tethered to the rest of the world, something his mother is always grateful to her for.

Lost in thought, sitting and staring up at what amounted to a closet in the middle of the woods, Jaime had failed to notice the dwindling daylight. Dusk came earlier now, bringing with it a sudden chill to the late afternoon air Jaime hadn't considered when he entered the woods. He had to hurry if he wanted to beat the creeping darkness… and avoid the wrath of Mala for being late picking her up from after school detention, or technically, her *double* detention.

For as little trouble Jaime gets into, Mala more than makes up for on her end. Just like freshman year, sophomore year, and junior year, she has already booked the second month of senior year with after school detentions. The rest of the school year will likely look much the same if history repeats.

Mala isn't a bad kid, she's just resistant to rules, be it passively, aggressively, or both. She doesn't *follow*. Whether a simple and obvious rule, like wearing shoes to class (she elects to not) or getting into heated debates with her Sociology teacher (to the point of being asked to leave), or her habit of walking out of class midway to go to the girl's lav, or any other violation, she has an innate tendency towards non-compliance.

Ironically, most of her teachers love her. Sure, she exasperates them, frustrates them, and tortures them, but she does it all with a smile and a laugh and the darn nonchalance they have to laugh and shake their heads... as they send her off to Vice Principal Tohr, who assigns yet another detention for her ever growing list of infractions.

To her credit, she always takes her lumps with nothing more than a perfunctory grumble of complaint. When her teachers, Mr. Tohr, or her parents, ask why, *why* doesn't she just do what she's supposed to do? She shrugs, gives a puzzled look, and says, "Um, because I don't want to?" Leaving them as frustrated and baffled as before.

Once, in their freshman year, Jaime asked her the same question, she gave a classic Mala response. School bored her to death, the rules were silly, and it amused her to pieces to do what she did. It was simple for her, and she laughed at attempts to over scrutinize her behavior.

Some people suggested she acted out because her older brother was a high achiever and she felt she couldn't compete, so she rebelled instead. She considered it. For five minutes.

Her conclusion, offered with characteristic aplomb, was, "Huh. Maybe. But you know what? I have way more fun than him."

She was right, too. Her brother was the one with the weight of everyone's expectations on his shoulders, while with Mala they prayed she'd at least show up. She was a free bird, and he was caged.

As far as she cares, the detentions are a reasonable price to pay for doing whatever she wants. Her father, always stern and serious, had drilled into her head actions had consequences, and she agrees, understands, and expects. So, when she weighs the consequences of her actions, she shrugs her usual shrug and figures, *eh, not so bad. I'll take my lumps.*

How can Jaime, or anyone, argue with that? By the middle of sophomore year, they'd all stopped asking and accepted the fact as she had. Mala won the battle, if not the war. Now, here they are in their fourth and final year of high school, and the usual routine has started. Mala will walk out the cafeteria doors—ending yet another double after-school detention—and head down the long west wing corridor, then stroll out the school's front entrance expecting to see Jaime leaning against his motorcycle, just like he always does. But he fumbled with a strange door in a darkening wood and cursed his mismanagement of time. He pictures her leaning against the brick pillar at the school's entrance, checking the time on her phone and for a text message from Jaime.

A text. He almost palm smacked his forehead. Jaime yanked the cell phone from his back pocket out again. He typed out:

Got sidetracked, b there in 15. Sry.

As soon as he hit send, he saw zero bars. He had no cell reception in the woods. This time he really whacked his hand against his forehead, cell phone and all. Giving the door one last shove to close it, along with one last look before turning back the way he came, Jaime made his way out of the Everwood, holding his phone up and out to catch enough of a signal to send his text to Mala.

Another forest anomaly they'd long since stopped pondering and accepted: they never got lost. Or they never got lost going out of the woods. Every time they went in seemed like the first time, never knowing for sure where the vague animal beaten paths would lead them, should they stray further than the first fifty yards, as they often did. Jaime's compass didn't work, backtracking wasn't an option, nor was mapping a possibility.

When it was time to leave, they started walking, and by some inexplicable means they always ended up near where they'd started. They also had never made it to any other side, making it seem like only one way in, and one way out existed. They went into the clearing that paralleled the apartment complex and came back out into the same. Every single time.

As Jaime sprints through the trees, shrubs, rocks, haphazard stumps and fallen logs, along a path not the same he came in on, he doesn't question it. Though it seems impossible, *no one* questions it or even acknowledges it. Except Mala. She has long insisted it is a magical forest.

To her, a mysterious door amid a forest would erase all shadows of doubt, were she to have even one. But Jaime has opened the door and found nothing save a bark facade and cobwebs to boot. Nothing fantastic happened, nothing unusual to see, and nothing magical occurred. The finding would only intrigue, then disappoint her.

Just as Jaime bursts through the clearing, a mere yard or two from where his bike stood idle, he decides to not tell Mala about the door. What good will it serve? The odds of coming across it again are against them, thanks to the strangeness of the forest. This time he had ventured deep, deeper than he'd intended when he had first set out that afternoon. As if the woods led him to where it wanted him to go.

He rolls his eyes, laughing a little. That is something Mala would say. The forest does not have magic powers. To him, no matter how inexplicable things are, it's just a forest. And to Mala, it is pure magic, a place where anything may happen.

Therefore, telling her about an unexpected intrigue in the Everwood, one found without her, and likely to never found again, can only upset and dishearten Mala. Jaime refuses to be the source of her disappointment, let alone her outrage at such a loss of perceived adventure.

By the time Jaime straps on his helmet and jump-starts the bike, he has decided on a most decisive *hell, no* on telling Mala about his find.

Twenty minutes later he explains in minute detail every aspect of the door sighting, unsure of both how he thought he could keep such a thing from her, or how she got the information from him as fast as she did.

Before he even gets off his bike—apologizing for being late as he does—she accuses him of being up to something.

"Spill it, Cromwell."

She snatches his helmet from his hands and holds it behind her back as ransom. She cares not one bit if dusk is upon them–despite being forbidden to be on the back of Jaime's motorcycle after dark–and waits for his answer.

"All right, all right." Jaime exclaims.

His initial, "It's nothing, I was just hanging out in Everwood, geez," receives only a raised eyebrow, her trademark expression of disapproval. So, with a sigh and an eye on the sky, he tells her what he's found deep in the woods.

Downplaying the details, he calls it a random door to nowhere, nothing exciting about it at all, then adds a casual whatever shrug and reached quickly—but not quickly enough—for the helmet still held behind Mala's back.

"Hmm, so if it wasn't anything interesting, then why are you almost forty-five minutes late? And why do you look so guilty? Oh, my God, tell me you took some pictures."

His second literal palm smack to the forehead that afternoon. Pictures. Why didn't he think to take a picture? If they ever find their way back to the door, it'd be by pure luck. Of course, Mala would at least want a picture.

She all but throws the helmet at Jaime. As she grabs hers from the back end of the bike, she yanks it over her long hair and gives the unmistakable signal of *let's go*.

Even though she glares and stomps, she hops on the bike. They have fifteen minutes of acceptable daylight left, barely enough time to get to the apartment complex where they both still live, and not a moment to spare. It isn't himself he is concerned for, but Mala. It took until senior year to gain permission to ride on the back of Jaime's bike, after a year of begging, pleading, sneaking rides, and cajoling for her parents to give in. The condition is daylight hours only, no exceptions. Mala agreed, Jaime's mother made him take extra training classes for passenger riders, and everyone is happy. Well, Mala and Jaime are. Their respective parents, not so much. Jaime pulls into a parking space in the side lot of their apartment buildings closest to Mala's unit as the streetlamps flicker on and Mala's cell phone chirps. It is her mother, checking her whereabouts, right on cue. With an exasperated sigh, she responds with a one-word text.

Here

She mutters something like *ohmyfrickingGod…* something she wouldn't dare say in front of her mother. Her mother is equal measures strict on some things and lenient on others. Disrespectful tones, words and attitudes were a stringent no. In matters concerning Jaime, leniency oft prevails, as he has proven to be consistent and genuine, trustworthy and reliable. Qualities Mala can be taken to task for whenever not with him.

Jaime makes unnecessary intense study of his fender, waiting, hoping, and fearing what Mala might say, or if she'll say anything at all. Maybe she'll stomp off and leave him out of sorts for the rest of the night, wondering how long she'll stay mad. She, too, is slow in returning her phone to her purse, re-locking her helmet onto the back of the bike, adjusting her backpack. All steps usually done in a blink.

Several minutes of mutual silence follow; one in which the usual neighborhood sounds fill the air. Elderly Mrs. Fritz admonishes her little white cairn terrier, Charlie, to come along in her heavy German accent as they go on their nightly stroll, Little Robbie's mom calls from their front entrance in her sing-song bird voice just like she does every night at dusk, trying to lure him back home from the playground and his friends. "Robbieeeee, Robbbbberttttt, Robbbbbieeee…" The *thwack* of a tennis ball hits racket strings on the tennis court echo off the brick buildings as a couple play an evening set under the flood lights.

All the sounds of home, comforting to both Jaime and Mala under normal circumstances, but tonight they are jarring and magnified by their silence. Mala speaks and the unexpected sound startles Jaime into dropping his keys.

As he bends down to pick them up, she says, "We *will* find the door. Tonight."

His hand hovers over the brown leather key chain, the words sinking in. He recognizes that tone all too well. It is the one she used the summer they were six-going-on-seven, best friends already. Mala decided she was a pirate and the tallest of the pine trees lining the backside of the property would be the perfect pirate ship, and the uppermost branches would be an even more perfect look out.

She had announced, in much that same tone, "We're going to the top of that tree."

She'd gone halfway up before he shouted. "Wait. That's not safe."

In his six-year-old mind he had no choice but to follow her up to top of the sap covered monstrosity. While he clung for dear life as they swayed, she sang at the top of her lungs, "Yo, ho, yo ho, a pirate's life for me…"

It was the only line of the song she knew, so she repeated it over and over until Mr. Stevens—their gruff but lovable neighbor from four units over—came out to see what and where the ruckus came from. Jaime watched from above as his salt and pepper color head turned in every direction but up.

Mala tried to get Jaime to not give away their hiding spot, as she called it, so instead of calling out and incurring her wrath, the terrified boy let out a fake sneeze, and when Mr. Stevens looked up, spotted them with wide bespectacled eyes, and ran for a ladder from his basement storage bin, he nearly peed his pants with relief.

Jaime promised ashen-faced Mr. Stevens he would not climb the trees again, but Mala required bribes and incentives—cookies and a promise to teach her how to ride her bike without training wheels—to elicit a pinkie promise. Only Jaime saw her cross her fingers behind her back, making the promise void without repercussion.

Jaime lets out the breath he'd been holding. She'll want to go look for the door. He knows it as he does his own name, but tonight? Implausible. Impractical. Entirely unsafe. Even as these thoughts come to mind, he understands saying them will only make her more determined to forge ahead. It also means she'll drag him along for the adventure—as she'll call it—whether he wants to go or not.

He opens his mouth to speak, and those raised eyebrow of hers glare back at him.

"Set your alarm, 11:55. I'll be at your door at 12:15." She flicks her sun-streaked hair over her shoulder and walks toward her apartment door without a second glance.

He calls out. "But it's a school ni—" the slam of her back door cuts him off.

Jaime sighs and heads in the opposite direction, around the building unit she lives in, and toward the front entrance of his apartment, which faces her front entrance. He ducks under a low-hanging branch of Mala's favorite crabapple tree as he rounds the curve.

As nine-years old, they'd once found a live bat in the shade of the very tree, its leathery wings folded so tightly against its body it appeared to be a fuzzy brown ball. They stared at it, baffled and curious, for about ten minutes, and arguing over who would be the one to touch it.

Mala had broken a branch off the tree and with one end gently prodded the fuzzy object despite Jaime's nervous warning of the risk of rabies. At first nothing happened, but the second time, when she attempted to flip it over, the creature unfurled its shiny black wings, emitting a shocking screech as he did so. The sound sent them both screaming and running as far and fast as they their legs carried them, heading for the playground at the other end of the complex. Hours later they tip-toed back to the spot under the tree, half hoping and half fearing what they'd see there, so it was with mixed relief and disappointment when they found the bat long gone.

Jaime gives the low-hanging branch of the old tree a swat as he passes by, knocking several crab apples free as he does, and then kicks the loose fruit as he stalks home, the weight of his unease heavy on his shoulders.

5 MIDNIGHT

At 11:47, Jaime sits on his bed, wide awake, and stares at the ceiling. He hadn't needed to set his alarm, as Mala had all but ordered him to do because he never goes to sleep until well after midnight anyhow, and even if he did, there's no way he'd get any sleep knowing two buildings over, Mala is paces around her poster lined room. No doubt she's already dressed and ready for what she considers being a grand adventure.

Jaime does not share her enthusiasm, nor does he feel any of the apparent confidence they'll find the door again. All logic goes against such a rediscovery. That it's the middle of the night only compounds the situation. But Mala is like the proverbial ferocious dog with a bone when she sets her sights on something. Once she has an idea or a notion in her head, there is no dissuading her. Ever.

He had spent the past twelve years trying to be the voice of reason to her impulses and ideas, and she has spent the same number persuading and cajoling and downright bullying him to follow her down her many roads of folly and fancy. He smirks at the last thought. Mala as his pint-sized bully, Mala as his medium sized bully, and now Mala as his almost grown woman bully. Always a full head shorter, she either glares up at him or smiles sweetly… whichever means to meet her end.

Bully is too strong a word. Mala never *really* makes Jaime do anything he doesn't deep down want to do. It's a matter of course, in his mind. He'll follow her lead, no matter what or where it takes them.

6 FROM THE MEADOWS

At eleven-fifty-nine, Mala perches on the edge of her unmade bed, retying her hiking boots for the third time. They were fine the first two times, but she's already gotten everything ready for their search and has nothing left to do but wait. Flashlight, charged cell phone, water bottle and snacks, all tucked into various pockets of the old gray cargo pants she'd taken off her brother's Goodwill pile and thrown on. She had to belt and cuff them to make them to stay up, so she won't trip, but otherwise they are perfect for heading out into the Everwood on a chilly fall night.

Over a black tank top, she wears her favorite thermal shirt, the one with holes in the cuffs—through which she sticks her thumbs—expecting it will keep her warm enough,

33

especially once they are moving. Her hair hangs down in a loose braid she hastily twisted, knowing she'd have to redo it once the branches poke at it. She is beyond ready to go.

She checks her phone for the umpteenth time. Twelve-o-two. Eight more minutes until she tip-toes out the back door, closes it behind her, and dashes around the back of the building to the front, ducking as she passes her front window and bee-lining to Jaime's front porch.

Every front covered entrance of each unit in The Meadows Apartments has an old-fashioned lantern style porch light that stays on throughout the night, casting a dull glow over the steps, the closest shrubs and walkways, so Mala will have to stay far enough in the shadows to avoid being spotting by any night owls who may look out their apartment windows at just that moment, including her own parents.

At twelve-o-nine, Mala creeps out her bedroom, opens her door in increments and squints out into the dark hallway. Once her door hits the half open point, she has to squeeze through. The next fraction will cause it to creak. That would wake her father, a light sleeper. Years of practice—and getting caught several times—taught her where to walk and which floorboards to avoid, so before her phone's clock hits twelve-ten, she steps out the door and onto the dew-wet grass.

She gives an involuntary gasp at the sudden brisk night air, a stark contrast to the warm apartment. A split second of doubt flits through her at the mission she is about to drag Jaime along. But then, on the same crisp breeze comes the smell of autumn. The decay of brown leaves and damp earth, grass, and night. Everwood calls to her with its scent. Without another moment's hesitation, she is off.

Jaime will be watching from his living room window; the outline of his shadow perceptible in the glow cast by the stove light his mother always leaves on at night. She pictures his head pressed up against the cool glass, his too long hair curling at his neck, and his fingertips on the window frame. Waiting for her.

How many times has she gazed up at him like that? Countless. She knows his outline, his stance, posture, and the details of his face. The scar she has traced with her fingertip when they were eleven, then kissed when they were twelve. It was an impulse, the kiss. One which had surprised them both and almost paralyzed them with awkwardness. They did what any twelve-year-old would do. They pretended it never happened and moved on.

Still, she's thought of that moment often, and as she rounds the corner of the brick building, looking up at the dark window of his second-floor apartment, she recalls it again. As always, the recollection sends a wave of heat to her cheeks. Sure, they'd been teased since forever about being a couple, and everyone assumed they were together. Neither admitted, confirmed, nor denied, and never had they spoken of it. Mala still doesn't know what they are. Best friends? Yes. Something more? Yes... no, ugh, maybe?

Jaime is always there, calming her with his sweet smile, amusing her with the crease between his eyebrows whenever she frustrates him—which is often—and being her steady rock, always there to help her. Even when she refuses his help, he'd stands by just in case. She might be a handful, but he puts up with her without complaint. Okay, with a lot of complaint, some resistance, and a fair amount of annoyance. However, Jaime is not as innocent or victimized as he pretends to be. He dishes as much as he takes. Sometimes he teases her mercilessly in her opinion and behaves in a most casual and indifferent manner, which makes Mala insane, as it causes her to feel insecure and un-tethered. She suspects he does so on purpose, and when she once accused him of such, he turned to her with a suddenness and such an intensity in his eyes. He took her upturned face in his big hands and whispered, "Never. I would never do that to you."

That moment—when even the wind through the trees stopped—took Mala's breath away, leaving her for once speechless. By the time she'd recovered from the shock wave of his intense proclamation, he'd already slipped through the low brush into the wood, setting them off on one of their more solemn treks into the Everwood.

They'd walked for what seemed like hours in silence; both lost in thought, both at a loss for words, as they trampled twigs and crunched leaves beneath their feet, trusting instinct to guide their way. The birds chirped, the squirrels and chipmunks burrowed and foraged, and all other life in the Everwood went about their business with no interest or bother with the brooding tall boy and the golden-haired girl who tried to keep up with his long strides.

Two months have gone by since, and like the kiss five years prior, has not been spoken of since. Still, Mala senses a change—one imperceptible to the casual observer—in their relationship. As always, Jaime waits for her each morning to go to school, leaning against his motorcycle, hands in the front pocket of his worn jeans and shaking his head as she bursts out her back door in a riot of almost put-togetherness as she shouts a perfunctory, "Sorry, sorry." or "I know, I know," as she walk-runs towards him. They still eat lunch together every day. Or rather he eats lunch, and she writes in her journal and turns her nose at the gray and brown matter that constitutes school dietary provisions.

As usual, he picks her up after her almost daily detentions. They camp out in oversized leather chairs in the adult department of the library on rainy Saturday mornings, eschewing the teen department in favor of the more sophisticated quiet. They take long walks together in the Everwood with a blanket and food for picnicking on any clear day and chance they got, and still hang out in each other's apartments, listening to music, watching TV and bothering their parents for food, and then more food. Now something hovers between them.

Mala feels Jaime's eyes on her when she isn't looking, as surely as he feels hers on him. Where he once wouldn't think twice about climbing over her to get the TV remote control, he now stands up and goes around her. If their hands brush, he jerks away as if scalded and then laughs it off and gives her a playful shove. She notices details and changes in Jaime she'd overlooked before.

His arms have gotten more muscular, his shoulders wider. When had a shadow of a beard started? Not bad, but different. Noticing him causes her to linger in front of the mirror, and rather than a quick glance, she instead tries to see herself as he might see her. Her rarely styled hair flows long and sun-bleached. She only has two looks. Down and messy, or up and messy. Her clothes? They are for comfort first, trends, not at all. Drawstring pants and tank tops, or slouchy sweaters and leggings are her staples, and the dozen or so loose summer dresses she paired with either cowboy or combat boots.

That is as exciting as it gets. Her smile, in her opinion, spreads too wide for her narrow face, and her teeth look like piano keys. Her laugh sounds too big, her hips too narrow, her chest too small. Overall, though, Mala determines herself to be average at least, with points either for or against quirkiness and individuality, depending on opinion. Not to worry, there is plenty of opinion to go around at Rocky Knoll High. Just ask Janie Walker.

She was the first girl in school to develop in all the right places the summer between junior high and high school, and according to some of the more catty and jealous girls in school, she seemed to enjoy the attention it brought her. The only one who seemed not to notice her, was Jaime, and not for lack of effort on Janie's part.

There are plenty of girls in school with crushes on Jaime. Though they have been mooning over him since junior high, it wasn't until recently Mala compared her looks with theirs, rather than laughing at them. Jealousy and envy has crept under her skin, and she doesn't like it. Her thoughts confuse and irritate her. She wants everything to be normal between them, and not this weird vibe. They have to talk about it; this thing between them and what it means. Just… not yet.

Standing at the edge of a shadow in the sharp October air and staring hard up into the window above, Mala is ready to turn all her attention to finding the door Jaime saw eight hours before. A strange, magic door. She won't accept his claim it leads nowhere. Sure, Jaime saw nothing. Yet, the hair on the back of Mala's neck stood up when he described the details of the door. She'd have made him take her there that second, had she not already promised to go straight home from school.

Like Jaime always said, promises were her Kryptonite. If one can be extracted from her, she keeps it.

But jailbreaks have a statute of limitations. This justifies a midnight trek in her mind. It may be their only hope of rediscovering the door. She only hopes his hike from earlier is still fresh in his mind, and they can retrace his steps. It doesn't matter that attempting to revisit the same spot twice has never worked. At least, she tries to make it irrelevant. They have rediscovered locations visited in the past. Just... not on purpose. This time, *this* time they will find what they seek. She wills it so, or at least tries to with every fiber of her being. Just as she uses the force of her will to make Jaime hurry down the stairs and slip out the front door so they can be on their way...

7 Into The Everwood

Fifteen minutes later, at twelve-thirty a.m. on the dot, Mala and Jaime stand where the clearing meets the tree line. They adjust and check their gear and make sure their flashlights work as their rapid breath forms clouds that drift and disappear back into the night. A three-quarter moon shines down, and there's a flush in Mala's cheeks from the chilly air. He can't stop staring at her.

"You look like something out of one of your fairytale books."

He means the ones lining her bedroom bookcase

"Like a nymph or something. I think that's what they're called."

All the times Mala has talked about those characters and figures throughout their childhood, pulling out book after book to read and re-read passages she loves, and he can't recall what they are.

"Gnomes, maybe? Sprites?"

Mala looks up, not hiding her impatience, only to see consternation on his face. He directs his furrowed brow at her. The moonlight—high above and behind him—casts a luminous glow like a halo or an energy field, around him reminding her of the angel from her childhood dreams. She startles. It has been years since she's thought about the strange dreams, the guardian-like figure who stood in the corner of every dream. When did the dreams stop? And why?

She forces the memories and the comparison from her head and focuses on Jaime. He is her guardian of sorts, not some dream visitor. Jaime always protects her, even when she doesn't want or need it. The two—with their brows creased at one another—stay locked in silence until the hoot of a nearby owl breaks the spell. It jolts them into action.

"Ok, you lead. I'll shine the light for both of us, so we don't waste both batteries," says Mala.

Jaime gives a sharp nod and steps though the shrubs. Just like that, they are out of the clearing and into the Everwood. The first twenty minutes are quiet, save the sound of their footsteps and the night itself. The still branches high above rustle now and again, beginning from a distant part of the forest and then approaching like a wave onto the shore, then dissipating once again, leaving a hush in their wake. Within ten minutes, Jaime has removed his hoodie and tied it around his waist, and Mala has pushed her sleeves up. They are moving fast, and their body temperature rises enough to counter the chill. Mala lets Jaime lead, a concession she rarely makes, but it is a matter of course he'll be the one to guide them towards their destination. After grilling him again for details, she learns he had wandered deeper than usual into the woods, following what he believed to be a deer path wherever it went. He had walked for about an hour and a half without pause, and noticed little aside from the unusual quiet, which he attributed it to his own disruption of nature.

Jaime moves through the woods with ease, his long strides confident. Mala loves his quiet self-assurance. Not that she'd tell him so, though. He navigates the changing terrain as well as Mala, balancing and shifting his weight as he pushes and holds aside the low-hanging branches for Mala to pass through unscratched. Despite the ever-changing nature of the forest, they both move through it as if dancing on a ballroom floor. Years of traversing through thicket and brush, bounding over fallen logs, or tramping through shallow streams has made them as adept and sure-footed as if they'd been woodland animals in another life.

Jaime stops. Mala smacks into Jaime's backside. He is like a brick wall. Mala bounces off him and Jaime grabs a hold of her waist and pulls her to his chest. Her cheek presses against him, the vibration of his laughter tickles her ear. Her own laugh sounds breathless. Mala pokes him in his ribcage before the moment becomes more intense, and he jumps as if cattle prodded.

They are once again just Jaime and Mala. Nothing else, nothing more, and it lightens both their moods. He stops to say he is unsure which direction to head. There seems to be only two semi-beaten paths to choose from, and straight is not one of them. Should they veer left, they'll find lighter, more sparse vegetation. If they curve right, they'll head into a line of tangled shrubs and trees in which a tunnel the width of a beach ball gapes, and through which they must crawl.

Mala chooses the challenging path, and Jaime, for once, agrees. Though the less overgrown way looks way more appealing, his instinct tells him to go toward the thicket. Where he'd found the strange door had been surrounded by ancient growth, so if they found it again, this would be the likelier way. Without further discussion, Mala has already skipped ahead and crouches to walk-crawl through the natural tunnel.

Thanks to Jaime's size, he must army crawl. He shakes his head at her reckless abandon and disregard for safety. Not that she sees his dismay from her angle… nor would she care one bit. Sighing a big, defeated sigh, he stomps his way to the opening.

He stoops down to start the undignified crawl through the small leaf and branch canopied opening, feeling like he is following Alice into the rabbit hole. He's never read Alice in Wonderland. Thanks to Mala, he knows the story well enough, though. The passageway is short, if not spacious. Jaime feels the scratch and scrape of bare branches against his scalp, arms and back, some hard enough to leave several cuts that will later welt and sting. He is grumbling a complaint when an audible gasp and exclamation from Mala cuts him short.

"Oh."

She has already cleared the other side and stands upright. Jaime, alarmed and helpless to help her, curses as he rushes on all fours up and out of the exit, ready to defend and protect her. He is mindless of the last branch which catches him below his right eye, drawing a bead of bright red blood. Mala turns back and gives a terse laugh which turns into another 'oh' at the sight of the gash on his cheek. Like a mirror reflection, they copy each other's gesture. His hand reaches down to her hair, extracting a brown papery leaf from the nest her hair had become, as she reaches up to wipe away the thin line of blood from his cheekbone. Something over Mala's head tears his gaze away from her. Less than a few yards behind her sits what has elicited the surprised exclamation from her lips.

The door.

It stuns him. Jaime had no real expectation of finding it again in the middle of a moonlit night, no less. He thought he'd entertain her flight of fancy, then lament along with her at their failure. Although Jaime's disappointment wouldn't compare with hers. He'd already seen the door, opened it, and found a big fat nothing.

The awe and excitement radiate from Mala like a heat wave irritates Jaime. She'll be disappointed when they reopen the damn door and find nothing but damp bark, dirt and spider webs, and Jaime knows all too well the only thing worse than a despondent Mala is an angry Mala.

That's it.

He'll get her angry at him, angry enough to distract her from the letdown of their strange but un-magical find. It will be worth the pouty silence from her, to not see the light go out of her eyes.

He'd used the tactic before, tricking her out of the self-sabotage she is prone to, so he could do it again. Mala, for as much as she pretends to be a cynic and a realist, is a dreamer. Only Jaime understands; few others ever get close. They all take her at face value, and her face gives nothing away to the world. But Jaime, who has grown up alongside her most of his life, knows well the long bookcase that up the length of one full wall in her bedroom, and the books, videos, and trinkets which line those shelves. C. S. Lewis, The Narnia Chronicles sits central and proud, their spines creased and worn from being read and reread many times over. The same goes for her Wizard of Oz series, assortment of fairy tales, Peter Pan figurine in flight, a replica of the Dark Crystal, even childhood classics from Beatrix Potter held court in a low corner. Roald Dahl took residence alongside Neil Gaiman, and J. K. Rowling leaned up against George R. R. Martin, who leaned away from Lewis Carroll.

The only one of her collection she convinced *him* to read is The Talisman, by Stephen King. Jaime had devoured everything he wrote, so it took no arm twisting to persuade him. As with Mala, it became a favorite, each of their respective copies bore the telltale signs of a well-loved and oft read book.

Her bookcase is the window to her soul. To see the contents of those shelves for what they represent, is to understand *her*. She is a dreamer, and her dreams are filled with fantasy, fairies and folklore. Between the covers of those books, and the movies in their pristine cases, live the world Mala wishes for. A world less ordinary.

She *wishes* it to be real with all her might. And now, as they stand mere yards from the peculiar door, Jaime senses Mala standing on an emotional precipice. There will be, if not for his imminent intervention, two defining moments. The moment *before* they wrestle open the door, and the moment *after* it opens; revealing the nothingness Jaime already knows it holds. Mala's fragile shell of youthful wonderment and wistful, wishful childhood flight of the imagination will crack and crumble for the last time. Her naivety will blow away like dust and the cynical facade will become reality.

Jaime has a foreboding the moment might break the Mala he knew, and a version he doesn't know at all will replace her. He cannot allow it to happen. He can't deter her though.

Distract her.

Since she is never more distracted than when angry at him, it seems the logical plan of action. He must hit her where it hurts the most, no matter how it pains him to do so. He braces himself and then says in his most taunting tone possible, "So, let me guess. You think you'll find Tinkerbell on the other side of that door? Or maybe Mr. Tunnis?"

He adds a pointed laugh for good measure. As expected, Mala spins toward him, her reverie broken. Her brow creases and visible even in the moonlight; an angry flush colors her face.

"First, it's *Tum*nus, Mr. *Tum*-nus, so get it right. Second, I don't expect any such thing. It's just a door, you said so yourself. So, whatever."

Jaime knows the name of one of her all-time favorite book characters. When they were younger, she used to draw pictures of those characters and label them, then toss them aside as not good enough for keeping. Jaime, unbeknownst to her, had pilfered several of them and kept them. Mr. Tumnus in fact, sits at the top of the stack of drawings in his bottom desk drawer.

He now has her on the defensive and he must keep going, regardless of the aftereffects. It is a psychological mind game he is not proud of playing, but believes it is for her benefit, and so continues.

"Oh, c'mon, now. Admit it. You think there's going to be some magic world on the other side. One with dragons and castles maybe?" He laughs, then adds, "Hurry, let's go open the door. Dorothy and the Scarecrow are waiting on the yellow brick road for you."

He's laying it on heavy and he cringes. Still, it is the best way to lessen the blow of disappointment she'll feel regardless of anything he says or does.

"What the hell, Jaime? Shut *up*. I don't think that. I just want to see the stupid door for myself."

Mala is embarrassed-angry. Caught out in her fantasy world and now has to save face. Exactly what Jaime is going for. Next, she'll insist on opening the door to prove to him how little she cares or believes there is anything special about the entryway in the middle of a forest.

"I'm going to open the dumb thing and look inside and then we can go home and be done with it."

She shrugs off her backpack, and dislodges the flashlight from her waistband, dropping it on top of the bag, and resecures her hair in a quick ponytail, all in rapid succession as she marches toward the door.

Jaime follows her partway, then sits on gray and mossy boulder, propping his boots on the small log that has fallen in front of it, making a perfect footrest.

"Okay, Little, have fun in Never-Everland. See you when you get back," he calls out, using his pet name for her to aggravate her even more. Her response involves a one-finger salute.

Jaime watches as she approaches the door, tilts her head in puzzlement at its odd handle just as he'd done. She reaches out to grasp it, but then pulls back her hand—just as he'd also done—before taking a hold of the orb, which once again is cast in rose gold light. This time it comes from the moon and not the sun and is less blinding and more luminous. Thanks to his detailed description how the door should be opened, she bypasses the metal appendage for the less creepy knob.

Lucky her.

This time the door gives and grazes the forest floor with a sound like a broom's sweep. Mala glances back at Jaime, who waves her on with a smirk intended to reignite her anger at him. Her returned scowl assures him his aim is true. His target is her pride, and he's pierced it.

Without a second glance, she steps through the arched frame of the doorway, turns back to him, and gives another one fingered salute right before the door closes, leaving him on the outside and her on the inside.

"Well. That was dumb," he shouts. "Guess I'll just sit right here and wait for you to get back from Ninia."

He waits for a muffled, *"Narnia, you idiot,"* to come from behind the closed door, but there is only silence.

Fine, I can wait her out. She won't stay in a tight, damp space for long. The first spider web that touches her face will send her toppling out the door, for sure.

Five minutes later, he is still waiting, but becoming more impatient by the minute. Now she is just being stubborn. She wants him to open the door, so she can either jump out and try to scare him—*ridiculous, will not happen*—or point and laugh at him for his concern, and exacting her revenge for *his* teasing. Well, he won't do it. No way, no how. He can be as stubborn as she is. He'll wait all night if need be.

Not that it will take long, though. As stubborn as she is, Mala is impatient. His denial of her instant gratification will grate on her nerves, so at any moment she'll be busting out of the enclosed space with an indignant scowl.

He imagines her jerking her backpack over her shoulders and stomping past him towards the rabbit hole opening from where they came, but still, ten minutes later, and nothing.

8 MAGIC LANDS DO EXIST

Is he kidding me right now?

That's the first thing Mala thinks after he teases her. Every snide thing he'd said is what she hopes. Well, not Tinkerbell per se, but yes. Something magical. There must be.

He made her feel silly and outright foolish. The thing she hates most is being made to feel foolish. Embarrassment is a mortal wound, something she avoids at all costs. She must save face and counter his claims with stark and adamant denial.

She flips him the bird, and the next thing she knows, she is through the door, but not before feeling the strange heated pulse emanating from the orb when she touches it. In fact, her palm and fingertips still tingle from the shock wave, and she stares down at her hand, half expecting to see a red mark. Two things hit her at once. She sees without having her flashlight, and the door—that heavily scarred and fabulous door—has closed on its own.

She is still processing this when a suspicion strikes her. There is no bark wall behind me like Jaime described.

Her heart palpitates. Her entire body pulses with each beat. Like a mannequin on a turnstile she turns a slow half circle, anxiety and excitement mounts at whatever she is about to see.

After saying for her whole life—or at least for as long as she'd begun reading fairy tales and fantasy novels—Magical lands exist, fairy tales are real, she chants in her head, this isn't real, this isn't happening. Even though in her heart of hearts, she knows. This is happening.

Once she faces the space where wall should be, her brain refuses process what her eyes see. The bark is translucent, shimmering and wavered like a like a mirage or a sheer curtain in a lazy summer breeze, and behind it there is something much more. It looks, for as much as she could tell, like the clearing, but now it is in full daylight.

Mala takes one step toward the bark/curtain then looks behind her at the door. She should turn, open the door, and call for Jaime to come see what she sees, but he is being a jerk, so he can wait out there a little longer while she peeks at the other side.

Her decision made; Mala steps to the quasi-wall and brings her shaking hand up to touch it. As she'd hoped and feared, her hand goes through.

"Holy shhhh…"

First her hand, then her arm, and next her shoulder pass through to the other side. The air warms her outstretched arm, a definite contrast to the cold damp air inside the compact space.

Once again, she pauses, thinking of Jaime who undoubtedly is still sitting with an amused expression on his face and waiting for her to come out. Although, by now, he must be impatient and even annoyed, thinking she is trying to trick him.

By now, he'll have his arms crossed over his chest, one long leg bent, with his old work boot jacked against the large gray boulder, the other leg stretched out long. He'll be keeping a wary eye on the door, all while pretending not to care. He probably has already called out some flip remark, unaware she cannot hear him.

She smirks at the image in her mind. He can wait a few more minutes. She'll take a quick look on the other side, then go back and get him. She takes a deep breath and walks through the wavering screen and onto the other side of the Everwood.

9 TIME'S UP

After the first ten minutes of waiting her out, Jaime's backside hurts from the rough boulder, so he hops off and paces the leaf and dirt covered ground, kicking then stomping acorns his heavy boots. After seeing the flicker of light through the door frame minutes before, he knows for sure Mala is sitting in there playing with her phone or her flashlight and waiting for him to give in and open the door.

He refuses to fall for it. Her willingness to stay in there despite the spider webs impresses him, but he can be just as stubborn. They have several hours of night before they have to be back.

The moon and starlit sky, along with the crisp October air carrying the scent of fall leaves, pine needles, and fresh earth, is enough to curb his annoyance and allow him to enjoy the solitude and beauty of a nighttime forest. Jaime looks up into the cloudless sky. The blue tinted moon peeks through the swaying branches. Stars twinkle and sparkle, peppering the sky as far as his eye can see. This is his heaven, out there in the Everwood. It is no trouble at all to be out there, *no sir-ree*. In fact, this is a great time to grab some snacks out of the backpack Mala left behind in her impulsiveness.

"Ha, ha. Well, lookie here. Now guess who has all the food? That's right, I do. Must be getting hungry in there, but oh, well."

Okay, so he can't resist taunting her one more time. He smirks and strolls over to her backpack, behaving as if she is watching him from inside the closet-like space.

As he lifts the backpack by one shoulder strap, Mala's black flashlight tumbles off and falls to the ground. It rolls away and stops at the base of the fallen tree truck he'd used as a footrest. Jaime's eyebrows creep upward. He'd assumed it is still on her belt.

Ah, then it is her cell phone she is using in there to chase the shadows.

Well, that battery won't last forever. His is already low— only ten percent battery life displaying on his screen—so he powers on sparingly.

He carries the backpack, straps dragging in the dirt, over to the log which halted the flashlight's escape, and sits down on the ground, using the log as a backrest. He digs into the bag in search of the granola bars she'd packed, but his hand wraps around a hard rectangle object. Without even seeing it, he knows it is Mala's phone.

She has no phone and no flashlight. Yet flashes of white light sneak through the cracks of the door frame. What else does she have on her to illuminate the dark? How long ago had he noticed the flashes? He checks his own phone, now at seven percent, and figures it was at least ten minutes prior.

He reconsiders his stubborn stance. Perhaps he'll go listen at the door. Maybe even knock, tell her enough already. He doesn't want to admit it, not even to himself, but a seed of concern has sprouted in his chest.

Crap.

He jumps up and walks toward the door, brushing the dirt and pine needles from his pants. He presses his ear to the battered door. The rough wood pokes his lobe and cheek and he listens. All he hears are unilateral sounds from the surrounding forest, and nothing from inside. Soon, he discerns a different emanation coming from where his ear presses. It is more of a sensation than a sound. A steady pulsing, like a vibration. It tickles his ear.

Jaime jerks his head back and rubs his earlobe to get the tickle feeling out. It reminds him of the slightly hysterical feeling he gets when a bug flies at—or worse—into his ear. That buzz discomfits him. It isn't right, nor is it explainable.

There are no electric currents to speak of in the woods. No train tracks to send vibrations through the ground and out the door. Mala left all her electronics in her backpack. So why does the door feel as though there is energy rumbling through it?

"All right, Little. You've had your fun. Time to come out."

Jaime's voice carries more of an authoritative tone than what he feels. What he *actually feels is* an inexplicable anxiousness. Harder to admit, though, is he loathes touching the door again. The continued silence from the other side gives him no choice. He exhales, forcing out a cloud of steam that billows and disappears into the night.

He slings Mala's backpack over one shoulder after re-depositing the flashlight in the side pouch and merging the contents of his backpack with hers.

I have no reason to empty my pack into hers. Nope, none.

He imagines Mala answering him.

"Ha ha, yeah there is."

"No there isn't."

"There totally is. You believe there is something on the other side of that door."

"I do not. I most definitely do not."

"Mhm, then why are packing up the backpack as If you're going somewhere?"

"I am going somewhere. In the stupid closet. To get you. I'm taking the bag so no one, um, steals it."

"You think the door is magical."

"No."

"Yes, you do."

Unbelievable. She argues with him even in his own head. There i*sn't* anything strange about the door… other than it is a door in the middle of the woods that leads to nowhere, and vibrates oddly, and… fine, there is *a lot* unusual about the door.

Slicking his shaggy hair back from his forehead, Jaime says, "Okay *fine*. Maybe there *is* something weird here. Something *weirder*. You win, are you happy now?"

He purses his lips and grabs the orb—ignoring the heat radiating from it and through his palm—and pulls the door open. The same dank darkness, the same musky moldy smell wafts out at him as the first time he opened the door. A smell not exactly pleasant, nor *un*pleasant either, to be fair. However, there is no light, and there is no Mala.

10 We're Not In Rocky Knoll Anymore

As Mala looks around, the first thought that pops to mind is, "Toto, I've a feeling we're not in Kansas anymore."

She is not Dorothy, there is no Toto, she's not in Kansas, and this most definitely is not Munchkin Land. At least, she doesn't think so.

At first glance, it looks like the clearing at the apartment side of the forest, but the more she peers around, she notices the trees are different. Weeping willows where pines should stand, trumpet vines in place of wild grapevine, plus others not identifiable.

The clearing is different, too. Instead of October straw-yellow tall grass waves soft looking, late spring, knee-high shamrock green grass. Oversized dragonflies helicopter about, resting on the wildflowers that dot the field. Even the birds that sing and chirp sound unfamiliar to her ears.

"Jaime is going to freak." She grins. "I'll go get him… in one more minute."

A lone billowy white cloud interrupts the endless cerulean blue sky. Through it, the mid-day sun flashes in and out like a child playing peek-a-boo. The cloud thins and dissipates as she watches, mesmerized. All at once the sun shines down again, and she smiles at the warmth on her skin. Her scalp tingles from the sun's heat, and the last autumn chill leaves her body.

Mala likes autumn well enough, but summer is her favorite. Now, this strange place is giving her another taste of it. She stretches her arms wide, palms up, and tilts her head up to the sun-soaked sky again, welcoming it on her smiling face. The sweet-smelling air fills her lungs.

A tickling weight upon her right palm startles her. It is the same weight as Sasha, Jaime's mother's parakeet. Ever so slowly, she turns her head. Her eyes meet those of the largest dragonfly she's ever seen. Mala holds her breath and cocks her head.

The fabulously colored insect mirrors her movement, as curious as she is. Its long, iridescent double wings tremble, ready for flight should it find Mala to be a foe and not a friend. *Or flower.*

Though the dragonfly stare-down engrosses her, she notices a low buzzing sound, one that multiplies in magnitude and volume. Breaking her gaze from her new little—*not so little*—friend, she raises only her eyes, allowing them to refocus on her surroundings, and looks for the source of the incessant buzzing.

One slow sweep of the immediate vicinity is enough to answer her curiosity. All around her, sitting on twigs, grass and flowers, some on rocks, others hovering, are hundreds of dragonflies.

They come in every color, many are even multicolor and in combinations she'd never seen. Scarlet dotted with ultraviolet, emerald green striped with electric blue, pumpkin orange with fuchsia zebra stripes, and so many more.

But none resemble or is even as comparable in size as the one still resting on her outstretched palm. Though it gives a slight tremor, she hesitates to lower her arm, or do anything to alarm the incredible creature. However, her muscles decide for her and her arm lowers. The dragonfly stays put, still watching her with its unusual eyes, head now upturned.

Risking its flight, she raises her hand in front of her face with great care. The girl and the insect are now eye to eye, and still the dragonfly is unfazed. It looks her up and down, reminding her of teenage girls as they pass each other by, taking in every detail, judging, comparing. To the grand insect's credit, it appears more curious than judgmental.

Mala, too, absorbs every detail of her new friend.

"You *are* a friend, right? Not going to attack me, I hope." She forces a slight laugh through her nose.

The eyes are most curious of all, perhaps. It is not the compound eye she learned about in biology, and not the eyes of any human she'd ever met. With a start, she realizes what they remind her of. Once, several years back, her family had gone on a vacation in Florida, where they'd taken a kayak ride through one of the many natural springs. As they drifted down the clear water, they came upon a long-necked bird that looked like a cross between a goose and a crane, a Cormorant. Nothing, save its size, seemed remarkable until the moment it looked up. A quick jerk of its long beaked head revealed an eye so spectacularly a shade of teal that Mala gasped in delight. As they passed the teal-eyed bird, they locked gazes until out of sight. She had forgotten about the magnificence of those eyes until she observes those of the unique dragonfly.

Its body—a delicate, long, and velvety torso in shades of ivory—is no less fascinating. There is intricate rose gold pattern that weaves and dances over the entire body. The sunlight causes it to glint and shine like a wedding band in the sun.

Mala's gaze drifts from the dragonfly on her palm to the field of buzzing miniature living helicopters. They all appear to be waiting, as is Mala. So, she does what any girl who's read every sci-fi/ fantasy book she's ever gotten her hands on. She speaks.

"Um, hey there? So, uh..." she chuckles, "what, uh, do I... what do we do here?"

That did not come out well. *Seriously, my whole life has built up to this moment, and that is all I have?* Lame, so lame. The dragonfly king—*or queen*—opens its mouth and... *oh my God, it's going to speak, it is going to speak...* lets out a strange cooing sound.

Oh.

How anticlimactic. The dragonfly seems to think so too, because—and Mala will swear to this—it bows its head, gives the are-you-for-real head shake, and looks all out exasperated with her.

Despite the annoyance at her thick-headedness, it appears the dragonfly might try again. Once more, it turns its teal-green oversized eyes to her hazel ones and lets out another melodic coo. This time, however, it adds—again, Mala would swear to this—a head nod out and over the field of dragonflies.

"Oh. You want me to introduce myself? Is that what? Um, ok, sure, sure thing."

There is no responding coo, or even a head nod in assent—just the steady big-eyed and patient gaze to let her know she is correct. But it *feels* right, and based on her years of fantasy reading experience, it seems the most logical next step.

So, channeling her inner Dorothy—*no munchkins here, folks, just some cooing bugs is all*—she turns toward the field of dragonflies, while on her hand the regal king/queen perched its furry footed body on her hand. Together they face the congregation, and Mala—feeling more than a little silly—announces, "Hello. Uh, greetings. I am Mala, from Kans… um, Rocky Knoll, and I come in peace."

Okay, so that was Dorothy mixed with earthing landing on Mars. And stupid sounding. At first, there's no perceptible reaction. The same drone of batting wings continues, the settled dragonflies stayed settled, and the king/queen holds court on her hand.

Then the cooing begins. Starting from what is clearly their leader, it spreads out like a wave, until the air fills with the dove-like sounds, all varying in pitch and coming from every angle.

The weight on her hand lifts as the lead dragonfly rises above the rest, flitting away from Mala and then back again several times. Mala suspects this creature expects her to follow, for each time it approaches, it's little—but big for a dragonfly—head tilts as those teal eyes bores into her own. It darts back toward the wood line so similar but different from the one on the other side of the door.

Wait. The door.

She's been so enthralled by her discovery she forgot all about the door and Jaime waiting behind it. How long has she been there? The sun seems to be in the same place as when she first arrived, but it *has* to be later. She reaches for her cell phone in her cargo pants, only to realize she'd tossed it in her backpack before crawling through the hole earlier. And her backpack sits as slumped over as Jaime probably is by now on the other side. She has only one correct choice. Return to the other side to get Jaime, so he can see the amazing sights, too.

"So, I'm guessing you want me to follow you, huh?"

The cooing amps up a notch in reply.

"That sounds like a yes. Thing is, I've got to head back, over there, through the door, and get my friend Jaime. He's gonna freak when he sees…."

The sentence dies on her lip as she turns to point out the doorway. It's not there, where she thought it to be. In fact, it isn't *anywhere*.

"No, no, no, no, *no*. Not happening."

Classic fairy tale slash fantasy novel rule number one. Never Lose Sight of the Portal. And what does she do? She *loses sight of the portal*. Great. She squints into the open space where the doorway should have been, then she remembers those pictures that, when looking directly at it, appeared to be thousands of dots. But if you *un*focus your gaze, you see the shape of whatever you are meant to see. So, maybe that's the trick to seeing the entrance. *Or exit, depending how you look at it*. Mala lets her eyes drift off and stares into the distance.

Nothing. Nothing appears in front of her eyes, nothing appears in her peripheral, nothing at all except for what seems like miles of tall grass peppered with bursts of Goldenrod, Black-Eyed Susan, Chicory, and Cornflower, plus wild flowers she doesn't recognize in shades of crimson, violet and cotton candy pink.

Had this been her point of view on the *other* side of the door, she'd see the long row of brick face that is her apartments breaking the horizon, with only their multi-colored doors to distinguish each connected unit. Her family's apartment faces the field while Jaime's—whose apartment unit is around the other side—is not. However, since she is now on the other side of the door, it matters not one bit. There is no sign of any man-made structures here.

The dragonflies, whose unusual cooing now sparse and hushed while she turned away, peps right up again sounding like a field of miniature owls as soon as she turns back to them. Their behavior reminds her of old Max, and how his tail would wag, thumping against any nearby object the moment anyone made eye contact with him.

The head dragonfly hovers as Mala struggles with her internal debate. Perhaps she should stay here and hope for Jaime to come through once he became impatient enough to come after her. But what if he *can't* get through? All *he* saw when he stumbled upon the door was a bark interior. No shimmering curtain, no other side, just the inside of a tree. Oh, and spider webs.

"Well, I've always wanted an extraordinary adventure. I mean, it's, like, *all* I've ever wanted." She takes a deep breath and exhales. "So, lead the way little Dragonfly boss."

Needing no further encouragement, the big little dragonfly gives what sounds like a coo of relieved exasperation, as if Mala is a stubborn toddler it has to coax into doing what's expected of her, and arcs back once again towards the forest. As for the attentive audience, well, they seem exuberant. Their movements—dashing up, down and all around, hovering then zig-zagging away, all while buzzing and cooing—seems a good sign.

Though they get close, none are as courageous as their leader. They are still unsure what to make of this foreigner, and though curious, have a shy reserve. Mala must resist the natural impulse to swat at anything that buzzes too near and let them inspect her. She decides the best way to gain their trust by ignoring them.

She'd done the same with one of the many stray cats in the neighborhood years before. That one had found its way into a storage unit in the shared basement of the apartments. Mala and Jaime often snuck down there for no other reason other than that they could.

A heavy rain fell in torrents, rolling thunder and lightning bolts illuminated the sky, keeping them stuck indoors. They figured an old-school game of hide and seek was in order. Mala had found one of the storage units had no lock, making it a perfect spot to hide. She went in, closed the wire mesh & wood framed door behind her, and felt her way to the far corner of the bin. While there *was* light in the basements, they were often either dimly lit, or the bulbs had burned out and needed replacement.

There was a cloth-draped armchair, and Mala sat on it, curled her knees up to her chest and tried to make herself invisible. Her hiding spot was excellent. Jaime would have to give up and call her name out, but she'd make him wait until he stood in front of the chicken-wire door, when she could jump out and scare him.

A few minutes after Jaime shouted out the required *'ready or not, here I come'* warning, and in the silence that followed his footfalls—in the wrong direction—Mala heard a small noise. It was the sound of something breathing wetly. Like a miniature version of the sound their neighbor's six-year-old makes when breathing through one of his constant colds. The sound repulsed and scared the daylights out of her. She nearly jumped up from the chair and ran out the storage bin screaming, but then she heard its pitiful meow.

The skinny mewling kitten was skittish and distrustful, but also starving for food and attention. Every time Mala moved towards the timid feline, it receded further into the shadows of boxes and dust covered furnishings, only to peak out again with shy curiosity. Forgetting all about Jaime, Mala sat down on the cool concrete floor, angling away from the kitten, and staying still.

Within minutes, the kitten—lurking in her peripheral vision—stepped out of the safety of the shadows on wobbly paws and sniffed the air as it approached Mala's bent knee. A few minutes after, two white booted paws pressed down gently on her thigh. Next, the scrawny black and white kitten purred and jumped up to nudge Mala's chin, begging for affection. By the time Jaime's footfalls echoed off the concrete walls of the dim corridor, huffing and muttering *this was the last time he'd play this childish game with her,* Mala had already named him Boots.

Using memory as her guide, she decides these winged creatures are not unlike the kitten, and need time to warm up to her, so she disregards them and instead keeps her attention on the rest of her surroundings.

The scarlet flowers that resemble poppies mingle and sway with the tall grass catch her eye most of all, tempting her to reach out to pluck one. She bends closer, hearing the cackle of the Wicked Witch's voice in her mind.

Poppies, poppies will put them to sleep.

Their broad silky petals and ink black centers perch on delicate fuzzy stems. Mala notes they are much larger than any poppies she's ever seen, and though the centers of each are the same color as the ones from Botany class, these have small, yet distinct matte-black heart-shaped faces. Two shiny, round, black eyes sit above a lavender bowed mouth.

Mala's brain is not computing what her eyes see, and she wishes to stop and study the strange flowers, but it's clear the dragonfly wants her to press onward and into the forest. Perhaps, she'll pick the next one she passes and inspect it as she walks. She reaches out and…

"*Coooo.*"

This is *not* the gentle soft sound of earlier, but a loud exclamation followed by the intense buzz of beating wings. Mala jumps away, jerking back her hand to her chest. The luminous dragonfly makes several forceful flight patterns, from left to right, right to left, forward and toward Mala's face, then away and in front of the ruby red flower, then repeating the dance once more.

No explanation needed. The movements and meaning behind them clear. Do Not Touch the Flowers. Mala doesn't need to be told twice. She is not the girl in every horror flick that goes up the stairs and toward the scary sound. Nope, Mala is good with heeding warnings from a strange creature in an unfamiliar realm. Or is it another universe? A parallel one, maybe? Since no one is talking here yet, she has no way of knowing.

Giving the flower one more glance as she passes by, her jaw drops at the sight of the sweet little heart-shaped face scowling at her. Would it have bit or stung her? She has no desire to find out. Mala continues to follow the dragonfly toward the familiar yet different forest, and she takes her first step over the natural threshold of branch and bush, under the swaying canopy of weeping willow. Or its parallel universe counterpart.

Dorothy's voice in her head announces, "Now I know we're not in Kansas anymore."

11 Odd Everwood

Well, this version of Everwood is a winner for strangeness. At home, Mala has never seen weeping willows *inside* the forest, they hold a lax sentry *around* the perimeter, sure, but mingle in with the oaks, pines, and cypress? Never. Over in not Everwood, they dominate the woodland. Their draping branches still display the deeper green leaves of summer, rather than those on the other side, whose leaves are now a golden yellow and beginning to drift to the ground.

While the golden etched dragonfly weaves and zooms between the long branches with ease, Mala must often part the pliable wood strands so she might pass though. If the buzzing chief feels slowed or hindered by her less agile pace, it gives no sign, and forges ahead, alighting on branches and peculiar shade flowers until she catches up.

It would be a lie to say she is unconcerned about her situation, or that she's entered the forest with no misgivings or trepidation. But, if every single one of her books, stories, and movies has ended well, then why wouldn't *hers?* So, she sets her mind to enjoy the unexpected adventure, and will worry about finding her way home later.

The sights and sounds of this new forest keep her head on a swivel, and she longs to stop and inspect every detail and nuance, and curses herself for leaving her phone behind, and having no chance of taking photographic proof.

Not that she'd share it with anyone other than Jaime. She's read enough to know how the story would go. She'd share the amazing pictures of a magical land, people would go nuts and invade and destroy it with their greed and pollution, and this beautiful untouched place would become a wasteland of tourist attractions and vendors selling trinkets and trash emblazoned with things like, 'My Grandma Went To A Magical Land, And All I Got Was This Lousy Shirt'

Or maybe:

I Left My 🖤

In Magic Land

Along with spinning light-up toys made in China and sold at a three-hundred percent mark-up, balloons shaped like colorful dragonflies—the likely trademarked symbol of the newly inhabited land. No, she will not cause this untouched land's destruction.

Though she has yet to spot any living creatures—besides the dragonflies who seemed to lose interest in her and droned about their business elsewhere in the forest—she suspects their presence. The rustling of leaves and slight snaps of twigs under foot tells Mala she's not alone.

Once or twice she felt certain she spotted the telltale flash of something, perhaps a deer, from the corner of her eye, but when she turned, it was gone again. If even there.

She guesses she's been walking a while; an hour or more, yet the sun hasn't shifted in the sky, and still peeks through the swaying branches, causing the light to flash and flicker. Mala had dressed too warm for the weather on this side and has to remove her ratty thermal in favor of her simple black tank top. She keeps moving as she peels off the outer shirt, then knots it around her waist, all the while marching along and parting branches like they are curtains.

In this wood, there are actual paths, ones worn away to the dirt below. They stretch out in every direction, winding their way out of sight and around different bends. The long-branched willows are dispersed between oak-like trees blanketed in silvery sparkling moss. It reminds Mala of a picture she once saw of a famous southern plantation lined with majestic Spanish moss-covered oaks, and whose heavy branches form an arch over the mile-long road. She'd obsessed over that photo, and ones like it, fascinated at how the gnarled branches twisted and fought their way up to receive the sun's rays, adorned with strands and curls of gray moss, like they were elderly high society women, raising a toast with arms laden in jewel crusted bracelets.

Ever since she was a small child, she's loved trees and imagined the people they'd be. For instance, her beloved crabapple tree was like a pouting teenager with two of its thickest limbs crossing each other in an act of defiance, while all the other taller branches grew wild. The line of pine trees, once doubled as her pirate ships, made her think of a line of sentries standing an imposing guard against intruders. Their own lone weeping willow reminds her of a wise and ancient wizard, under whose shelter she'd hide and gaze up into with awe when she was little, writing wishes on strips of lined notebook paper, folding them into small, tight squares, and leaving them wedged into the bark, in hopes the Willow Wizard would grant them.

Though the bits of square paper vanished each time when she returned, her wishes never came true. She sighs at the memory, then smiles. Here she is, walking the woods of a magical forest on the other side of a magic door. Her biggest wish of all has come true.

12 Fine, I Believe

At first, Jaime stares dumbstruck. Jaw-dropped, wide-eyed, and straight up struck dumber than dumb by what is before him. Well, what *isn't* before him. Or anywhere near him. He looks around the small space. Had he closed the door as Mala had done, he'd find himself squashed without enough room to turn around. But he has no intention of closing himself in there and doesn't care if it makes him a chicken.

He does, however, tap on the bark facade, first up high, then low, then all around, listening for a hollow sound somewhere that might reveal a hidden passageway. It is the only logical explanation. He exits the small dank space, drops the backpack down on the ground, and walks to the left side of the door. It is a tremendous, broad tree trunk whose lowest

73

limbs curve all around the door, and whose whip-like branches twine with its neighbors on either side.

She must've somehow snuck out.

The twin sentries are so wide in circumference that even with Jaime's long arms, he cannot put them all the way around. He searches for access through the thick overgrowth of the quasi-closet and acknowledges he's never seen trees like this one anywhere else before. Dispersed among the surrounding bushes and shrubs, are every thorny vegetation he's ever known, and ones he doesn't. Holly and wild rose, thistle and blackberry, and others he guesses Mala can name, if she wasn't playing a childish revenge game and hiding from him.

It is like a wall of foliage, determined to keep him out. Funny enough, he doesn't recall it so formidable earlier. Yet another mystery of the Everwood. If Mala is behind there somewhere, she realizes the only way back unscathed is through the door again.

Resigned, yet somewhat triumphant at the last thought, he returns to the open door, and debates whether to wait her out, or bang on the walls insisting she come out. Jaime checks the time—*crap, four percent battery life*—it surprises him to see it is past three a.m. In an hour, the sky will be lighter, the stars dimmer, and the moon fainter.

They need to wrap this up and head back home, pronto. Jaime gives the wall several fisted thumps, accompanied by a curse-peppered warning he's had enough, and is leaving with or without her. No response.

"Okay, I warned you. Here I go… One… two… three… I am NOT kidding here. Four… five… six… I swear to God,

I'll leave you here to walk back yourself. Seven… eight… nine…

SLAM

Okay, more like a *whoosh* and a solid *thunk* than a slam. Regardless, the result is the same. Jaime is closed inside the weird closet, in the dark, in the middle of the forest, with less than four percent battery life, and two backpacks holding two flashlights, *outside* the door. Why? Because he hadn't planned on shutting the door and being trapped in the dark in a space where he couldn't turn without smacking an elbow or a knee.

Blindly—he is not ready to use up his remaining battery life—he gropes the damp walls and turns an awkward semi-circle until the rough wood of the door grazes his fingertips. His hand slides down for a door handle. All the while, he listens for Mala's laughter to come from the other side. The moment he is out from the claustrophobia inducing space, he'll lay into her for this latest prank.

The problem is, there's no laughter from the other side, nor is there a door handle. Just deafening silence and weathered wood. *Well what the…*

"Hello?"

This is ridiculous.

Even as he rams the door with the side of his body, he knows it wouldn't open. Just as he knew—before they'd even left the lamp lit sidewalk and crossed the parking lot separating the apartment complex from the field—that going to the Everwood in the middle of the night was a shitty idea. In his same trying-to-be-calm way, he understands Mala is not playing a game. She is not there at all, but somewhere *else*.

When they were younger, Mala had indoctrinated him into her fantasy world, so much that he'd even believed in the possibilities. But then they grew up and put away those silly notions. At least Jaime did. He'd locked away every childhood dream and tale Mala had planted in his head a long time ago.

He'd buried them down deeper and deeper into his subconscious with each passing year, and his Spock-like logic overrode his secret hope that magic was real, that Mala was right all along.

He *thought* he'd thrown the key away many years ago, accepting the world was as it appeared at face value. Sure, there are beautiful things, moments and places. He appreciates all of them, perhaps more so than expected of a teenage boy, but *magic*? Magical places, with magical creatures?

It can't be.

Or so he has told himself, all while indulging Mala's flights of fantasy and wild imaginings. She has trusted him with her wishes and dreams, and he knows too well what the mockery and ridicule from someone you love can do to your soul. He will not be the spoiler. He will not take it all away from her, not dim her light, or allow anyone else to do so.

And so, this is how he finds himself. In a closet-like space in the woods, in the middle of the night, trying to make sense of something which makes no sense at all. His tendency towards logic fights against a small voice in his head— Mala's—saying, *just believe.*

Jaime hears her, "*C'mon Jaime, just believe with me,*" like she's beside him.

She never said, '*pretend* with me.' It was always *believe.* So, Jaime tries. The moment he does, he felt a tingle, a small burst of elation, a lightness… a *letting go* and giving in he's not experienced since they were small children. A time when he would follow her lead—with reservations, but still follow—and she would take him on grand adventures fueled by her imagination. God, they had so much fun.

A slow smile creeps across his face, and Jaime shakes his head in willing defeat. He waves the white flag and accepts what Mala has sworn to believe all along. He is so lost in his revelry he doesn't comprehend what his eyes are seeing, or rather that his eyes *were* seeing. The utter blackness of seconds before has changed from charcoal to thunder cloud gray, from gray to fog. It isn't bright, but there is now some visibility where before there had been none.

Once again, he shuffle-turns, his arms folded against his torso to spare himself more painful whacks. Once turned, he stares in astonishment at the bark... or what is left of it. The cracked and rough wall is no longer. Instead of solid immovability it shimmers and wavers in and out of focus, revealing glimpses of field and perhaps more forest on the horizon.

Jaime raises his hands, holds his breath, and presses his fingertips to the wall that is only sort of there. There is first the firm coldness of the tree and then nothing but warm air as his hand passes *through* it.

As if scalded, Jaime jerks his hand back in shock. The wall solidifies, and the tiny space darkens again.

"No, no, no... Hey, hey. I believe, I do seriously, I do."

All bravado gone, his defenses stripped, and his acceptance of the surreal tangible, Jaime *believes.* For the first time in a long time, he believes in magic. As if on cue, the room brightens, and the wall becomes transparent again. Risking no further hesitation, Jaime stretches his right hand though, then his left. The image of Frankenstein's monster comes to mind. He toes one boot over the line, and while holding his breath again, he ducks his head and pushes through the opening, praying it wouldn't switch back while he is midway through.

Jaime—all of him, is through to the other side of the doorway. He looks about the field, expecting, or at least hoping, to see Mala. Instead-to the left and to the right-he sees more of the almost knee high tall green grass in which he stands. It stretches out for miles, and runs parallel a forest just like Everwood, but yet different. He turns to look behind him. His gut tells him the door will not be there, and it is right. Jaime is already playing by what Mala would call "Fairy Tale Rules," and the rules of any fairy tale are:

1. Expect the unexpected
2. Anything can and will happen
3. Things are rarely what they seem
4. Magic is everywhere
5. Doors are usually portals and will probably disappear leaving you stranded in a strange land all by yourself.

Okay, so the last one isn't one of the rules but it fits right in. Jaime half expects flying monkeys or a talking rabbit to run by, but it seems for the moment at least, he is alone with his thoughts.

He imagines Mala's reaction, equal parts exuberant triumph and awed elation, and smiles. How he wishes he could've seen her face. He'd offer a '*yes, yes, you're right and I'm wrong*'. But what she *wouldn't* have known? He is glad to be wrong. Though he never admits to her, she'd enthralled him with her daily regaling, and it saddened him when stopped.

Like all children, there had come the point when they stopped believing in all those things children accept as true with wide-eyed, wonderful innocence. It happens at about the same time girls develop and boys *notice* them develop. Dolls and superhero toys go into storage, while posters of musicians and celebrities go up on bedroom walls. Girls sneak their mother's lipstick and the boy's voices crack. A time of abject awkwardness and confusion.

For Mala, shutting down that part of her life was like someone trying to slam a door against a windstorm. The wind kept trying to push against the door to open it, and she leaned back just as hard so it couldn't. Still, dust coats the bookshelf, figurines sit untouched, movies unwatched. But like the figurative windstorm outside the door, her attachment to those mementos of childhood gone has never died. They've laid dormant, waiting for their revival.

Their discovery vindicates her; her proof she isn't wrong or silly, and everything she dreamed and hoped for *is* real. Mala's wish of all wishes has come true. There is only one problem Jaime needs to solve—aside from a missing portal—and it is... Where *is* Mala?

13 Big Birdie

Despite the thrill and exhilaration of the strange unknown land and its inhabitants, exhaustion seeps in. Mala's now been up for over twenty-four hours, and it is catching up to her. Her eyes feel sandy, her steps are sluggish and robotic, but still they press on at her little insect friend insistence.

When she can walk no further, they hit a spot where the paths fork. One route winds around the most breathtaking lake (or river; she can't see where it leads) with sparkling water in a shade she equates to robin's egg blue.

Trees that look much like those oaks she'd seen in pictures grow close to the banks, their moss laden branches reaching out low over the water. On many of those drooping and gnarled limbs perch bright lemon-yellow birds that call to mind Great Herons or egrets. As she stares, slack-jawed and awestruck, one of these fabulous yellow birds alights and takes flight, making its way across the lake. Mala hears the heavy flap of wings as the bird comes toward her. They sound like the flick of a wet blanket on a clothesline in the wind.

It lands at the edge of the bank nearby. It hasn't spotted her yet; its long beaked head is bent, and it navigates the bank's uneven terrain. Mala stands as still as her tired legs will allow.

The closer the bird comes, more of its body is in view. It is much bigger than she first realized. It is—thanks to both long legs and the long graceful neck holding up its downy head—almost as tall as Mala.

Mala, despite her resolve to remain still, takes an uncertain step backward as the giant yellow bird approaches. It is less than a yard away, and still not looking at her. She looks for the mighty dragonfly, but it has disappeared, leaving her alone and uncertain with yet another unusual creature to contend with.

From the orange and black-trimmed beak comes, "All right, love. Here we are. Shall we get on, then? Oh. You're not Merris. Curse my eyesight. Now, who might you be?"

Mala, with her volumes and volumes of fairy tale, fantasy, and fiction readings under her belt, does what comes naturally. She faints. When she comes to, she believes she is in her bed, wrapped up in her down comforter. If the twitching and ruffling of the 'comforter' doesn't set her straight, then the piercing blue eye staring down at her does.

"'ello, now. You won't be dropping out on me again, yes?"

There it is again, the funny tutting grandmother voice, coming out of the long and pointy beak of the huge bird.

Despite her disorientation, or perhaps because of it, Mala laughs as the Sesame Street theme song pops in her head the moment she thought 'big bird'.

The bird conveys a multitude of emotions. Confusion, concern, dismay, and more than a hint of impatience. So, despite still feeling out of sorts, Mala sits up to discover herself cocooned her within two downy wings, her cheek up against the billowy chest of the great egret-like bird.

The bird waits for her to say something. She stammers. "Oh, no, no—I'm okay now. I—you just, well, I wasn't expecting you to speak."

The bird jerks her head back and tuts, "Well now, wingless one. What'd you think, we haven't our manners here on the Mere? Someone putting an ugly word in your ear? I'll have you know we Audris are a class group. Not like those *lower* Audris down in the Tarn. No, *that* lot hasn't a single manner to split between 'em."

Mala struck a nerve. The last thing she wants to do is offend a sharp beaked, talking creature in the middle of a magic forest, with no way out and nowhere to go.

She apologizes. "Oh, no, not at all. I meant, well, where I come from, birds don't talk like people do. Well, *some* birds can talk, but they only repeat phrases, not, like, have conversations. I think your manners are lovely."

At this, the mollified bird puffs her chest out more than what seems possible. In fact, she's outright jolly, and totally over the perceived insult to the Audris of the Mere, as she called her kind. Mala loathes to announce they've not introduced themselves to one another, for fear of mortifying the proud bird in their mutual etiquette fail, so she instead takes the blame for the oversight. Mala *did* cut her off mid-speak when she'd fainted, and the bird had attended to her so well, it is likely she had been mid introduction when Mala *dropped out* on her.

"So sorry, I-I think I fainted before I caught your name. I'm Mala, by the way."

Gesturing with one long wing, as if to say 'a*ww, come, now*' motion, she laughs—a most unusual sound, something between a twitter and a caw—and say, "Oh, right. Right you did, indeed. I'd just about gone and said we should get on with it, saw you weren't a'tall who I thought you were, an' when I went to tell ya my name, *Blat*. Down you went. I had half a mind to laugh, I tell you, but like I said, we Audris of the Mere are a mannered bunch, we are."

Mala stares at the Audris. After a pause, which involves the bird trying to stifle another twitter and caw at Mala's expense, she hops.

"Oh, right, right. Yes, now, my name is Ardaelie. But you can call me Ardie, everybody does."

Mala nods. Ardie gives another long-winged gesture, this time to say, 'come along'. With slow deliberation, the Audris marches her wide webbed feet back down the riverbank, and Mala trudges along after her.

Once at the bottom of the ledge—which is steeper than she expected—she sees the water is even more stunning up close. With her boots touching the lapping water, she spies schools of colorful fish darting about under the surface. Fascinated, Mala bends closer to catch a better glimpse.

Though nothing should come as a surprise to her anymore, she startles when a plump little fish breaks the surface below her down turned face and gazes at her with wide puppy-like gray-green eyes.

"Well, hey there, little guy. What's your name?"

She speaks to the little blue and orange striped fish, who wags its hind fin, once again reminding Mala of an excited puppy. A raucous burst of laugher—caws and twits—erupts behind her. She turns to see several of the large yellow birds congregating behind her.

"I say, Ardie, I say. Does she think it'll answer her?"

Caw, caw, twitter, twitter.

"Imagine that, would ya. Talking guppers. I never. Have you ever?"

Caw, Caw, Cawwww, Twit, twitter, twitter, twit...

"Aw, now looky, we're embarrassing the funny girl-bird. Enough now, enough."

The caws and twitters die down to snickers and snuffs, but Mala still feels put out. How is she supposed to know who talks over here and who doesn't? And did Ardie call her a bird-girl? Time for wide-eyed wonder to take a back seat and get some clarity.

"Um, excuse me? *Excuse* me?"

Their laughter subsides. The bickering and bantering like a bunch of old biddies screeches to a halt. Another time, maybe, their raucousness *would* have amused her were she not the source of their entertainment. More so—were she not so mad—she'd have laughed at the comical expressions on their pointy faces. Until she'd raised her voice, they'd forgotten she is standing there at all.

They all freeze in place, staring round eyed at the bird-girl. A few mutters of w*ell, I never* and *impolite, her kind* are sprinkled with several *right, right's* escaping from behind their wing covered beaks. Audris are terrible at whispering.

She waits for their grumbling to stop with her hands on her hips and a raised eyebrow. Jaime—if he were there with her—would've announced to the gaggle of tall birds, *Uh oh, now you've done it,* at the sight of that arched brow.

In a gentler tone than she feels like using, she says, "Please excuse me for shouting. I'm not from here, so I don't know who speaks, and who doesn't. I didn't know there were biting flowers here. I don't know where I'm supposed to be going, how I'm supposed to get there, and I *definitely* don't know how to get back to where I came from. So, if you'd be so kind as to help me out here, I would be most grateful."

Okay, so her tone is not as gentle as she tried to make it, and her inflections are sharp, even to her own ears. But she is tired. Exhausted. And as thrilling at this exotic and beautiful place is, she is in it alone. Being tired, alone, and lost—even when in a magical land—can wear on a person after a while.

"Oh, now," tsks, Ardie, "the poor dear isn't at all right, now is she? Let's get you settled in for the night, right now?"

They all begin a new chorus of *tsks* and *tired, is all* followed by directives and orders to *fluff it up good and right for it, now. Right, right* as they busy themselves with preparing... a nest. For *her.*

"Oh, I—did you say, *for the night*? It can't be later than noon, right?"

Again, intent on their own conversations, they take no notice of Mala. She sighs and gaze at the clear blue sky. The sun is overhead still, the cloud that had threatened to mask the sun when she'd first arrived, is long gone. Night does not look likely to be falling any time soon, based on that sky. Still, a quick *nap* can't hurt, can it? And, she must admit, that nest looks inviting.

14 Not Impressed

Like Mala, Jaime assumes that the only way out is *in*. As far as Jaime sees, there isn't another living thing around for miles. He hears no buzzing, no chirping, no rustle of leaves or telltale snapping of twigs under furry feet. He seems to be alone.

He notes the differences from back home. A midday late spring/early summer sun high and warm overhead, tall emerald grass leading to a forest flush with shades of green, and wildflowers abound. The odd sight of willows leading into the wood makes him grin. He bets Mala has delighted at those elegant wistful branches as much as she had the one at home.

Home. He had known without turning back to look the door was gone. That's the way these kinds of things went in Mala's fairy tales, isn't it? It's not a question of going back, at least not yet. It's a question of where Mala is, and is she safe?

The most probable direction, knowing her as he did, is into the forest. Therefore, it is where he heads, looking first left, then right, then left again, as if readying to cross a street, and not through an empty field. Or rather, a tall, grassy, wildflower filled field that stretches to either side of him for what seemed like an eternity. But other than *that*, empty.

He looks for signs of previous travel, but no remnants of trampled grass or disturbance of any kind are visible. She may have come through some time ago, or perhaps not at all. Jaime bites his thumb nail. What if the doorway leads to some place different for each that opens it? It happens in some of those stories, so why not this one?

He shouts. "Because *this*, this is not a *story*. This is *real life*."

If he expects a reaction or a response, he remains unrewarded. Still, he surveys the field for signs of life, noting only on closer study the centers of the little red flowers— *Poppies, you Neanderthal*, Mala's imperious voice inside his head—dotting the landscape resemble little angry doll faces. But that freaks Jaime out, so he doesn't stare long.

He's so busy ogling and contemplating that it is with sheepish embarrassment when it dawns on him to call out for Mala. However, now that he *has* thought of it, he feels foolish. What if she is right behind one of those huge sentry-like willows, watching him and giggling as she waits for him to do something like that? He envisions her doubling over with laughter, mimicking him, and asking if he's scaredy-cat, afraid to go into the woods.

Nope, nope, and nope. He will not fall into her trap, not this time, damn it. He is going march straight into the forest and find her and then get them the hell out of that place. Because Jaime has already learned some not so nice nuggets of wisdom long before the tender age of seventeen. Nuggets like: Anything that looks too good to be true, probably is. And his favorite: Believe nothing of what you hear, and only half of what you see.

Sure, the last one doesn't seem to apply *yet*, given there has been nothing to hear, but time will tell. Now is the time to make his way towards those willows, and into the woods that lay beyond.

15 The Greenwood

Mala, despite having felt silly climbing into a giant bird's nest, gives only the most perfunctory resistance to the motherly nudging of the group of birds as they direct her to the down and leaf filled nest. The bunch who'd been boisterous, are all gentle murmurs and ruffling, coaxing the overtired girl to take respite in the sun-warmed nest.

As Mala curls onto her side in the plush feathery bed, the lazy summer sounds of the forest envelope her. The cicadas—similar but louder—sound like tiny alien spaceships with their slow & steady crescendo. The delicate chirp of small birds and the irregular buzz of insects all became a soothing lullaby.

The birds stop speaking and perch along the perimeter of the nest, surrounding the near-sleeping, blonde-haired human.

Each plump yellow creature, while standing on one long leg, unfolds their expansive right wing, touching their neighbor. From above, it must look like a bright sunny yellow umbrella, but underneath, only a few filtered rays sneaking through the sparser wing feathers, with bits of dust catching like sparkles as they drifted through the hazy beams, resemble more of a dome tent.

Once they complete the chain, each bird tucks their considerable beak under their still folded left wing, and within moments all she hears from the cocoon-like bedding is the gentle hushed sounds of breathing, occasional sighs, and at least one not-so-dainty snore.

As Mala drifts into a deep sleep, her last conscious thought is of a childhood memory. Unlike her older brother, Mala loved nap time when she was little. The routine was soothing in its familiar regularity. First, lunch while watching reruns of old television shows. Peanut butter and jelly, with a glass of milk, or grilled cheese and tomato soup. Then her mother would shuttle her off to her bedroom, lower the shades and turn down her covers. Mala would hop in and get sandwiched between the cool sheets, wiggling around until they warmed from her body heat.

Once tucked and settled, her mother closed the door until only a sliver open. Through the crack Mala listened to the mid-morning game shows and the clink of plates and glasses as her mother washed them in the kitchen sink. Sometimes she overheard her talking on the phone over the other sounds, or the gentle knock on the back door followed by hushed laughter that meant Jaime's mother had come by for a cup of tea and gossip.

In those days, Jaime's dad was still around. He'd lost his job and was home during the day a lot. This, Mala gathered from eavesdropping, and not from Jaime. He never talked about his father, and both he and his mother spent a lot of time avoiding him. Mala only remembers him as being a tall, handsome but cold man who rarely talked and smiled even less.

Jaime's mom visited with Mala's mom, and his dad stayed in their apartment with him. According to Jaime, he read the comic books stashed under his mattress and never napped. He and his dad didn't spend that time together bonding. Each would stay in their respective part of the apartment until the front door opened, signaling the return of the mother and wife, their buffer.

Over in Mala's apartment, things were different, yet somewhat the same. Her father worked long hours, but when he was home, the mood in the small apartment would change, going from fun and light to tense and quiet. It was no wonder the two women bonded on that first day of their children's kindergarten class. Sharing a mutual but unspoken discontent, relieved by a couple hours a day of laughter and conversation while their children napped, was probably what got them both through those long-ago days. All things that a six-year-old child wouldn't understand.

All *she* knew at six was that she *loved* to sleep. Even with all the household noises, Mala always napped because she loved to dream. Almost always, she had vivid, epic imaginings that, upon awakening, she'd had a compulsion to recreate them in drawings, or as she got older, in writing.

So, as she sleeps like a snug gosling in the feathered nest, strange but befitting dreams flit through her mind. Birds as small dragonflies, dragonflies as big as birds, talking flowers, Hoggle, from the movie Labyrinth guides her down the yellow brick road, and the wizard from Harry Potter appears as the Great and Powerful Oz. None of which rouse her from slumber.

What wakes her is the part of the dream where she'd been mowing the lawn dressed as Big Bird, the steady drone of the lawnmower buzzing louder and louder until she startles awake. There is an actual buzz, but not that of a lawnmower. It's the golden trimmed dragonfly doing an aerial dance in front of her face with the deliberate intention of waking her.

"I'm up, I'm up."

Thpppittt.

A bright yellow feather sticks to the corner of her mouth, and she sputters and swats it away, looking about her surroundings in confusion at waking in an unfamiliar place. The dragonfly disappeared as fast as it had appeared. But before she gives it much thought, the sight the bird wing-canopy above her head distracts her. The feathers, leaves and nest, are enough to bring back to mind all that had transpired, and she jumps up, rousing the still sleeping birds.

At once the nest is a chaotic cacophony of wings squawks and caws, *beg your pardon*'s and *do you mind*'s as they bump and topple over one another. It's comical, yes, but for Mala— who is central of their bedlam and getting batted in the face by a flapping wings, being knocked about, and even stepped on by stumbling webbed feet—her funny bone is not tickled.

Once again, she struggles to gain their attention. They are busy admonishing each other for clumsiness, poor manners, and general all-around faulty birdsmanship, so she yells. "Hey."

She gives them no chance to start their litany of etiquette reminders and launches straight into talking business.

"Thank you for your attention. Now, I need to know where I should go, and who it is I need to see, so I can find my way back home. Oh, and what *is* this place? Can any of you help me with that, or not? Ardie?"

Again, with their overlapping chatter, they try to give suggestions, ideas, and recommendations at once, sounding like game show contestants on Family Feud, each shouting out their best answers for the team leader. Mala silences them with her hand like a traffic cop.

She looks again to Ardie, since she'd been the first of their kind she'd met and waits.

"Oh. Oh, well, right, right. I suppose I could bring you on down to see the Pond kin. Though I can't say how much help they'll be. Not to bright, you know, and fewer manners than smarts, bless their feathers."

Mala doesn't know what or wherever on earth this *Pondkin* is, but she is glad for any kind of progress and movement since she still has no answers to the many questions in her head. She tries again, starting with the simplest question.

"So, where are we? And what are Ponkins?"

She regrets asking. As predictable with this lot, they all blab at once, each trying to talk louder than the next, none offering an answer to her questions, but repeating them in various forms.

From one. "She wants to know where we *are*?"

From another. "What kind of question is *that*?"

Several. "Where we are, right, right."

And then a different one. "Ponkin? Did she say Ponkin? What in the…"

Back to the first one. "I say, what does she mean by that, I wonder?"

Mala's patience ends. She is done, finite, bye-bye crazy birds. Without another word, she pivots on her booted heel and walks back up the embankment.

Near the top, she hears, "I say, I say. She's gone off an' walked away, right, right."

Another. "Oh, how rude."

Another one. "Not even a good-bye."

"Now, now," says Ardie. "No need to run off. No need. Be a dear and let your Ardie show you the way, now."

She slows enough to let the flustered bird catch up. Thanks to her long spindly legs, Ardie is by her side in seconds, her wide triangular feet patting the ground with steady *twacks* as she matches Mala's pace. She gives the bird a curt nod but keeps walking despite having no clue which direction to go.

"Ehh, er- you may want to follow that path over thataway, there. If you wish to pay a visit to my kin over in the Pond, that is."

Oh. Pond kin. Not 'pondkin'.

Well, that makes more sense. Curiosity overrules her intent to hold a grudge, and she asks Ardie all the questions she's been dying to get answers to. From her, Mala learns that the baby blue colored body of water they were leaving is named the Great Kaleidi Mere, the largest (but not only) body of water in what they call the Greenwood, the fraternal twin to her and Jaime's Everwood, it seems.

"Now, we, over in the Mere, are the Audris of Mere, and my kin are the Audris of the *Tarn*. The Mere is much bigger than the Tarn. There's a-a few minor… distinctions."

At this, Ardie darted a nervous side eye at Mala, who is too busy being enthralled by the exotic insects and smaller, hummingbird-like birds flitting about close by her, so she added a muttered, "But nothing of any concern, no, none whatsoever."

She continues, saying that the two Audris differed distinctly. The Audris of the Mere are elegant and graciously mannered specimens of beauty, whereas the Audris of the Tarn are a step above savages. At this, Mala smiles, but says nothing. She's already had a taste of what Mere bird manners are about. How much worse can Tarn birds be?

After what seems like hours the sun is *still* where she first saw it. Despite her best explanation of what 'time' is to Ardie, she stares at Mala with those pie round eyes as if she's daft. All Mala can surmise is time is different here.

Ardie at last announces, "Well, now, well now, here we are."

Only there is no pond, or lake, or lagoon. Just another enormous droopy willow smack in front of them. Puzzled, Mala looks from Ardie to the tree and then back again. Ardie looks at Mala, and tips her long beaked head at the tree's mighty trunk.

"G'wan then. Peoples first."

Mala offers an arch smile to the anxious bird and waits out her protestations and deferments until she runs out of words and agrees to go ahead. Muttering under her breath— and with an exaggerated blasé attitude—the great Ardeil-something teeters toward the willow, but instead of stopping once she reaches it, she keeps going. Mala cringes, expecting the hard thud that is about to occur as bird meets bark, but both the ancient looking bark and Ardie shimmer, just as the tree wall had done when she came through the door in the Everwood. Surely, nothing can surprise her anymore in this strange land. She is wrong.

16 TURTLEDOG

If Jaime knew the adventure Mala is having and could compare it to his own—or his lack of—it would disappoint him. Sure, it is crazy and pretty cool to be in some kind of weird alternate world, and yes, he is pretty impressed by it all. But he's been wandering through the strange forest for what feels like hours. Although, he has no way of telling. His phone battery has long since given out, and the sun seems to have not moved an inch since he first stepped over into the foreign clearing on the other side of the now gone door.

He is getting hungry, and as the initial adrenalin rush at finding himself in unknown territory subsides, exhaustion is setting in. Unlike Everwood, this forest has many paths that wind and twist every which way. There is no signage, so he follows his best guess and lets his feet guide him, for lack of a better idea.

Jaime figures, after a time of guarded suspicion, Mala will not be jumping out from behind any of the many willow trees that line the dirt paths, or any other tree. It's not in her nature, nor her ability to postpone a surprise for longer than a few minutes.

No, it's clear to Jaime that he must search for her, and only hopes she is not in danger. It reassures Jaime for the moment to see nothing as he looks around. For lack of a better idea, he sits on a large humped boulder and stretches his tired legs out in front of him. He tilts his head skyward, hears and feels the stiff muscles in his neck pop, and closes his eyes against the sun sneaking through the green leaves and spindly branches.

The sun warms his face. It's a pleasant contrast to the cooler forest interior and Jaime can't help but smile. His skin prickles and the hairs on the back of his neck rise at the sensation of being watched. He's experienced that feeling enough over his school years. He has almost a sixth sense for it and doesn't doubt for a moment that it is real. Jaime rights himself, not wishing to startle or alarm who or whatever is watching him.

Without warning, the boulder beneath him shifts. The unexpected movement topples him backward, and he lands on his back. His long legs lean against the boulder, pointing upward. Dumbfounded, sore, and with the wind knocked out of him, Jaime watches the boulder move again, away from his supine position and toward the path.

A turtle. That is his first impression until it turns to face him. What Jaime sees next might only be believed by Mala.

Rather than the face of a turtle—as he'd expected—the 'boulder' has the face of a dog. Or at least, that is the closest creature it resembles, with its long furry gray ears, round doleful gray eyes that look down a stout little snout, complete with a shiny black nose. It's dappled gray feet are furry, dog-like paws, with wide pads like a basset hound.

Jaime and the turtle-dog blink at one another. Jaime can't presume to know what it's thinking. So, he does what he imagines Mala would do in the same situation. He introduces himself. "Um, hello there, little—err, big fella. What's your name?"

Tinkling laugher erupts from the surrounding bushes, from above in the tree branches and from behind their broad barks. The dog-turtle blinks again. Jaime jumps up, twisting this way and that, searching for the sources of the laughter. It sounds like the laughter of children, and along with the boulder guy, it is his first encounter with anything or anyone alive since crossing over the threshold of the strange doorway.

"Who's out there? Come out and show yourselves. I promise, I won't hurt you."

More laughter. *Okay, I guess they're not afraid, then.* Maybe *he* should be afraid, but then, those are the sounds of children. How frightening can they be?

As if in prophetic answer to his question, Jaime feels a sudden poking sting, like that of a large bee, on the small of his back. Before he turns and swats it away, a small voice announces, "None of that, big one. Stay put if you know what's good for you."

"Easy now, buddy, easy. I'm not here to hurt you."

Jaime attempts to pacify the little person. Or whatever it is. He reminds himself of the rules and regulations of fairy tale worlds. There *are* no rules and regulations. Again, the sounds of laughter, now bolder and louder, ring out from the forest. The boulder-dog blinks at Jaime.

"Okay, okay. Guess that was funny. How about this, you don't hurt me? Let's try this again. My name is Jaime. Now who might you be?"

From behind the tree closest to Jaime comes another of the small voices.

"Mateo, he looks harmless enough. I think you can relax now."

At once, the incessant sting at his back ceases. All around him emerge small upturned faces, calling to mind a scene in one of Mala's favorite movies, The Wizard of Oz, when the munchkins revealed themselves to Dorothy at the Good Witch's persuasion.

However, these are not the faces of small adults, they are the faces of children who look only ten or twelve, with some looking as young as seven and eight. They also are not the brightly clothed, jovial villagers of Munchkin Land. These small people appear disheveled, cloaked in combinations of furs and leaves, and wear cautious yet curious expressions. Parts of their exposed skin—arms, legs, necks and faces— have a fine coating of delicate green moss, like that growing on the trees in the forest, but lighter in density. It justifies Jaime's failure to notice them. They've camouflaged themselves to suit their environment.

"We will see, Aedina. We will see," states the gruff boy at Jaime's back.

He turns to the boy the way a fugitive faces a SWAT team. The boy—Mateo, they called him—eyes him, unsmiling.

He repeats the girl's—Aedina—declaration. "Hey, there buddy. Your little friend is right. I *am* harmless. See, no weapons. Nothing."

Jaime stretches his long arms out on either side of his body, turning his hands over. *See, nothing in my hands*. Still, the boy steps back, raising his spear, as Jaime now sees it to be, as if expecting attack.

"I am not this buddy you say. I am Mateo of the Virescent, Guardian of the Greenwood. My 'little friend' is Aedina, leader of the Guardians of the Greenwood."

Jaime resists the urge to laugh at the solemn boy-man, his haughtiness has lost some of its effect with the childlike quality of his voice. It is like being scolded by Mala's six-year-old next-door neighbor. Although, the neighbor never carried a sharp spear, Jaime is quick to remind himself.

Mustering as much reverence as possible, he gives a curt nod to Mateo, and a sweeping bow to Aedina as he announces, "Good day to you all. I am Jaime of… um, Everwood, Senior of Rocky Knoll High, and I come in peace."

Okay, so that was a bit of overkill, but they seem impressed. Or at least, accepting. Tiny Aedina, with her long auburn hair and almond-shaped eyes set in a pixie like face, approaches Jaime, much to Mateo's obvious consternation. She stands waist high of his tall frame, yet still has a commanding presence. He had been mistaken and misled by their size; she is older than what her stature suggested, and likely the same age as Jaime even.

She, too, holds a hand-crafted spear, however, hers bears a rawhide string holding several feathers of various shades and patterns. They dangle and wave in the breeze she creates as she stalks around Jaime.

As she circles him on her small bare feet, Jaime remains still, following her only with his eyes. The rustle of leaves and sticks all around him and the dozen or more greenish children tensing their now visible spears serve as fair warning. They are not playing.

"Tell me, Jaime of Everwood, how is it you come here, to the Greenwood?"

Jaime explains how he arrived through the strange door—noting the quick darting glance Aedina shoots to Mateo—and then tells them of Mala, in hopes they have seen or even met with her and can bring him to her.

"We have not seen your Mala. Tell me again. This *door*… what does this mean?"

Jaime, surprised at first by the question, describes it the best he can.

"A door? Oh, a door is—well, it's made from wood. Like a tree, you know? And um, someone cuts down a tree and uses the wood to make a rectangle shape that opens and closes, and like, separates one place from another."

He is about to explain what hinges and locks and doorknobs are but stops at the collective gasps and expressions of horrified disbelief on the faces of Aedina, Mateo, and the few greenies who've peeked around tree trunks.

"You *kill* trees?"

Aedina asks in the same way one would ask if you murder puppies, so Jaime is quick to clarify,

"Whoa, whoa—not me. I don't kill—trees. *Other* people do that, not me."

Aedina eyes him with skepticism, then strides toward him, spear pointing up and under his chin. He retreats, taking small steps backward, until the boulder/turtle/dog's solid presence behind his legs stops him. It seems the odd animal has exhausted itself by walking ten steps and is now asleep in the middle of the pathway.

Jaime totters, then plops on the back of the boulder/dog/turtle, waking it with a *oof* and a grunt. He watches, frozen, as it extends its long neck, bringing its wet snout right to Jaime's stunned face, and sniffs; once (wetly), twice (wetly again), and a third time (very, very wetly). Deciding Jaime is friend not foe, it licks his face in a sloppy, turtle-dog kiss that both repulses and amuses Jaime. He laughs despite the danger he senses with Aedina's sharp spear still aimed in his direction.

The bizarre creature takes his laugh as invitation for more soggy attention and licks his face—and hands since Jaime had raised them in self-defense from the exuberant onslaught—in earnest. Once Jaime wards off the beast, he notices all eyes are on him.

17 AEDINA

Aedina, despite her outrage at Jaime's callous disregard for the life of a tree, can't help but chuckle, too. The sight of the handsome giant as he laughs and struggles against the affections of his new friend amuses her, and she studies the human with a less hostile eye. Perhaps this oversized being is as harmless as he claims to be, or perhaps not. Either way, Aedina intends to find out.

She waits a few moments longer, enjoying Jaime's mixed delight and disgust, then releases a sharp whistle and declares, "Murphius. That is enough for now."

The boulder/dog complies with slow obedience, tongue hanging out of his grinning mouth and floppy ears perked at the sound of her voice. Jaime stands, sputtering and swiping at his wet face with exaggerated dramatics. Aedina lifts a hand up to stop his thanks for rescue and presents him with a conditional offer of help.

"Jaime of Everwood, Senior of Rocky Knoll... High, I welcome you to the Greenwood. As Mateo mentioned, we are the Guardians of the Greenwood, and we invite you to join us in our return home. Come with us now, rest and eat. After we will help you find your Mala. Murphius will gladly join you on your travels, I believe."

Aedina smirks as she ignores both Jaime's uncertainty and Mateo's scowl, and walks ahead, secure that all will follow her, just as they've always done.

Though she isn't arrogant; she knows she is a capable leader to her companions, that the Elders have chosen her with a confidence gleamed after much watching and testing of her. She has proven herself as the fastest, most nimble hunter, and a compassionate and patient community member. Who else to bring in the wildlings and encourage them to adapt, then one who once was a wildling herself?

These are the thoughts inside her head as they trudge along the forest floor. Truth is, Aedina is trying to convince herself that the human is safe, and that bringing him to their shelter is a reasonable idea. For the first time in ages, she is unsure. She *likes* the human. Mateo, who knows her well, senses it. She knows *him* as well and senses his doubt and mistrust of both the human and her judgment in bringing him into their refuge.

But Aedina also suspects Mateo of jealousy over the big human boy, who is so different from them in every way. Another, more guarded truth—one that she admits only to herself—this found human is just the distraction she needs from the swirling thoughts that have been her constant companion.

The pull of the wild tugs at Aedina. The freedom, the abandon of all that is ordinary and familiar. The routine and constant presence of the Virescents and other Guardians make her feel captive once again, confined by their need and dependence upon her for guidance and training, and for *survival*.

A sigh escapes Aedina's lips, and from the corner of her eye, she sees the human boy—*Jaime*—looking at her profile. Beyond him is Mateo, with his permanent scowl as he stares hard at Jaime. All around them, in the trees and through the thicker parts of the Greenwood, are the sounds of the rest of the Virescents moving from branch to branch, tree to tree, under and around brush, following their leader without worry or fear for what is next. Worry is their leader's burden, and fear of the human is laughable compared to the fears of the beasts that will soon come again.

With an eye to the sky, she hurries her pace, encouraging the others to do the same. Even with his long legs, the boy is not as agile as they are, although he seems sure footed. Still, Aedina doubts his ability to scale the treetops with any proficiency. She has to stifle a giggle at the image that pops into her head—the clumsy mammoth supine on the dirt, Murphius sloths away, his expression—but the repressed chuckle becomes an involuntary snort of laughter that breaks the silence.

"May I ask, mighty Aedina, what's so funny?"

Jaime stops in his tracks, a bemused expression and cautious smile lighting his face, affecting her with in a most unexpected and unfamiliar emotion. Aedina, for the first time, is flustered. So flustered, in fact, that she didn't realize that she is staring up at the crescent scar deepened by his smile. He lifts his hand to it.

"My scar, hmm? It's a doozy, I guess. I fell out of a window when I was small and—oh, a window? Ah, well, that's a square thing, with glass, and it's in a hou—umm, never mind. I fell. A long time ago, and this is my reminder, in case I ever forget."

Aedina nods at his strange story, understanding only that he was uncomfortable. This puzzles her, as the Guardians view scars as marks of honor and pride. She has many and can give the story of each one. She gathers the bulk of her thick hair and pulls it aside, showing him her most pride worthy mark. A once angry jagged line courses the length of her ribcage, from underarm to hip bone, now as silvery and taut as the one on his face.

Jaime lets out a slow whistle and reaches to touch the scar, an impulsive move that mortifies them both. From behind, the ever-watchful Mateo makes a guttural sound yet says nothing. Instead, he catches Aedina's eye and motions for her to come to him.

Aedina, ever the stately leader, withers him with a cool stare and only lifts her eyebrow—in a gesture that, to Jaime, is very Mala-esque—to say she is not his to command. Mateo, duly chastised by a mere glance, approaches the pair, cutting his eyes in Jaime's direction, who gave another regal bow and stepped away to give them some privacy.

She watched, wearing a slight smile, as the gangly human sauntered over to old Murphius, who greeted him with delighted licks and snuffing. But her smile faded into a frown as she turned back to Mateo, her irritation clear.

Through gritted teeth, Mateo whispered, "Why are we helping him? His kind cut trees, for Ray's sake."

Aedina resists the urge to strike him, though her hand flexed and clenched with the temptation. Instead, she used her calmest, most condescending voice.

"Well, Mateo, we are not *yet* helping him. We need to know more about him and his kind. The Elders have passed down our laws and rules for ages. Bring back any willing wildling, forage for food, and should we come across a foreign being, we must bring them to the Elders. Or have you forgotten?"

The hard set to Mateo's mouth turned from a scowl to a frown. He grunted his assent and reclaimed his place. Aedina returned her attention to Jaime. Based upon *this* human, his kind could never be a Viscerent, let alone a Guardian. If all his kind lacked the stealth inherent to a Guardian of the Greenwood, then they'd never survive the rigorous tests and trials put to them. Let alone survive life in the Greenwood. Plus, his skin is the strangest color. Not a trace of green. How odd.

Those thoughts led her to wonder how it is Jaime survived in his Everwood. Surely, he could not hunt with any success. His heavy footfall would scare everything with fur away for miles. Though, she had to admit as she observed him, he did not appear starved. No, Jaime, Senior of Rocky Knoll High—whatever *that* is—had not gone hungry in his wood and had even managed to cloth himself in strange, dyed skins unfamiliar to Aedina. Perhaps the Elders would know these ugly odd garments and might shed light on how not one, but two humans had slipped into the Greenwood.

The Elders, with a wisdom gained over their many years, had told Aedina of humans in existence. Then, they bound her to uphold the Oath of Unspoken Promise, as each Chosen One swears to at the at the Acceptance. The Unspoken Promise is that last in a series of vows taken by a leading Virescent, and it is a promise to go to the Elders if ever they encountered a human. Aedina would do one better. She would bring one to them.

18 New Friends

"What the…" Mala blinks away the mud to see a flurry wings and cackles before her. She flips over onto her back and raises her arms to shield her face and head from attack, and when none comes, she lowers one arm and peeks out. Many pairs of marble-round, pale blue eyes stare from tilted downy heads, down long pointy beaks at her.

Lowering her arms, Mala surveys her surroundings and assesses her situation. What just happened? One moment she is pressing her hand against an ancient willow—one that Ardie had disappeared through seconds before—and the next she is face down in mud and muck with beating wings and flapping beaks all around.

"Well, I'll say, Ardie ole girl. You sure brought us a funny looking bird, now didncha?"

Again, with calling her a bird. What is wrong with them? Have they never seen a person before? *Oh. It is more than possible they haven't.*

"Oh, now, now, give it some space, will you? Scarin' it half to death. Ardie, dear, does it talk?"

Mala gathers her wits and sputters, "Of course, I can talk, and I am not a bird. I'm a *person*."

A few gasps and *oh, my*'s erupt from the crowd, along with some knowing head nods and nudges accompanied by *tsk, tsk*'s.

"Now, now, cousins. Remember your manners. Right, right. Give the person-bird some air."

Ardie's ministrations causes the rest of the birds to step back, but not without the over-talking and blustering that Mala realizes as their natural behavior.

"Says she's not a bird."

"Not a bird? Indeed not, I suppose…"

"No, no, those wings haven't a feather to speak of."

"Person? What kind of bird is that?"

"Not one I've ever seen the likes of, right, right."

"Don't ya listen you old hag, she says she's NOT a bird a'tall"

"Who're you calling an old hag? I'll give you old ha…"

And with that, they set off again in a flurry of wings and beaks, batting and swatting one another. Ardie is in their midst, and Mala *still* sits in mud, dazed, confused, and filthy. This is *not* how she imagined a visit into a fairy tale world. Not. At. All.

She brushes herself off as best as possible, and tiptoes away from the chaotic scene toward the nearby path. It is not the same one she'd been on, on the other side of the tree bark, but does it matter at this point?

It isn't until she's rounded the bend that follows the Tarn, that she no longer hears the cacophony of the arguing yellow birds, who look only slightly different from Ardie in that they were smaller and paler. Otherwise, they are just as oblivious, ill-mannered, and loud, *and* useless in helping her.

***

As for Ardie, once she notices the strange bird-girl gone, she shrugs her winged shoulders and mutters, "How rude. Well, I hope the little bird-person went back to the Mere side. No telling what she'll meet up alone on the Tarn side," before abandoning her atrocious relations and their ill-bred foolishness for the soothing calm of the Mere.

Giving a doubtful glance behind her, the great yellow bird waddles back through the willow trunk herself, and on toward the Mere without another glance. Audris are notorious for their forgetfulness, and Ardie is no exception.

***

Mala has already stopped thinking about the crazy Audris, too. After a wary glance at her surroundings, she kneels at the edge of the pond and splashes water on her face and arms. Her mud-caked clothes will have to wait; Mala is not stripping down to her underwear here, no way.

There is much to see along the Tarn, more than she had during her walk to the Mere, for certain. The smattering of deceitfully delicate red poppy-like flowers in the clearing are now in abundance around the Tarn, and they sway in her direction as she passes by. This time, Mala is mindful to keep her hands away, wary of their bite. Or might they sting? Either way, she has no intentions of finding out; the ivory and gold dragonfly gave clear enough warning.

Finally, she spies fresh proof of life. *Thank God.* She's had enough of rude birds and cooing dragonflies. A small cream-colored rabbit hops and totters across the path and twitchs its nose at Mala, who's stopped in her own tracks to gape at the cute bunny so unlike the wild rabbits of home with their drab dabbled gray/brown fur. This plump little rabbit is anything but plain. Throughout its creamy coat are flecks of gold from the tips of its ears to the fluffy tail on its backside, and the eyes, so familiar in their startling teal coloring, observe her.

The rabbit waits for her, so for lack of a better idea, Mala walks toward the wee creature. As she approaches, one hand out as peace offering, the tip of its nose and long whiskers twitch again as it sniffs the air.

The dragonflies from the field, or at least similar ones, buzz around, alighting on flowers and hovering over the gray-blue water of the Tarn. Birds of different varieties call and sing to one another, and she even recognizes the familiar harrumph of a bullfrog hidden in the marshy bank. The rabbit is silent and motionless, save the slight twitching.

"You know, what, bunny? You resemble a certain little dragonfly I met earlier. Same coloring, same eyes. Coincidence, or not? Well, guess what, buddy. I don't believe in coincidence."

Something else is at hand here. It *is* a magical land, so they *can* be the same. Mala has already witnessed enough impossibilities to prove her theory true.

"Um… hello? Do you, uh, talk, by any chance?"

She darts glances all around to see if anyone is watching her talk to a rabbit and hopes she doesn't look foolish, like she did when talking to the fish, thanks to Ardie and company's mocking. A flick of one long velvety ear and the sight of the rabbit's backside as it hops away answers her.

With a sigh, she rests her hands on her hips and looks around. The rabbit, though further away now, sends her twitchy side eye glances as it nibbles on the tall yellow-green blades of grass along the path. Across the pewter-colored Tarn, water bugs and mosquito dimple the surface, along with the exotic dragonflies hovering and zipping about. The willows and oaks dip into the edges of the still water, large sleeping and preening birds upon their twisting branches, and the endless mid-day sun shines down. Her first impression is it's a serene and beautiful place; the kind where curling up against a shady tree with a book or peaceful thoughts is made for. But it is almost *too* still, too quiet. As if on pause, waiting for something.

This is also a place of strange sights, hidden dangers, and the *unknown*. An odd sense of disquiet envelopes her, and all at once Mala considers perhaps it is all an illusion. What if this peaceful looking haven is not what it appears? Here, trees are sometimes portals, and birds communicate— excessively—and dragonflies coo like doves and flowers bite. So, there *has* to be more than what meets the eye in the Tarn.

Her gentle reverie and wide-eyed awe turns to a suspicious eye and doubtful study of all that looks innocent. Is she being watched?

In the back of her mind, the voice of Jaime's mother speaks up, as clear as if she is standing behind her. In classic Peggy style—or at least the Peggy style that developed after she kicked Jaime's dad out and began taking self-defense classes for which she became certified in and taught—she states, "Know what, Buttercup? Trust your gut."

Peggy, at only five feet tall, has fast become the neighborhood's resident badass of the apartment complex. She is the one the other women go to for advice, pep talks and all-around motivation, and Mala is no exception. She's even taken Peggy's self-defense class—using Jaime as her sparring partner, much to his chagrin—and passes along what she's learned to the younger girls in the apartments, earning her high praise from Peggy.

Peggy starts every class with, "Know what? Trust your gut."

The only time she ever varies that saying, is when she says it to Mala, who'd she'd always called Buttercup. She tells her story—the condensed version of it—to every new group of women she empowers. She met a tall handsome man when she was an inexperienced girl of seventeen. He was on the quiet side, didn't seem to have a lot of friends, and his family wasn't close. Peggy was just the opposite, and she convinced herself that she could get him to come out of his shell. She was wrong. Her heart wasn't listening to her gut. Her gut insisted he wasn't right, and it sent her lots of red flags and signals she didn't want to hear.

Next thing she knew, she'd moved away from everyone she loved, married to an increasingly angry man, and raising a little boy mostly on her own. She saw her family on holidays and birthdays, and only if they came to her. Peggy became someone she didn't know and didn't much like either. Then one day, she woke up, looked at her boy—handsome like his daddy—and all her love for him came out like the sun through the clouds after a day of rain, and she thought *no more.*

There is a lot more to it than that, but she keeps it to the point, and her point is always *trust your gut.* So, Mala does exactly that. She trusts her instincts, and they tell her all is not what it seems. She is being watched.

As if on cue, a cloud—the first she's seen since her arrival through the door—passes over the sun and the temperature drops. The change agitates the placid birds. Several fly off in a huff and noisy flap of wings and beaks—Mala is certain she hears cries of, *I never* and *right, right* from across the water— and a strong breeze blows cold through the trees, strong enough to whip the long strands of hair that come free of her braid in front of her face, obscuring her vision.

She gathers her hair to secure it again, but the sight that materializes before her stops her. It is the biggest, blackest bird she's ever seen. It stands as tall as her, with eyes as black as coal, wings and body blacker than night and as shiny as satin. The only spot of color on the enormous bird is its beak, which reminds her of fire.

Mala and the ebony bird eye each other. She with trepidation and fear, it with a sly and knowing side-eye stare that further unnerves her. Everything around the Tarn has either gone silent or disappeared. Even the mosquitoes and water bugs vanish. She takes this in while not taking her eyes from the massive creature who hasn't looked away from her.

A grating, frigid voice punctures the stillness.

"Human."

It is both a question and a statement, coming from everywhere and nowhere. The vulture-like bird never moves, its beak never opens, yet the voice comes from *him*. Though the voice is inside her head—it sends reverberations through her ribcage—it is a word spoken like a beat of a drum.

Her voice shakes. "Y-yes."

The horrible yet lustrous bird remains statue still. After a pause, it says, "Girl."

This time, Mala nods yes in response. She asks, "Who are you? *What* are you?"

A pale, almost transparent eyelid swipes across the black eye. It speaks inside her head, "Friend."

Another voice, in another part of her mind whispers, for the second time, "Know what, Buttercup? Trust your gut."

The voice that sounds like gravel and ice inside her head grinds, "*Friend.*"

The coarse sound is loud enough to make her wince and take a step backward, inciting the bird to mirror her movement. It takes a wide step forward with one thick webbed, sharp clawed foot as it ducks his head and narrows his eyes. There is menace in those eyes, no mistaking. It frightens her, and fear makes her anger surface, and she reciprocates his stance. Her arms tense and bow at her sides. Like the warrior Peggy had taught her to be, she is ready to battle, even if she does not wish for it.

Almost comically, the vulture-like creature jerks back his downy ink black head. Though he does not back away, he approaches no further. They stood their ground, waiting for the other to make the next move.

"Girl. Them."

She does not understand what this means. She blinks and the vile creature takes a jerky step back as if stung.

Inside her brain, the scraping whisper again. This time, it is less commanding. "Girl. It. My."

Through gritted teeth, she hisses back, "Go. To. Hell."

At that, the girl-sized beast opens its beak for the first time, revealing a shock of red mouth, from which it emits an ear-piercing caw. It echoes across the Tarn. As much as she wants to recoil from that ugly mouth, gaping at her from only a mere two feet away, she stands her ground and glares back at the atrocious creature.

With a great gust and flurry of its immense wings, it rises from the ground, fanning the powdery, sickly sweet stench that emanates from its body into the air. The thing glares a last hateful look at Mala and flies off toward the once again cloud-free sky, beating wings as long as Jaime is tall, and sounding like boat sails in a powerful wind, cracking and snapping.

Mala watches the bird fly up and away until the sun breaks away from the single dark cloud and blinds her. When her eyes adjust, the creature is out of sight and heaves a sigh of relief. It is only then she felt her legs buckle and her blood race up to her eardrums. Her heart pounds in her chest.

Looking around—now with a suspicious eye—she notices the winged monster's departure has signaled to the Tarn inhabitants that it is safe to return. Gradually the birds fly back to the tree branches, the insects resume their water dances. All the while, the sun shines down. From across the way, Mala spots two animals that looked like a doe and her fawn approach the water's edge. As the fawn drinks from the still water, the doe watches Mala; ears pricked, and body tensed. When Mala makes no movements, she takes a quick drink.

Closer by, on the bank near her, a turtle lumbers out of the water, not giving her any discernible attention as it attempts to scale a fallen log jutting out over the water. After watching the slow struggle for a few minutes, she scans the area the deer were, but they've already gone. They, along with the awkward turtle, are the first normal things she's seen since crossing into this strange place and she is sorry to see them go.

The water itself look cool and inviting. Mala has an urge to wash her face and hands. She approaches the water, kneels, and leans forward. Her reflection in the still surface startles her. Her eyes. They are not their green hazel color, but teal. She springs backward, away from the water's edge, and scrubs her eyes with her fists. When she dares to look again, they are back to normal. She must have imagined it.

Sure, that's what happened. You imagined it.

Mala ventures another look around. It is as if the episode with the vulture never occurred at all. Mala has no one to acknowledge it to—even if just to say, *can you believe what just happened here*—or to pat her on the back for her bravery, and there is nothing but the smell lingering in her nostrils to prove it. Except...

One black feather, wide as her hand and blacker than black, lying stark against the green grass. The grass underneath has turned brown and crisp, as if burned from the contact with the errant feather. Though it repulses her, part of her wants it for a souvenir—proof of her time here to show Jaime and add to her bookshelf. She reaches to pick it up and—

"I wouldn't do that."

A small, solemn voice, coming from a distance. Mala looks up, then around. There is no one. Had she imagined the voice? Perhaps it is her inner voice, warning her from danger? She looks down again at the feather, this time with a doubtful expression, biting her lower lip.

"I'm tellin' you, you'll be sorry if you do."

Again, the small voice, sounding like a miniature version of a tired old man. Again, her head jerks up. Then around. Nothing.

I'm not in Rocky Knoll anymore.

This time, she looks *down* and around.

The source of the tired old man voice… is a bullfrog. Leaning on a toadstool, standing upright, his flat webbed feet planted on the ground, and his big pale belly paunched out like a green Santa Claus, no less. Mala laughs. And laughs and laughs.

All the while, the bullfrog observes the hysterical, funny looking creature and waits for her to regain her composure.

He wonders if this is one of those mythical humans he's heard tales of, and decides if it is, it's nothing like what he's imagined. *Much* less stately than one would've thought if one were to believe in human tales.

Once she regains her senses, she sits down, or more like plops down beside the bullfrog, and says, "Well, hello there, talking bullfrog. How do you do?"

"And hello to you, talking… human? I am called Adalbert, and I do just fine, thank you. You are…?"

"Ahh, Adalbert. Well, Adalbert, I am called Mala. And, yes, I am a human. Pleased to meet you. Do you prefer Adalbert, or Bert, or…?"

"Oh, Bert'd be just fine, just fine, indeed."

They chat about the weather (*quite nice, isn't it*) and the beauty of the Tarn (*oh, lovely indeed*) and even blueness of the sky (*ah, such a delightful shade of blue, for true*).

"So, Bert… what's up with that feather and the nasty beast it belonged to, hmm?"

At this, Bert fidgets and darts glances skyward and sideways, scratching at his neck with long knobby webbed fingers, then at his shiny head. When it appears as though he will not answer, Mala draws out his name, like she does with Jaime when he's dodging a question.

"*Bert…*"

"Ahh, oh. Yes, the um, the… oh? Right, the, ah, beast, as you called it? Ah, right. Nasty business that one. Best not even speak of it, you know. Come now, you must be tired, after all your adventuring."

Adalbert pushes off the toadstool with a great *harrumph* and, using his small waist-high stick, hobbles bow-legged toward the path, making a wide berth around the feather still lying in a patch of dead grass, not glancing in its direction.

Mala, despite his assumption that she would, does not rise and follow along, and instead stares at him as he totters away, He is talking the whole time.

"Suppose you might be hungry…"

"Mind you step, there…"

"Pesky biters, the red fellas…"

"The missus will round you up somethin' tasty I'm sure…"

"… though I'll not be supposing you care for cricket stew."

"… merciful, it is warm today..."

"Now do you…"

After about a few yards, the curmudgeonly bullfrog realizes she's not answered a single question, nor is she even following him.

"Well, I say. Human, have you gone daft on me? Look, here. The missus is expecting us. Well, me at least, and you don't want to keep the missus waiting, if you know what's good for you."

"Bert," begins Mala, "I've come through a magic door into a strange world, been led into the forest by a giant dragonfly, harassed and insulted by talking yellow birds, fallen into a puddle of mud, nearly attacked by a creepy humongous black bird, and now I am *talking to a toad*."

By the end, her voice has risen to an unnatural octave. Bert's wide mouth puckers and purses several times as he draws himself up to full height—all impressive fifteen and one-half inches of it—puffs out his throat and releases a low baritone honk. Or moo. Well, something in between the two. Either way it is loud enough to startle. The bullfrog slaps one flat, webbed hand over his plentiful mouth in dismay, and his already round green/gray eyes stretch rounder.

His thin lips quiver as he tries to regain his composure and keep *his* temper. As she's about to learn, calling a frog a toad—and vice versa—is high insult indeed.

In a shaking voice that borders on croak, he stammers, "Madam human, I will have you know I come from a very long and distinguished lineage of Bullfrog. I served on the Seven's council, as did my father, my father's father, and his father before. Perhaps, wherever it is you come from, Bullfrog mix with common toad, but we do *not*, thank you very much."

Well, there it is.

Just when she thought she'd seen it all, two-legged walking, old man voiced talking, crotchety bullfrog is, of all things… a snob. It gets crazier and crazier here in not-so-Oz or No-Flippin'-Way-Land, or whatever they want to call this place.

She swallows all this down, apologizes to the bullfrog, and agrees to follow him to heaven knows where to meet God knows who and eat whatever the hell they feed her.

19 THE VAGUE

It stares out from blackness… at nothing. It *feels* nothing. It is nothing more than hunger and thirst. It has no eyes, has ownership of no form. It borrows from the minds of its prey. It is everything indiscernible—a taste that defies description, a smell familiar but implacable, a sound pleasantly unpleasant. It is utter apathy and disinterest. Until the girl, that is.

To the *It, Human, Girl*, it appeared as a giant black vulture-like bird. Something from a childhood nightmare that her conscious mind had long forgotten. The Vague, in its wretched way, has a talent for absorbing and using hidden or forgotten fear. When they see the reflection of that fear it paralyzes them. At least, it is supposed to.

She is not afraid. She didn't look away, in fact she stared into the blackness with an intensity that made the Vague… *feel*. What *is* this 'feel'? It accesses the thoughts with something akin to a mathematical mindset. Having no heart, no soul, no body to speak of, the Vague cannot, *should* not feel. It is an *absence*, not a presence. And yet…

"Human. It. Girl."

It tastes the words.

"My."

A pause. Aloud, into the air, "It. My. Human. Girl…"

The Vague has the word for its feel. *Want*.

20 JAIME

He admits it, he likes it in the Greenwood. It is beautiful, serene, and—though he'd never use the word aloud—enchanting. Aedina, when not ready to stab him with her spear, is pretty cool, too. Even kind of cute for someone who is a little green. Literally. When he asks Aedina how old she is, she gives him a puzzled look, and he has to explain birthdays and aging. The conversation is odd and not very enlightening.

"So, um. Every year—that's, like, twelve months—you get another year older. And you have a party to celebrate, where you have cake and get presents and—"

Aedina blinks at him.

"What? No? Nothing? You mean to tell me you don't know how old you are? Any of you?"

Jaime sweeps his arm wide to extend his question out to all the Greenies (*ahem, Virescent*) he both sees and cannot see up in the trees, behind trunks, and bushes as they follow Aedina and cranky Mateo toward their home.

"We have not this *birthday* you speak of. We are just here, each day of Rays, each day of night. We have celebration when the day of Night has gone and when we return from a journey. This is all."

Day of rays, one night? Must be their way of saying day and night. Although, it *does* seem their days are much longer than his. The sun remains locked in its place where it had been since he'd arrived, with only a couple passing clouds.

"Ok, but when you were a baby, and your parents—"

She interrupts. "What is parents?"

Oh boy.

"What *are* parents. They're um, the people who raise you, you know? Like, they bring you into the world and love you and take care of you."

Though baffled and skeptical of Jaime's testimony, Aedina nods. She processes everything he's told her in silence. She stops with a question on her lips, and when she does, everyone stops with her, including Jaime. The only one who fails to notice the halt in their procession is Murphius, the boulder-turtle-dog who is now Jaime's best friend, trailing at his heels as they make their trek toward the Virescent home.

His rock-solid shell bumps up against Jaime's backside, sending him sprawling for the third time. As he rights himself, the sloppy tongue of the funny beast catches him square in the mouth, causing him to sputter and gag. The wood alight with laughter—giggles and outright guffaws from some—at Jaime's revulsion and comical pose. Their conversation forgotten, Aedina reaches out a strong, helping hand.

Not for the first time, Jaime notices her copper-colored eyes matches the sun streaks in her hair. He is discomfited by their steady gaze.

It is Mateo who breaks the momentary spell with hissed whisper. "Ahead. Guardians, be watchful."

Faster and quieter than Jaime would've thought possible, the Virescent all make themselves invisible by blending with the environment. All save Aedina and Mateo who, with rabbit quickness, band together in front of Jaime. All three see the flaw in their maneuver. He towers over both, obscuring him from whatever is coming not at all.

He feels absurd being protected by two people small enough for him to rest his elbows on their heads, but his heart thunders and his hands are damp in expectation of what is coming. He has no idea what else lurks in these woods, and is not keen on finding out, based on their palpable tension.

The moments tick with only the steady sound of Murphius' panting alternating with low wheezing as he looks up at each of them. Jaime is losing his sense of urgent alertness as the seconds keep passing with no sign of anything amiss.

"Um, guys? I don't think there's anyth—"

"*Shh.*"

Reprimanded and silenced not by one, but two little green hued elf-like people.

Great. Bet the girls back home would really have the hots for me now if they could see this.

As he muses over the scene playing out in his head, a sudden tremor in the air—like a wave of heat without the actual heat part—stops him cold. He looks up, out toward the path before them in time to see a sight hard to describe.

The path—all of it, trees, dirt, rocks, and bushes—ripple like a still lake after someone tosses a stone. Rings of air emanate from the center, expanding as they spread out, and then vanishing. In that central point, where the rings were most concentrated, a shape solidified. Something like an elephant's trunk pokes through. It wiggles and flicks from left to right to test the air. It snaps to center—the exact location of human boy, Virescent lad and Virescent leader girl—recoiling as if smelling something foul before sniffing harder.

Though Jaime tenses more at the freakish sight before them, he notices the other two lower their spears and wear matching amused expressions. He, however, is not ready to drop his guard, saving his trust for proof of good intent from the creature still deciding whether to come through the opening it had created.

At once the trunk like appendage retracts, almost disappearing into the ripples. But before Jaime can blink, the entire enormity bursts through with a dainty 'pop' sound. The momentum sends the beast forward, almost on top of the three—well, two. Jaime has backed up—and would have crushed them had it not come to a graceless stop.

Jaime's head cocks sideways at the animal. It has a trunk like an elephant, only shorter. It slopes up to a head most like a rhinoceros—complete with a horn perched between long-lashed eyes—than anything else. The body is a whole other story. It is hippopotamus-like in its girth and mottled pink coloring. It resembles a composite of all three pachyderms, mixed up as one intriguing beast.

"Hel-*looooo*! How are my darlings this fine day of Rays?"

It talks. Of *course,* it talks. Also, it talks like the fat lady from the opera with a head cold, because how *else* would a large, hippo-pink, elephant-trunked, rhino-horned creature speak? Jaime is near reaching the exhaustion *plus* magic overload induced hysteria.

In fact, the only thing keeping him from losing it, is Aedina, whose copper-penny eyes are watching him. He will *not* lose it in front of her, and not in front of moping Mateo, who waits and looks for any opportunity to make him look foolish in front of her.

Obviously, the little green guy is in love with her; anyone with eyes can see *that*. It's easy to see how any guy could fall for her. Sure, there is the obvious. She is beautiful, even with the greenish skin tone. But for Jaime, there just is nothing more attractive than a strong-minded, confident girl that does her own thing instead of following what everyone else does.

He supposes it is because Peggy Cromwell is his mother. She had the courage and tenacity to get them out of a bad situation, away from his dad, despite being afraid and alone in the world. Peggy made a life for the two of them by the force of sheer will and determination. Considering that, how can a girl whose biggest worry is whether her lipstick matches her dress appeal to him?

What drew him to Mala is *her* tenacity—something he also calls it stubbornness and pig-headedness. A carefree girl whose peers call her strange, or weird, whereas he sees the truth. She is unique and unafraid to be herself, regardless of what others think or say. When they were little kids Jaime once imagined her as a warrior in search for battle. It is an image that never quite disappeared from his mind, and he pities whoever's misfortune it is to become her foe.

Jaime knows he is fortunate to have such influential females in his life. Peggy has never shied from telling him how proud of the steady kind-hearted man he is, and Mala—for as much as she teases and torments him—loves him. If she is his warrior, then he is her rock steady—if not reluctant—cohort.

However, her reluctant cohort would dismay and embarrass Mala now. He hasn't made a single move since the apparition solidified into actuality, and is in fact, rooted to the spot.

"Eh, what's wrong with that fellow? Is it sick? Ahh, and *ahem*, what exactly is it? Does it not speak? I do say, it's rather large to be a Guardian, yes? Oh my, it's lost it green as well? Dear me."

The strident blast of verbiage from the short trunked animal ceases. It takes a deep, wet breath and continues. "What on Greenwood is it *wearing*? I've seen nothing like it. Have you? No, no you haven't. Where are you taking it? Oh, my, it hasn't been taking *you* anywhere, I hope. Should I be frightened? Oh, in a thousand Rays, I never thought I'd become a captive. I am a delicate soul, as you can see. I just cannot be—"

Aedina, who's been looking back and forth between Jaime and the blabbering creature, has had enough. "Camillia. *Milly*. Stop, stop, it's all right. Everything is all right. We are not being held captive, nor are we holding him captive. This oddly adorned one is Jaime, he comes from…" Aedina hesitated, "the east Edges. He is our guest, and we are bringing him to Havenheart. I swear, you are in no danger. For true. Just look at him there."

Well, now that tone is unnecessary.

Two-ton Annie (okay, Milly) scared of *him*? The other way around is more justifiable, after all the mammoth beast *did* just bust through thin air right in front of them with no warning. Big shot Mateo sensed something, so he one upped him there.

Feeling foolish, he steps forward, not looking at the now smirking Mateo, and says, "Hello, Milly, you can just call me Jaime. Pardon my rudeness, I, uh, I'm not from around here. You see, I came through a do—"

"He came through a downpour on the Edges, Milly. He's been eh, knocked in the head, so he's not all together right. We're in a hurry to get home, so I'm afraid we won't have time for chatter this day of Rays."

Jaime shoots her a quizzical look, which she pretends to not notice. Instead, Aedina keeps talking to Milly the land whale, and gestures for him to walk again. He follows instructions but plans to ask questions later. Nodding to Milly, he side-steps and skirts the stammering behemoth, who still managed one trunks-worth of a close sniff of Jaime's neck before Aedina guides her attention away by saying, "My word, Milly, have you been to the Springs? Your skin looks positively radiant."

This is enough for Mateo and Jaime to scamper ahead. Murphius has once again fallen asleep and will follow along after Aedina. At least, Jaime hopes so. He's grown attached to the ridiculous looking thing, even if it is slobbery and slow and always tripping him up somehow.

He and Mateo rounded a bend, putting them out of view of Aedina and Milly. The operatic cadence of Milly's loud voice still carries, but the words are incoherent. After a moment, Jaime senses the hard stare from Mateo at his back. Sighing, he figures he has to befriend the little guy and let him know he is not in competition for the affections of the mighty Aedina.

"So, Mattie, how long you been a Guardian?"

"I am called Mateo. Always."

Okayyy, not a good start. Try it again.

"Always, huh? That's a long time. So, even when you were a baby, you were a Guardian?"

He isn't being sarcastic, just curious. Okay, maybe a little sarcastic.

"I hear you speak of these *baby* with Aedina. I do not know what is this. I have always been of the Havenheart. There is no 'baby' you speak of, no parents and no bird's day."

"Bird's day? Oh, you mean *birth*day. Okay, so you and Aedina and all the other Virescent become Guardians? Just like that?"

At Jaime's mention of Aedina, Mateo looks toward the bend, where she remains with Milly, and furrows his brow. He seems uncertain whether answer. Perhaps because she has yet to appear, he say, "Mateo is Virescent. Not Aedina. She is… *was* a wildling. Before Soji brought her to the Havenheart."

Well, that means nothing to Jaime, but it matters to Mateo. For the first time on their journey together, Jaime sees something other than what he had perceived as a lovesick green boy. His tone is resentful. Hostile, even. He concedes he might be wrong, but then, as his mother is wont to say, *trust your gut.*

As if sensing Jaime's misgivings, and knowing more questions were to come, Mateo retreats behind a wall of silence, shutting down Jaime's attempt at learning more. To both of their relief, Aedina at last rounds the curve, motioning them to join her. However, now he watches the Virescent's display of obedience with a new and more suspicious eye than before. As for the Virescent, wary unease and darting glances replaces his smug superiority. He realizes he's opened a curtain for Jaime to peer past, and now that it is open, cannot be closed.

If Aedina notices a change in their dynamics, she shows no sign, as the suspicion that preoccupied *her* involves Milly's toward Jaime. As she directs them off the path and into the dense woods, she explains.

"She went along with our story, but she's a crafty one, that old yabber. Not everything is as it seems here, Jaime of Rocky Knoll, you mustn't tell anyone else of the… *door* that brought you here, for your own safety. We must stay off the paths now, for she will smell your odd scent."

She shoots the offended Jaime a smirk, lessening the sting just a little bit.

"I'll have you know my grooming habits are above average thank you very much. Sure, I've been out her for a while, but I took a shower, washed my hair, and put on deodorant today. Or was it yesterday? Either way, I am fresh and clean, something you all might try, I might add."

Aedina lets out an abrupt laugh, noting *that* is exactly the problem. "Well, now Jaime of the Everwood, there lies my proof. You do not smell as though you belong here. You stand out like a red feather on a Great Yellow Audris. We must do something about that, quickly. Mateo take him to the Archeia Waters, then to the Havenheart. I will have to meet you there. It is time the Elders know of our guest. Best they hear it from me, rather than Milly."

In a blink, she disappears. Not vanishes, but near enough to make Jaime step back in surprise at her speed and agility as the gust of wind left in her wake tousles his hair. For the first time since meeting, the two males shares an equal emotion.

Mutual dread. The prospect of more time alone together looms like a lead balloon.

The questions Jaime has for Aedina, will now have to go to Mateo, who is like the proverbial brick wall. But somehow, Jaime will have to connect with the curious Virescent if he is to learn anything at all about this intriguing place and its unusual inhabitants.

For the moment, though, he must train all his focus to navigating the thick forest as he trails behind the impatient Mateo, who Jaime has slowed down excessively going by the sighs and huffs every time he stops for Jaime's sake.

"Is this how humans travel through woods? It is very slow, and you are very noisy. How do you even hunt with such noise?"

Mateo's tone is unsurprising. Jaime expects no less than disdain from the greenie. However, the attempt at conversation—albeit laced with contempt and scorn—catches him off guard.

"Tell you what, my friend. You answer my questions, and I'll answer yours. Sound like a fair enough deal?"

Mateo pauses, looks up ahead, then twists in Jaime's direction and offers a curt nod, signaling his assent to Jaime's proposal.

"Once we reach the Archeia Waters, we may speak. Now, we walk. You are too slow as it is and talking slows you more."

Ah, yes. Wouldn't be a complete conversation with him unless an insult got tossed in for good measure, now would it?

Jaime ignores the baiting comment and takes the high road. Mainly because he needs the little guy. They've gone deep into the woods, with no way for Jaime to find his way out.

This gives him pause for concern. Is this angry green boy dangerous? Is he resentful enough to *accidentally* lose or worse, harm him, deep in the woods with no one to see or hear to contradict his story? He knows nothing of these people (or whatever they are) and now feels foolish and gullible for trusting them. Aedina herself warned him.

Before his thoughts turned to an escape plan, Mateo startles him by announcing, "We are here."

Jaime says, "You're kidding, right?"

The stony Guardian stops before a massive willow set higher than the other woodland trees and stands alone. Jaime, for the first time realizes that the bark of the ancient looking willow trees resembles that of the strange door that had led him and Mala to this paradisiacal land.

Mateo grasps a handful of silvery green trimmed wispy branches the same way Mala gathers her long hair, sweeping them aside in a grandiose wave of mock chivalry as he motions Jaime to go ahead.

"Um, dude… what? It's a tree trunk. Where do you want me to go?"

Mateo, true to form, rolls his eyes and gives a look of, *Duh, what do you think*. Either way, Jaime is not about to be the source (again) of Mateo's mockery and amusement. He will not walk smack into that tree as Mateo expects him to do.

"Oh, no buddy, I wouldn't dream of it, you go right ahead and go first."

Ha. Got him there. Jaime expects Mateo to give a sheepish 'oh-well-I-tried' shrug and be back on their way to this Archeia Waters, but he has also learned to expect the unexpected here in bizarre-o-land. So, while what happens next doesn't entirely shock him, he *is* awed and impressed.

Mateo shrugs, but instead of stepping down and away from the giant tree trunk, he takes an exaggerated sideways leap and disappears into the tree. Somewhere in the back of his mind, he imagines Mala arm smacking him at his lack of outward astonishment, and like always, thinking of her spreads a dopey grin across his face. Where on earth—or in Greenwood—*is* that girl?

Jaime resigns himself to follow the other boy through the tree truck, for lack of better ideas. At least this way, he'll have a chance at getting his many questions answered and led (or at least sent in the direction) to wherever Mala might be.

Not without the mandatory trepidation at preparing to walk through an inanimate object, Jaime approaches the trunk, brushes aside the same feathery cascade of silver-green willow branches as had Mateo, and stands before the rough bark as he determines the best way to proceed. For instance, should he step right through, as one would a doorway? Perhaps it is wisest—and on the right side of caution—to poke his head through first. But then he'll risk exposing his unprotected head to the unknown other side. Of course, he can put his hands through first, but that—

His hypothesizing ends when a sinewy hand reaches through the tree, grabs the front of his hoodie, and yanks him through to the other side. There, a sight that renders him frozen with shock meets Jaime.

21 TORTANINE

"Where'd everyone go?" The gentle Tortanine yawns.

He looks around, blinking. His human and his Virescent are gone, and even the ghastly shrill Rhinello is nowhere in sight. He smacks his lips and debates whether another nap is in order, or if he should set off to find the others.

A shadow passes overhead, bringing with it the chill. He shakes and pants inside his rocklike shell, opening and closing his mouth in almost yawns. His tail wags in short spastic bursts, sweeping the leaves and debris from the path behind him, and then stops as a black form descends from the sky. With wide doe-like eyes, Murphius watches the shadow's descent. He emits an involuntary whine which drifts into a growl, and then back again. The shadow, known to all in Greenwood as the Vague, will not be passing by. This time it will pay visit to the last of the Tortanines.

22 ADALBERT

"I am telling you, Adalbert, she is trouble, that one. *Why* in Greenwood would you bring her *here* of all places? Sometimes I think your time in the service has left you addled. What am I to feed it, for Ray's sakes?"

It is hard for Mala to not overhear the heated conversation between the bullfrog couple. Whispering is not a strong suit of bullfrogs either. Still, she pretends not to hear them and instead busies herself with inspecting the tall cattails that grow alongside the Tarn's edge. She reaches out to touch one fuzzy brown pod and as she does, she loses her footing on the slick grass. In what feels like slow motion, her arms wave, and her legs buckle. She splats into the water with a fistful of cattails and no more grace than she had the mud.

The last thing she sees before a face full of water clouds her vision, is the two bullfrogs with both their mouths open in surprise; the missus with one hand over her heart and the other covering her gaping mouth, Bert with one hand on his hip and the other pressed between his bulging eyes and shaking his head.

The water is only tepid and shallow where she's fallen. So shallow, that she sits up with the water line only at her waist. As with everything in the Greenwood, the water is not like any body of water she'd ever known.

This water has the consistency of water mixed with gelatin just as it firms. It slips and plops through her hand. The odd texture mesmerizes Mala. She is oblivious of the bullfrog's admonishments to get out of the water. It isn't until she heard the distinct note of urgency in Adalbert's voice and realized that they were doing their version of whispering.

"Why are you whispering?"

Their pie round eyes dart over her shoulders and behind her back. Like a scene in a scary movie—the kind she never ever watches—she twists around to see what they gawk at.

Welting the gray water are dozens of black lumps, and they are on the move. The flat surface looks like an outbreak of mumps, and it moves closer. Mala needs no further encouragement to vacate the thickish water. She flails and struggles to upright herself, and bites back a hysterical laugh at the sight of Adalbert's outstretched hands as he offers his useless help.

The first wave of lumps are an arm's length away, and Mala's fevered glances back show her they are not featureless lumps of water, but creatures that are all eyes and teeth and mottled-gray mass. The sight is enough to propel her from the water and scamper to the safety of the bank. If water magnifies things below the surface, then these monsters are about the size of city rats, and just as vile looking. Everything about them is a stark contrast to the beauty of the Tarn, and Mala shudders with revulsion.

"What—what are those things? Are they fish?"

The two bullfrogs exchange glances, his questioning the missus, hers in resignation.

"Come on now, back with us and we'll get you straightened out. I suppose it's time we ought to tell you what you need to know about the Tarn, and Greenwood for that matter." After a pause, he adds, "Afore you get yourself hurt. Or worse."

Though Mala is listening, she can't take her eyes off the water, now returning to its glass smooth stillness, the gray monsters retreat makes the water appear like a wave in reverse. Once the last ripple rolls back and disappears, she allows the pair to lead her away. She returns a few mistrustful glances back toward the water, not altogether believing that the creatures are in fact gone.

Adalbert and the missus lead her to their little watery haven away from the Tarn. It is a section of lagoon like a small inlet—attached to the main body of water by a narrow connector allowing passage for only the smallest of aquatic creatures—and surrounded by an abundance of cattail, wildflowers and reeds, save for one flattened area to which they bring her.

The three sit on the matted grass and look at one another. Mala—chilled from her damp clothing—sporadically shivers but the ever-shining sun warms her back and dries her top. The heavier cargo style pants will take longer, but the odds of two bullfrogs in a lagoon having human-sized clothing are unlikely, even if they *are* talking bullfrogs. She removes her waterlogged hiking boots and her soaked socks, wringing them out and laying them in the sun as she stammered through her chattering teeth.

"S-s-so what's the deal with those things? What are t-t-they? And that other thing. That awful black vulture-thing. What, or who is that?"

Again, the pair exchange hesitant glances, resulting in the missus giving Adalbert a *go on* nod in her direction.

"What? Oh, me? Yes, yes, well, right then. So, you, eh, want to know about the grayscales, do you? And the, eh, the black vul— eh, thing, do, do you? Ah, well I—eh, that is, they—eh, that is, it is…"

"Oh, merciful Rays, Bert. Just spit it out already. Agh, never mind. Listen hear, girl. Those things, those monsters, and the thing that came for you, they're bad, bad creatures. Nothing in the realm like them, thank the ever-shining light. There are things best left alone, but I can see you'll not rest till you hear of it. I suppose it's best you do, all the same."

The missus drifts off at the end, seeming to lose her train of thought. Her thin, wide mouth puckers then grimaces. Bert darts his eyes about the sky, taps one webbed foot, and then blurts, "It's the Vague. The Vague, I say. Has it got you, missus? Dear, oh dear. It's got the missus, it has. Come back to me—"

"Oh, calm yourself you dotty thing, you. I is just collectin' my thoughts, I is. I wanted to tell her in a more delicate manner, I did, and now you've gone all kinds of *hysteronical* on her."

"Well, madam bullfrog, you gave me a fright, you did, off boggled-eyed at the sky, you were. Not my fault a'tall, it isn't. Why I…"

What is it with these Greenwood inhabitants? Are they all ill-mannered and scatter-brained?

Mala clears her throat and interrupts the bickering duo. "I'm sorry… the vague? What is that, and what does it want? Does it, like, kill you?"

This time, the pair talk over one another until the missus put up a webbed hand, silencing an indignant Bert.

"Ah, yes, yes. All in time, girl. Let me start at the beginning. A long, long time ago—before all our time for true—the Greenwood is quite different. Unlike what you see here now, with the flowers always in bloom, and the grass and trees aburst with greenery. No, before our time, the Greenwood warred. It is a place of conflict and ugliness, a place of beasts who'd make the grayscales look pretty. Chaos ruled… as did the night."

The plump bullfrog settles herself deeper in the grass. "They forced our kind—all the gentler creatures of the Greenwood that is—into hiding. They were no match for the likes that ruled, as they had no fight in them, being mild-mannered as they were. So, they stayed hidden for many years, deep in the thickest parts of the forest, gathering food and taking shelter wherever possible. It's is a low and sorrowful time for the creatures of the Greenwood, for true."

The missus heaves a big breath and crosses one of her long legs over the other. "Anyways, one day, as the story goes, seven strangers arrived. No one had ever seen anything like them. Seven luminous beings—three males, and four females—that exuded tranquility, peace, and compassion. Eh, they sorta looked like you dear, only specialer. Ah, no offense intended, now. Anyways, the warring stopped at the very sight of them, it did. The beasts bent their knees to the visage that had come before them."

Bert interjects, "It was like they cast a spell. I dunno, maybe they did. But what happened was this. The fighting stopped, just like that. Of course, it weren't so simple, as nothing ever is. As the missus said, maybe it was a spell the Seven cast, maybe they was just the stronger of the wills. But on that day of new Rays, and for ever more since, the gentle traded places with the warring beasts, the Great Rays came back, and the night retreated. Mostly that is."

The missus takes over, clarifying. "The Seven? Oh, they're called the Elders by the Virescent."

Mala opens her mouth to ask…

"Before you ask, Virescent are the Guardians of the whole Greenwood. Anyhow, the Seven gathered the meek and mild of the land, who came from all parts near and far to see and hear with wonder what the magnificent and foreign beings had to say. The smallest of the Seven, that'd be Endelyn, a delicate looking lass with flaxen hair that nearly touched the ground and a voice that sounded the way a breeze feels against your skin, spoke for the others, offering to the awed creatures their most desired wish. Freedom. However, freedom came with a price, as all things do. The Seven could not exile the wicked beasts, nor kill them, as it was not their way."

Bert continues, "Alas, they could only banish them to the north Edges—it's the farthest and darkest parts of the

Greenwood, with warning to never return during days of Rays. And that's that."

Mala asks, "But what about the... the Vague?"

"Right, right. Getting' there, dearie." The missus clears her wobbly throat, draws herself to her full fourteen inches, and continues, "There was one, however, that came after the Beasts, no one can say when or how or why it came, and in fact, a little foxy fellow—I forget his name at the moment— found the nasty thing quite by accident, he did. Turned his fur white on the spot, they say. I wouldn't know, acourse, I've never left our part of the Tarn, I haven't."

The missus taps her temple. "What was I saying, now? Oh yes, ah, now, it has no actual name, no true form, so we call it the Vague. My dear, it was the Vague that you saw on the bank in the form of a black vulture. It would seem that's some kind of change, none for the good."

The missus pauses and looks to Adalbert to carry on, she has exhausted herself. He collects his thoughts and continues for her in a contemplative tone.

"Thing is, no one around these parts has ever seen more than the passing shadow of the Vague for quite some time before *your* arrival here, let alone have a word with it. Gave us all a fright, it did, all up inside our heads. But, you—you weren't afraid a'tall were you? Brave girl, I say... or foolish. Either way, you've gone and made it mad, I reckon. Hard to say since we never have seen it ourselves before now, we haven't."

Bert stands and paces. "What I *can* say is, in all the times I've heard tell of that black foulness, no one yet has heard it do more than some mumble-mumble, certainly no bit of chasing around, like it did with you. Something has come to pass here in the Greenwood, and I reckon it's not of a good sort."

Mala still has more questions than answers. The most pressing questions are, "What *is* 'the Vague' and what makes it so frightening? And why can't the Seven—or the Elders—not banish it? And where are the Seven now? And *who* are the Virescent again?"

"Now, slow down, there slow down. I'll tell you best as I can, I will. You see, the Vague is... well, that's just the thing, isn't it? It defies explanation. It doesn't have a shape, or a face. For Ray's Light, like the missus says, it doesn't even have a name, now does it? It is... emptiness. Nothingness, is what."

He shudders. "Now, you may think that's not such a scary thing, but imagine being sucked into that vast nothing, where you *feel* nothing, care not at all. You become nothing, yet you live on. That's what the Vague is, and what it does. Up till now, that is. It seems that thing came to claim you, and you fought it. But more importantly? You won. Now, I don't rightly know what any of that means, just a bullfrog, you know. But I know who you need to find, and that's the Seven. Only they can help you here. At least, I think they can. Acourse, you must get past them Guardians of the Greenwood first, you know. Eh, that would be the Virescent, you recall the missus telling you about, now don't you?"

Bert sits, his spindly legs fold at his sides. He tips his head back and closes his eyes. She waits for Bert to continue and explain what these *Guardians* are—and how to get past them—but to her amazement, the bullfrog has fallen fast asleep and snores.

The missus chuckles and drags a lily pad behind her, which she flicks over her sleeping husband with the tender love of a devoted wife. She plants a loud smacking kiss atop his head, one which he rewards with another snort, then a contented sigh.

"Never mind him, now, dear. Not as spry as he once was, but then, neither am I. All right and good, it is. Here we are now, time for you to take a rest."

She studies Mala a moment before continuing. "You've a long way to go I suspect, and there'll be time enough for more explaining later. Must say, I'm quite sleepy myself. Haven't done so much talking since I don't know when." In a loud stage whisper, "The mister isn't much of what you'd call a conversationalist, he isn't. Not that I'm complaining, mind you. Peace and quiet, I like."

"Is it ever night here, or just day? The sun is in the same place as when I arrived, but it can't be, can it?" With a gasp, "Oh. Has time stopped here? Is that what it is? I suppose that would make the most—"

"Oh, light of Rays, no. Time keeps a moving here, just like anywhere, I suppose. I keep forgetting you're not from the Greenwood. Well, now, let me think here. Day and night, night and day, you ask. Hm, yes, I recall hearing it told that once there was equal measure of the two. But that's long since ended. I believe it was when the Seven arrived. Now, for all my lifetime, back through to my parent's grandparents time, it's been six days of Rays, one of night. If you haven't been here a night yet, well, you're in for something. Acourse, I don't recommend you being caught out there for that, I don't."

Missus raises a webbed hand to stop the next question on her lips. "Now, I mean it, you must get some rest. As should I, and we'll talk more after, I promise. There you go now, get comfy as you can."

Perhaps it is because she's had so little sleep at all, perhaps it's the warm sun on her back, or the missus soothing tone, or maybe it is all of that and more, but for the second time in the Greenwood, Mala curls up on her side and drifts into a deep sleep. Her last image before her eyes shut is of the motherly frog brushing her hair from her brow with a cool hand, worry pursing her thin froggy lips.

23 ARCHEIA WATERS

Jaime throws a punch at whatever yanks him forward and through—*Oh my God, I just went* through *the tree*—but because his aim is high and his target low, he catches nothing but air. His target, Mateo, has the advantage of surprise—and lack of height—and his return punch lands low in Jaime's gut, doubling him over and knocking the wind out of him, along with his pride.

When he straightens, Mateo tenses for another attack, but as much as it tempts him, the vision behind Mateo distracts Jaime. A wide, lavender-colored stream flows from a small jagged waterfall over moss green rocks in a curving trail. It ends in a roundish pool surrounded by exotic looking flowers which droop in heavy bloom. From the pool rises a fine mist like steam from a hot spring. The air is heavy, like a sauna. Long flat stones disappear into the frothy lavender water, as if stones intended as stairs.

Forgetting his surprised anger from just moments before, Jaime asks the still wary Mateo, "Is this real? I mean, it can't be, right? Places like this don't exist."

The green-tinted boy scoffs, and says, "It is as real as your Rocky Knoll, human. If you are done assaulting your host, perhaps you could do what we've come here for. You will find the Archeia Waters to be pleasant, I assure you, but do not linger for long. Their magic is powerful."

He wants to know more, but his stubborn pride won't allow him to ask. And as much as he doesn't want to strip down in front of his nemesis, he has little choice. Besides, the lavender pool is the most inviting thing he's ever seen, without doubt.

***

Mateo wishes to be anywhere but here, with the tall one. He stinks of—well, whatever those foreign smells are—and he'll be glad to be rid of at least them, thanks to the Archeia Waters. He searches his satchel for something that might cover the oversized human and finds nothing suitable. After a moment, an idea comes to him. Watching the human, he crouches down and snatches up the human's clothing piled beside the spring and dunks them in the water. Indignant and angry shouts burst from the stupid human.

151

"What the hell do you think you're doing with my stuff?"

Mateo, ignoring the human's comical, helpless ire, takes the saturated clothing and cut them with his short dagger—first the hood, then the sleeves of both shirts—and once satisfied with those, moves on to the heavy pants. He studies them with a cocked eyebrow, then runs his sharpened stone knife along the seams and across the legs. Last, he stomps and rolls the dismembered clothing into the dirt.

It isn't until he's laid the articles on a rock, now less than half their original size, tucked the clothing scraps into his satchel, and secured his dagger in a loop sewn into his tattered leather loincloth, that he speaks.

"I have orders to help you blend in. Now that you have the stench of stranger washed off you, you might have a chance of that. As for your dressing, no one is adorned as such. You stand out, and not just for your abnormal height. This is the best we can do," he waves a hand at the tattered and scant clothing, "for now at least. Your hair is too short, but there's nothing we can do for that."

"Ha. That might be the first time I've ever heard that."

Mateo gapes at him as if he's said the most absurd thing ever.

"I do not think I would like this Rocky Knoll you come from. Tell me of your Everwood. This sounds maybe better, yes?"

"Everwood? Yeah, it's great. I mean, not as great as your Greenwood, and not as great as… what's this place called? The Arc-ana Waters?"

Mateo gives his first non-sarcastic smirk since they've met, and corrects him, "It is the *Archeia* Waters. This is where the Archeia—the sylphs who once frolicked and played throughout all of Greenwood and enchanted all who gazed upon them with their magical voices and lavender auras—came to hide during the time of Wars. The legend says they dove into this very spring, never seen again in their authentic form. It is also said that if one remains for too long in the waters, the Archeia will rise and pull you under with them for all eternity."

At that, Jaime—who has been submerged for perhaps twenty minutes or more—bolts out of the steaming water and snatches what is left of his still damp and dirtied clothes. He hops and fumbles into them. Though the Guardian boy has already walked away, Jaime hears his low chuckle and must calm his temper once again. He needs answers from the boy still.

Swallowing both his pride and his temper, he calls out in his most conciliatory tone. "Ha, *ha*. Good one, you got me there. Didn't know you had such a funny sense of humor, buddy. So, umm, tell me…"

Jaime, whose back is to the spring, stops mid-sentence because Mateo—who now faces him—stares past him in disbelief.

"Ah, yeah. I see what you're doing there. You make that *Oh, my God* face, I turn around and see a big fat nothing, you laugh and laugh and laugh. Jokes on me, right? Well, nope. Not fallin' for it."

"No joke, human."

Raising one lean and muscular arm, Mateo points behind him and down at the water. Jaime sighs. He'll let the green kid get his chuckles again if it means he'll lighten up a bit from here on out. He turns around to look at the swirling lavender water, expecting to see a whole bunch of nothing, but cast his own disbelieving eyes on a whole lot of something instead.

Breaking the swirling frothing surface, hands—at least a dozen of them—feminine, long nailed and pale, reach up like zombies from a grave and reach for Jaime. No faces are visible through the lively water, but the tops of their heads crown, and their long hair sways and dances.

Mesmerized and almost paralyzed by the vision before him, he continues to watch as the apparitions rise higher from the water. At any moment, the faces will ascend through the plane and be visible, and anticipation roots Jaime to the spot.

For the second time, Mateo's strong grip clamps around his wrist and yanks him. Jaime is in too much of a fog to even be angry and lets the Virescent half drag him away.

"We must leave here at once. Back through the veil, now!"

Mateo's tone compels Jaime to follow, despite the overwhelming desire to stay and see the Archeia as they rise from the water. He lets Mateo push him through the tree trunk, back to the other side. The air, compared to the climate of the spring, is cooler and causes Jaime to shiver. It doesn't help that he is less clothed than before, either.

His brain fog lifts, and Jaime looks back at the tree—or *veil*, as Mateo called it—letting the surreal-ness of it all sink in for maybe the first time since he's arrived. He doesn't understand *any* of what is happening, or why, and he wants, no *needs* answers, and he will not wait another minute longer to get them.

"All right. That. Is. *It*. What the hell is this place? Who are all of you, and why the hell am I here? I want answers, Mateo, and I'm not moving until I get them."

"Move, human."

Yet again, Mateo looks behind Jaime, and this time Jaime feels no skepticism. He turns to see what lies behind him… and wishes he hadn't.

24 Aedina's Deep Thoughts

When she last saw the Elders, it was for her Chosen ceremony. Unlike Mateo, she hadn't wanted the responsibility—the *burden* of responsibility—for she's always considered herself a wildling at heart, and not a true Virescent. Wildlings are responsible for no one save themselves, and before Soji the Mindful had found her by the bank of the Tarn, she knew no other way of living.

Soji, the chosen Leader before her had also been her mentor. She was patient and kind, despite Aedina's stubbornness and mistrust. And wildness. She followed Aedina throughout countless days of Rays, and through several nights, too. Always staying far enough away to not rattle her, yet close enough for Aedina to become accustomed to her presence.

Wildlings travel, hunt, and live alone. They shun and avoid contact with other wildings and are even more expert at staying hidden than the Virescent. It is a task of the Leader to find these lone souls and encourage them to join the Virescent, but never to force them to do so.

Aedina never understood why the Elders insisted the wildings be sought and persuaded to join the Virescent, and the only explanation given is that it is for everyone's protection. This left her with more questions than answers. For unlike the others—both Virescent and converted wildlings—Aedina was not content with such plain response. Protection from *who*? Or what? The creatures of the Greenwood had reveled in several lifetimes of peaceful existence, with only the night to fear.

Out of six days of Rays, one of black night is a burden and a worry they all accept as fair exchange. They've survived for over two hundred years, yet the Elders insist the Virescent serve as Guardians of the Greenwood entire, and who can argue with the Seven?

Not a small green-hued girl, regardless of how quick witted and thoughtful she is. However, no matter how many times she reminds herself to be grateful to the Elders for appointing her the leader of the Guardians—a great honor never given to a such a newly named Virescent in the community—she still harbors misgivings about her place there.

Part of her still longs for the freedom and solitude of the Greenwood, despite her attachment for many of the

Virescent. Particularly the smallest of them. They are what tethers her most of all to the community, followed by her sense of duty to those who have chosen her. Aedina's enjoyment of riling Mateo, who tries to hide his resentment behind his stoic demeanor, may also play a part.

His hostility is understandable, and she doesn't blame him for it, though it makes her sad. Once they were friends, in fact he was her first and only friend when Soji first brought her—a wary and defensive wildling—into their home, the Havenheart. It was he who had taken her under his wing when Soji left them to join the hunt, leaving her feeling abandoned and overwhelmed.

The little ones that she found so dear now were of the greatest revulsion in those first days. Their need and dependence had appalled her; their vulnerability offended her. So, it was Mateo who seemed to understand her need for space and took her out into the woods to train for a place in the Guardians, hunt and even talk when she was willing.

Despite his own sound sense of community, he seemed to not mind her balking at their ways and had won her over. Aedina excelled in training; she was quick, fierce, and fearless. Qualities that caught the Elders attention and caused the rift between her and Mateo to begin. Though he tried to not show it, she saw his envy at the notice they paid her.

His face betrayed his thoughts. *It was he who trained her, he who guided her along, and he who showed her how to be a member of the community. So why was it she who became the chosen Leader, when he so much more wanted it? What was it they saw in this wildling they did not see in him?*

His bitterness grew, becoming less veiled no matter how he tried to hide it, and their friendship dwindled down to civility. When he challenged her nomination, forcing a competition between the two for all the—and the Elders—to witness, the last of the ties that bound them were broken. She was the victor, and the chosen. It only solidified the dissolution, making them Leader and First Guardian, but nothing more.

Had *he* have won, Aedina would have been pleased for him, and only mildly disappointed for herself. For despite her initial ambivalence at becoming the Leader, it was his outright hostility that fueled her need to lead the Guardians, and to suppress the urges to run towards the freedom and lack of responsibility of the wildling life. If only he saw how his behavior affected the outcome, then perhaps he would have controlled his temper and swallowed his pride.

Aedina learned well about managing pride and temper, *and* impulse and control, with thanks to Soji. For a long time, after Soji brought her to Havenheart, she behaved reckless and mean. She resented the uncomplicated way the others interacted, their comfort and even their sense of peacefulness. Aedina couldn't understand their ways, their happiness, or their acceptance of a life that seemed confining to her.

But over time, and with her trademark patience, Soji showed her a better way to think and react. She told her that life was about choices. Would she be a part of a community that needed her and wanted her, or would she choose her freedom and solitude? Soji clarified that the choice was hers, but to choose with mindfulness, with clarity and certainty rather than impulses based on lack of learning or fear, and to choose *after* she had given the Havenheart a chance.

By the next time she had seen Soji, many days of night later, she had decided. She would return to the wildling life. However, Aedina was in for a surprise. Soji had found and brought not one, but two wildlings with her to the Havenheart. They were the smallest of wildlings she'd ever seen and reminded her so much of herself with their wide distrustful eyes, their skin more brown than green, and trust in Soji, the only Virescent they'd likely ever seen.

How had ones so tiny survive? They had not developed the hunting skills, nor the sheltering skills necessary to take cover from the days of night. Something about these two waifs—one raven-haired girl, one towheaded boy—both waist high of Aedina's own slight stature—pulled at her heart. The words she'd prepared to say to Soji as she departed turned into an agreement to shelter with the pair as they acclimated to the Havenheart. Although, it was at Aedina's insistence rather than at Soji's request.

Just like that, she was staying, continuing Soji's work of teaching the new wildlings the words and ways of the Virescent people. Just as Soji had taught *her* on their travel to the Havenheart over sixty days of night before.

How things changed so fast is a mystery to her. From wildling to Virescent, from seclusion to population, from ambivalence to affection, from affection to competition, from all that to coldness. Still, she has Raven and Towe to return to at each hunt's end, and that warms her heart.

Thinking of the two, she suffers a pang of guilt at not first going home to Havenheart. However, she must reach the Great Willow and speak with the Elders before the next day of night's arrival. With only two more days of Rays, the night will be upon the Greenwood quickly, and she still has far to go before she reaches the sanctuary of the Elders. Perhaps, with their magic ways, they already know of the human boy and human girl and are testing her commitment to her vows.

Unlike the other Virescent, she does not fear the Elders. Not that she doesn't revere them or respect them. She is awed and humbled by their age and wisdom, let alone their great and benevolent powers. She trusts their guidance even if she challenges and questions them. They, in their ever-present calm demeanor, respond with an amused indulgence but also lead with firmness and check her impertinence when it overpowers her curiosity.

These thoughts and many more occupy her mind as she skips rocks and skims beneath low branches, navigating the terrain of the Greenwood as if familiar as an old friend. Her part of it, at least. The Elders claim the vastness of the Greenwood makes it impossible to know it entirely.

She often wonders what lies beyond the Edges—the border of the Greenwood. Who or what is out there? Are there more like her, like the Virescent, like the other inhabitants of their woods?

Perhaps there are animals and creatures by the likes which she's never seen, and perhaps even more humans like Jaime and the girl human. How is she, or anyone, to know those answers without venturing out into the unknown?

In her mind, Soji's voice tells her not every answer is theirs to have, and to be grateful and glad for the protection and relative safety within the Greenwood's boundaries. It is what she had said many times as first her mentor, then her friend. Though she does not agree with her kind Soji, she misses their many long talks almost as much as she misses her gentleness.

Aedina's losses are layered. First, with Soji's departure for the Peace Haven, then her rift with Mateo at her Leadership nomination, and last, parting with Raven and Towe for indeterminable amounts of time to fulfill her obligations. It leaves her with a once inconceivable void.

Despite her heavy thoughts, Aedina cherishes her solitary trek to the Great Willow. The earth beneath her feet and the familiar pull of the wild are a homecoming of sorts. She can pretend that she is responsible for no one, has no duty or obligation to fulfill… even if for just a brief time. As always when she reflects, she imagines her inner voice to be that of Soji. What would she say in response to such weighted thoughts? What fresh perspective would she give? Aedina imagines their conversation.

Soji would say, "For as much as you feel conflicted, and despite the things that make you sad, Aedina, you are in fact, happy."

Aedina's response would be, "Happy? With such contrary thoughts and ideas? With such different wishes and dreams? How can that be so when I want to be free and yet can never walk away from those who need me?"

Soji, with her kind smile and warm eyes would ask her, "My dear, do you think you are alone in such notions? You cannot believe it is only you who battles duty and desire? I have taught you better. We all have doubts and questions and want to know our place in the Greenwood. You must change your perspective if you wish to change your life, my wild one."

"But how? *How* do I just stop feeling? I don't even know where to begin."

"Oh, my dear, you never stop feeling, nor should you. You change your feeling a little at a time. You look with a different eye, is all. You believe your conflict is a burden, yet truly, it is a gift. You have been blessed with the gift of having lived in both worlds—wild and tethered. You have known both abandon and attachment. These are all gifts. But for everything we are given, there is a price to pay, and we must accept that heartache is that price."

"How did you become so wise, my Soji? This makes sense to me. I feel lighter already, just knowing it is all right to feel as I do."

"Well, dear one, since this is all in your mind, I would say that you now have the wisdom you seek. We chose you as much for your capacity for understanding as you were your agility. It is your task to cultivate your gifts so that one day you will pass your wisdom to the next Leader, as I have done with you."

And with that, Aedina becomes more peaceful. It is simple. Only *she* makes it complicated, and only she can change her perspective. It is up to here to decide whether to see her life as a series of gifts, or a layering of burdens, whether to be happy, or miserable.

The realization stops her in her tracks, and when she looks up, it startles her to see she has reached the Great Willow. It stands enormous and proud, bathed in the light of Rays with members from many Greenwood species on and around its massive long branches, walking or resting outside its canopy, and some even making their way under and through to approach the ancient trunk.

When the first sweet-scented breeze caressed her face, she lets go a breath that she hasn't realized she's been holding. The Elders. They know she is here, and they welcome her.

25 MURPHIUS

The shapeless blackness that is the Vague swirls around the quivering Tortanine. Murphius tries not to breathe in the sickly smell that emanates from the thing, tries not to look, but he cannot stop the voice of it inside his furry head.

"Give me it. The girl."

Murphius' fear and revulsion now mingles with confusion. What is *girl*? He only met the b——. He tries to stop his thought, knowing the Vague might hear it, but it is too late.

"It tell. What have you? Mine."

Even Murphius, in his simple gentle way, understands the rudimentary speech of the Vague. He wants his Jaime, and he wants the other like him. But Murphius cannot tell the Vague, even if he wants to (which he does not).

He'd fallen asleep by the time they'd finished talking, and when he awoke, they'd gone. He tries to push those thoughts at the swirling mass and hopes it will just go away.

For a moment, it hovers and pulses like a breathing creature, but it is not. Then it drifts backward, away from the frightened turtle/dog, and he thinks with relief, *It is leaving.*

But it is not.

26 MALA DREAMS

Bert and his missus gave her much to think about, but because she is asleep, strange and jumbled dreams tumble in her overloaded brain. This time, she dreams of her beloved old dog Max, but in the dream, he is the same ivory and gold trimmed creature as both the dragonfly and rabbit.

He has run up ahead to the edge of the forest while she stands stuck in the field. She calls his name. Max turns and runs back to her with his familiar deer-like gallop, but just before he gets close enough for her to touch, he morphs into the vulture. She recoils, falling backward into the field, squeezing her eyes shut.

Instead of the sharp stabbing of the hideous beak, the gentle nudge of a wet nose prods her. It is once again Max, in his true black and tan coat. Mala smiles at the familiar face, her heart fills with joy. He blinks at her, and his eyes are the magnetic teal of both the dragonfly and rabbit. It awakens her with a jolt. However, when her eyes open, she questions her wakefulness when she sees what hovers over her.

It is a woman, slight and with flaxen hair down to her feet, with a face that reminds Mala of an expensive porcelain doll; the kind children aren't allowed to touch for fear of soiling or worse, breaking. The angelic being smiles down at her, motioning her to be silent, and outstretches an elegant and dainty hand for her to take. Mala accepts the proffered hand, feeling clumsy and large in her presence. The moment their hands connect, though, every ounce of insecurity vanishes, and an overwhelming sense of lightness and peace radiate through her palm and into her entire body.

"Are you an angel?" she asks, awestruck and mesmerized.

"Not quite, my love, nor are you dreaming. I am Endelyn, of the Seven. And I welcome you to the Greenwood. We've been expecting you."

Endelyn.

"Expecting me? But how? I don't understand."

"Yes, this must be confounding for you, I'm sure. All I can tell you, is that I must seek the Vague, and *you* must make your way to the Great Willow, as quickly as you can. Time is running out, I fear."

"The Vague? But I've seen it. It almost came after me, but I think I scared it away. Wait. Time is running out for what? I need to find Jaime, do you know where he is, if he's even here?"

"The day of night will be upon the Greenwood soon, that is why you must hurry. I'm afraid I do not know of this Jaime you speak. He is not in the visions. The Vague... you say you have seen it, and it nearly attacked you? This is unheard of..."

Visions? Did that mean she sees the future? But if she can't see Jaime...

"But where are you going? Can't I come with you? I have so many questions, I..."

"And we will answer them, in the right time, but for now, I must leave you, and you must continue your journey."

With those words, the edges of the ethereal vision fade into a ball of rose gold light, so blinding in its intensity that Mala must shut her eyes to it. When she opens them again, it is to the sight of the oversized dragonfly hovering before her face, then darting off into across the Tarn. Mala watches until she disappears, then turns to the still sleeping bullfrogs. They'd slept through a monumental visit.

She debates whether she should sneak off while they snore, but then Bert lets out a snort that wakes both he and the missus with a jump.

"Hrmph! What, what! Who goes th—ok, right, right. It's just you, human girl."

"Yes, Bert. Just me. But I just met…"

Mala stops midsentence, deciding not to tell the pair about the mysterious visit from Endelyn. Instead, she continues with, "I was just wondering if you'd help me get to this Great Willow?"

Bert and his missus exchange another one of their looks, an unspoken conversation that speaks volumes— at least to them, it does.

He tells her, with the missus nodding beside him, he can take her only so far as the first veil, but then he must leave her to, "… return to the Tarn, as it is. Day of night will be upon us soon, I'm afraid. I, uh, I suppose, we should get you on your way now, I'd say."

Both bullfrogs lift an anxious eye toward the clear blue sky as if it is full of storm clouds and lightning bolts. Mala, too, looks up, puzzled.

"Bert, would you tell me more about this 'day of night'? And also…"

"Oh, yes, yes I will! As we journey, though, for you my dear human, have far to go and little time to get there."

The big bullfrog claps his flat hands with a *plat* sound and nods. Mala nods, too, and before long, she is hugging the missus goodbye and thanking her for the mound of dead flies wrapped in a green leaf and tied with a long blade of grass, *case you get hungry on the way.* She hides her revulsion well enough as she handles the parcel and contemplates the appeal of the one soggy granola bar still in the side pocket of her now dry cargo pants. Neither are appetizing, but given the choices… well, it is an easy pick.

They are on their way, away from the Tarn and toward the narrow path through the woods; one fair haired human girl strolling alongside one exceptionally large, upright standing, walking stick holding, talking, green bullfrog named Adalbert. Just a regular day in the life of a teenage girl, is all.

27 JAIME

Jaime watches the blackness approach. It is like a cloud of exhaust fumes from a diesel truck, but instead of dispersing into the air, it thickens as it advances. He can't look away, despite Mateo's hold on his arm and hissed warning to stay away from it.

"What the hell is *that*, Mateo?"

The black cloud takes new shape, and with it comes a familiar smell: James Cromwell's cheap cologne. *Impossible*. Even as he thinks the word, the smell intensifies. Drug store cologne, stale cigarettes, and pungent beer; the essence of his memories of his father.

Making it more repugnant to Jaime is the sight of this thing wearing his father's flannel shirt…

"It's the Vague. Do not touch it," hisses Mateo.

No worries there, that is that last thing he wants to do. His father's plaid flannel shirt—the one with the last button missing and the breast pocket coming apart at the seam—his worn denim jeans and even more worn work boots. But worst of all, he sees his father's eye's, the same shade of coffee brown as Jaime's, but empty and bloodshot.

He expects the baritone voice of his father to come out of that hard mouth set in his chiseled face—even at his worst his father was a handsome man—but a scratchy cold voice picks at his brain in a toddler like speech pattern.

"Human. Boy. Mine."

Um, hell, no.

"Human. Girl. Mine."

Mala. Does this thing have her?

"Have. Mala. Have boy."

Jaime's temper ignites. He yanks his arm out of Mateo's firm grasp and moves toward the black cloud that is also his father—not knowing if he could strike it—but more than ready to try.

"Do not touch it, Jaime. You cannot fight the Vague. If you touch it, it will take you and you will no longer exist."

Even in a rage, Jaime is no fool. He stops within inches of the apparition, fists clenched and breath heavy. He watches as the blackness swirls and pulses, blasting him with sickening waves of the smell of his father.

He shouts at the vile cloud. "Where is she? Tell me."

"Mine."

It whispers in his head. If not for Mateo, Jaime would've charged with blinding anger at the thing, but as it is, the Virescent commands his attention with one simple sentence.

"If the Vague has her, she is gone."

Jaime's heart stutters perhaps even stops for a moment. The rage, the fight leaves his body. He turns away from the blackness, walks to Mateo, and falls to his knees.

28 MATEO

Mateo is not the cold and heartless Virescent Guardian he appears to be. In fact, he is the opposite. But a Guardian must show strength always and not allow feelings and emotions to misguide. He has already dishonored and disappointed himself in his dealings with Aedina, and this strange being is not about to influence or affect him.

Yet, the sight of the human's abject grief moves him. He wonders at his earnest grief for losing his partner... and at his own position. For the first time, he imagines life without Aedina, and the thought sends a spear through his heart. He returns his thoughts to the boy beside him. Perhaps this creature is more than what *he* seems. More than a clumsy, self-satisfied tree cutter. His strange appearance and size, the way he walks and the odd way he speaks—all off-putting to the proud guardian—are merely different, and not bad or wrong.

It is this newfound compassion for the oversized boy that causes him to reach a hand down and place it upon his head as he sits
crumpled before him, the same way he would when consoling a small wilding new to the Havenheart.

This is a gesture of great significance in the Virescent world—equivalent to a hug in the human realm—one that signifies a blessing of sorts. The placing one's hand upon the head of another passes along peaceful wishes, hopes for safekeeping, and a promise of understanding.

Mateo doesn't bother looking back as he leads the human away. The Vague will not follow, it is a creature almost spider-like; waiting for its prey to walk into its web. But never has the Vague changed shape or spoken with anything more than monotonic simplicity. Something is changing in the Greenwood, and it is not for the good.

He glances sideways at the transformed human beside him. Gone is the swagger and nonchalance. His head hangs, and his glazed eyes blink at the ground at his feet. He follows Mateo with oblivious trust like a young Tortanine, less the jovial contentment.

"I think we much adjust our plans and go to the Great Willow. Perhaps the Seven—our Elders—can be of assistance to your friend, if the Vague does have her. Have hope, my friend."

His words seem to help somewhat, and for the first time since they left the black monstrosity, Jaime picks his head up, focuses on Mateo with wide hopeful eyes, and nods. He picks up his step a little more, and this relieves Mateo some, for they have a way to go, and may not make it before the day of night arrives. Mateo will need the human to be at his most alert if that happens.

29 The Great Willow

The closer she gets to the Great Willow, the more Aedina relaxes. Her tight muscles loosen, and the tension leaves her shoulders. Is it the Elder's magic at hand or the relief of arriving before the day of night falls upon them that calms her?

She supposes it could be a mixture of both. As she gazes around at the beautiful haven, she doesn't much care about how or why this place affects her so; she is just glad to be there at last. The tiny seed of doubt at the reaction she might receive upon telling the Elders of the human, and that she was allowing Mateo to lead him to their sanctuary without their permission gives her pause.

She *had* planned to bring him straight to the Elders. However, Milly the Rhinello, and her sudden appearance had concerned her. While Milly and her kind are not malicious by nature, they are prone to indiscriminate gossip. There is no question in Aedina's mind that word has traveled halfway through the Greenwood of the strange visitor from the Edges.

As far as it concerns the girl human, *if* she is even in the Greenwood, she makes no guess as to her wellbeing. Nor does she fret over it; a truth for which she is only marginally guilty over. For the first time, Aedina wonders about this girl that makes Jaime's eyes light up at her mention. Is she tall like him? Behave as he does? And, last, she wonders at her appearance. A strange feeling overcomes her, one she's never felt and had no name for.

She pushes all her doubts and worries and strange feelings aside and makes her way toward the brightly lit, wide parting of long shimmering willow branches. At the threshold, she hesitates, but the call of the Seven beckons her in unison with their melodic sounding voices. "Come, Aedina, we have been waiting for you."

The glow under the thick green canopy, rose-gold and emanating warmth, illuminates the vast entire of the cave-like expanse. After several moments Aedina's eyes adjust to the unusual light, and when her gaze lands on the Seven, her heart drops to the ground, though she cannot decipher what is wrong.

The Elders—whose ethereal beauty and tranquility radiating auras are as awe striking as always—sit inside the alcove of the tree's massive trunk, as they always have done when receiving guests. But something is not right. She looks at each Elder; first at Kaylen, her raven colored hair falling over her shoulders as she nods once. Seated beside her is an unsmiling Caryss, then auburn-haired and serene Elsabet, who also nods in Aedina's direction. Gabrien, perhaps the most handsome of all the Seven, smiles his welcome at her. Maxis, always serious and watchful, offers a curt bob of his blonde head, and looks to Tobias beside him. Tobias raises the tips of his fingers from his lap, a gentle wave of greeting.

Aedina realizes what her eyes missed as she looked to each Elder. Endelyn is not in her place between Elsabet and Gabrien. She turns a confused and questioning eye back to Gabrien, whose smile had seemed most welcoming of the six seated Elders. *Where is Endelyn?* His countenance changes ever so slightly, but enough so that perceptive Aedina catches the faint flicker of his faltered smile before it restores itself upon his perfect face.

"Endelyn has gone to seek a human girl that has made her way into the Greenwood. All is well, child. She shall return any moment, we are certain. Come, tell us what has brought you to the Great Willow this day of Rays?"

"You do not know? There is another human in the Greenwood, and he is with Mateo at present. They are moving towards the Havenheart as I stand before you."

The Elders exchange glances and unspoken conversations as Aedina looks on in consternation. Has there ever been a time when she's not seen the Seven together upon the dais? She is certain she has not.

Despite Gabrien's assurance, she cannot shake her unease.

Of the Seven, it has always been Endelyn to answer her curiosity and even her impudence with patience and good humor. Without her there, she must reserve her queries, unsure how the others might receive her.

After several moments, Gabrien and the others return their attention to Aedina and ask her to tell them everything she knows of the human she and Mateo discovered.

"He calls himself Jaime of Everwood, Senior of Rocky Knoll High, and claims to have come to the Greenwood through a *door*. His description of what the *door* is nearly cost him his life, I must tell you."

Again, the six exchange looks and nods. Then Kaylen speaks. "And what of this *door* did he tell you? Did he describe it to you and Mateo?"

"Yes, it sounds as though someone made it from a willow... one of the veils, by his description, and set in his Everwood. But how could this be?"

Ignoring her question, the six confer with each other in silence, giving her time to look about the rose-gold lit enclosure and admire the lush green canopy overhead and the intricate leaves on the branches arcing and twining together. It creates an expansive covering that reached all the way to the forest floor. The grass, where not cleared by a tidy dirt pathway, is of a verdant green, short and velvety looking. In fact, everything under the Great Willow is deeper and richer in hue, sharper and clearer in texture.

Sights and sounds from outside the Great Willow do not make their way in. No breeze or sunlight penetrates the heavy cover, so the only light is that which emanates from the tree itself; it is a veritable fortress.

The six majestic figures alight their matching teal eyes on her. Blessed with good intuition, she knows they will ask something of her.

Says Maxis, in his deep baritone, "Aedina the brave, we must ask of you a favor of great importance, one that will affect the safety of all the Greenwood."

Aedina is brave, the moniker was apt. She accepts their request without hesitation, regardless its entailment. Even when she hears the next words—spoken by soft voiced Caryss—she gives no pause. If the Greenwood and all who live in it are in peril, she must haste. It is her sworn duty.

"We were dishonest with you upon your arrival. It is Endelyn. We cannot…" A look to the others, then he continues, "sense her aura. We fear that perhaps she has succumbed to the Vague."

"This cannot be! How could one of the Seven fall prey to the Vague? You are the most powerful in the land, it is you who banished the beasts of the night and even the night itself!"

The six Elders smile down at Aedina's outburst of regard and praise. But it is Gabrien who corrects her, his hand raised to halt her speech, "Ahh, brave one. You are good to say such things, but remember, we have not banished night, or the beasts. We still must exist with their presence amongst us. As it is, the day of night will be upon the Greenwood soon, and therefore the urgency for your task is great. It is imperative that you hurry, however, we must give warning that you may very well be caught out in the day of night... unsheltered."

Despite herself, Aedina shudders at the thought. The day of night occurs after the sixth day of rays and comes on with a suddenness that could only be seen to be believed. In Aedina's lifetime, few have been exposed to the day of night, as the gentle creatures of the Greenwood take shelter underground at the first signal from the Seven.

The Seven are their keepers of time, makers of peace, and the only real protection against the Beasts that come out at night, for the night belongs to them. This is the arrangement struck with the Beasts all those eons ago, it grants the gentle creatures the day, the beasts, the night.

However, the Seven were more intelligent than the greedy Beasts, who—not understanding time—quickly agreed to the conciliatory offer of twenty-four hours of continuous night. Unbeknownst to the Beasts, this gave the best of circumstances to the kinder inhabitants of the Greenwood. When the Beasts realized the deception, it enraged them. However, the deal they had consented to bound them.

As they withdrew into their hiding places, they growled and grumbled and swore their revenge upon any creature that found themselves without shelter on their night of havoc, but retreated, nonetheless. The creatures of the daylight rejoiced and professed their boundless gratitude towards the Seven.

As for the Vague and where it came from, no one knew. Not even the Seven; a truth Aedina had gleamed from Soji after must questioning. It was perhaps the first and only time she had witnessed a slip in her calm and patient visage…

"Soji, when did the Vague come to the Greenwood? Has it always been here? Was it once a beast? Why did the Seven not banish it as well? How…"

"Aedina, my child, I do not have all these answers. As I have told you before, not every answer is ours to have, and you must accept the benevolence…"

"Yes, but, the Seven must know where the Vague came from?"

"… *of our* Elders with gratitude, and with fewer questions!"

"But, what of the day of night? How do we know what is out there if we have never seen? If we are the Guardians, then shouldn't we…"

"They do not know. And we must never venture out into the night. *Ever*. That is enough for today, Aedina. Now, please, go back to the Havenheart and continue your lessons."

After a pause, in which she gathered herself, she continued. "We will continue your training later. For now, I must rest."

But they never did. Without warning or preparation, Soji entered her time in the Peace haven, joining her predecessors, and where Aedina herself will one day, far from the present, enter. That was the last time she saw her Soji, leaving her with regret and sadness at such an unceremonious parting of ways.

She takes small solace in knowing Soji is not one to carry such feelings herself and would only wish her well. She would not have left her, had she not believed Aedina ready to face the challenge of leadership otherwise.

30 Endelyn

Endelyn wishes she could have spent more time with the human girl, for she is quite the curious creature. So much in her own likeness, that even *she* felt some surprise, despite the foretelling. She senses she would like the girl, given the chance to know her. As it is, it seems not within the realm of possibilities.

Flying over the Greenwood, in the dragonfly's form, she marvels anew at the beauty of the land they endeavor to protect and love. She believes in her heart they have done well, done *right* by those who call it their home, for everything they've done is for the best interests of those creatures.

Before the Seven, they had only known fear and darkness, but since the Seven, they've existed in relative peace. Endelyn and the other Seven learned from watching the creatures and their interactions there must be a balance of all things. Too much peace could be as detrimental as too much war. A truth Endelyn finds most ironic and hard to fathom.

Had she not seen it with her own eyes, she'd dispute the statement. But the earthly creatures have shown her their truth. One cannot appreciate joy without having known sorrow, peace without conflict, kindness without cruelty, and peace without fear. Likewise, day without night becomes meaningless.

The beings of the Greenwood do not differ from others they've encountered. This discovery dismayed the Seven but didn't surprise them. They could only hope their acts of compassion and munificence would become a way of life for all, just as it is for them. *They* have always coexisted in perfect harmony, so it stood to reason that, given the opportunity so would others. Alas, this is not the way, and the need for the day of night was born.

As timeless and utopian-like beings, they learned that, for creatures unlike themselves, balance is essential for coexistence. Though it caused them sorrow to do so, the Seven agreed amongst themselves that they would need to allow the Beasts to exist. The truth: they could banish them, send them far beyond the edges and into distant worlds for someone else to manage.

Hence, the Seven created the days of night. Their magic was impressive enough to make it so that on every sixth day of Rays, one full day of night would ascend; a time when the beasts roam and ravage the land.

However, the gentle Greenwood creatures would not be lambs for the slaughter. They had forewarning, and their fate would be in their own hands.

The first warning comes as the sound of a rolling crescendo of thunder, building up to a great *clap*. Next, blackness obscures the bright orange sun, and a screaming wind howls and shrieks through the trees. Most frighteningly, come the snarls and growls of hungry beasts, each one more terrifying than the last as they tear through bushes and splinter thick branches like twigs. The sounds of snapping, tearing, and gnashing keep the helpless creatures locked away in their hiding places, trembling with fear of discovery by the monsters above.

When the endless cacophony ends, the Seven sound their horn, signaling to the entire forest they are safe once again. They rejoice anew on each first day of Rays, hearts and minds filled with relief and gratitude that they and their loved ones have survived another night and reaffirm their trust that the Seven will keep them safe.

Since the days of Rays are otherwise continuous, the Seven pass one shadow across the sun to signify a fresh day, and help the creatures be mindful of passaging time. This is the way life has been for several centuries. Until the Vague appeared. The Vague is an entity of all its own, and unlike the Beasts, it is not of the Seven's control.

It perhaps had existed in a dormant state for as long as time, or perhaps snuck in from the edges, much as the two humans have seemed to. Regardless, it surprised the Seven, an occurrence that caused much consternation amongst them, for they were never *ever* surprised by anything before this thing they called the Vague.

A young fox named Reve—who'd been trotting along the Tarn in search of food—discovered the Vague by accident. It would be the little fox's saving grace that he could run as fast as a flash, and therefore got far away from the seething blackness that beckoned him with a cold emotionless voice inside his head, and went straight to the Great Willow to tell the Seven of thing he had come upon. So frightened was the little red fox, that his beautiful fur had turned white from tip to tail. The poor thing was never the same and remains no further than a stone's throw from the Great Willow.

Despite their efforts, they have learned little of the dark mass, only that it seems incapable (or at least unwilling) to engage in dialogue, merely reciting the simplest request or command—no one could be sure as it never changed it tone—and exists for no purpose other than to entrap any living creature inside its void. One haunting truth they uncovered: of those that fall into its trap, none return. But, because it seems without thought or even aggression, the Seven deemed the only action necessary for the Greenwood dwellers, is avoidance, a tactic that has always worked well… until present.

This, Endelyn learns by chance after leaving the human girl. As she glides and weaves over and through the land, looking at the beautiful landscape above and below her dragonfly wings, she spies a surprising sight: Another human. This one, a male, walks with surly Mateo, in what appears to be a companionable way. It is the *Jaime* Mala asked after.

For a time, she follows un-noticed above and behind them, observing the human boy's movements and gestures, trying to gleam as much of his ways as possible before approaching. In appearance, he differs greatly from the girl—tall and dark haired where she is slight and fair. Together, they are a fine representation of their race, thought Endelyn, who has no other reference aside the Seven themselves.

They are heading toward the Great Willow, and Endelyn intercepts them. She alights before them, changing back to her true form.

Jaime steps back. "What is that?"

"It is all right. It is better than all right, my friend. This is the great Endelyn of the Seven."

"Tell me, human boy, what troubles you so?" she asks.

Upon seeing the human boy's dejected countenance, handsome as it is, her gentle heart aches for him. She is glad, after hearing the cause of his grief-stricken face, to assuage his worries with assurances his human girl is well.

Mateo and the boy tell her of their meeting with the Vague, which disturbs and stuns her. Had they been mistaken or lax in not handling the concern of the Vague before this? Never had the Vague expressed… *anything*.

It is—or *was*—almost lethargic, lazy even in its attempts at soul seeking, its verbiage rudimentary at most, its projecting of feeling: none. But this encounter with the human is like nothing she's heard of before. There is only one thing for Endelyn to do. She must seek the Vague herself.

So, after quickly telling the two odd traveling companions all she learned, she assures them they are correct to head straight to the Great Willow. The command pleases Mateo, as it is there that Aedina will likely still be. Jaime appears pleased as well in the knowledge Mala is making her way there.

It pleases *her* to leave these two with lighter hearts than how she found them, although it may be short lived. Should she fail, then the Greenwood and all its inhabitants might be in for the fight of their lives, and the Seven may not be able to help them.

31 Day Of Night

Adalbert plops and flops along, humming a bit here and there, making a show of calmness that Mala sees right through. Bullfrogs are not subtle amphibians. At least this one isn't. Not that she's ever had a reciprocal conversation with one before coming to the Greenwood.

"Bert, tell me about the Seven and the Great Willow, would you? I'd like to know what to expect when I get there."

"Ah, the Seven, yes? Well, we've not long before we reach the veil… but I can tell you what I know. Let's see now; there's the four misses: Endelyn, as you've heard about, she'll be the one likely doing much of the talking when you get there, then there's Elsabet, she's of the red hair. Let's see, ahh there's Kaylen with the russet color hair, and then you have Caryss. She's got a head full of black hair. Anyhow, that's how you'll tell them apart, otherwise they look much the same! Did I mention those eyes of theirs? Oh, they are a something."

Mala notices Bert is now talking faster, fanning and patting his waddly neck as he does.

"What is it about their eyes that—"

"Now, for the gents, there's Gabrien, he's got wavy brown hair. Maxis, he's the one with the long hair- dark blonde. Last, there is Tobias. He's got the pale hair, like Endelyn. All same color eyes, each with different color hair. Now lookie here, this is what we call a yum-yum tree, the most delectable…"

"Bert, you said you've never left the Tarn, right?

"Right, right, very true. Over here we have the prickly-"

"So, if you've never left the Tarn to go see the Seven, then that means the Seven have come to you. How long ago was that? Bert… were you waiting for me by the Tarn because they told you I was coming?"

Adalbert Bullfrog stammers and stutters, then gives up and gives in.

"All right, all right! Yes, I knew. It was Endelyn that came to see us, said she needed us to keep a watch over you until she comes to see you for herself. She just had to tell the others about your presence in the Greenwood. Said to us she saw you in a vision, but it was very hazy, so if we could just keep you put until she figured it all out… and well, there you have it."

Bert wrings his webby hands together. "I've been stalling you, miss. Waiting on Endelyn to return for you, but the thing is, she hasn't yet. But I can't keep you round the missus much longer, what with the Vague an' all. So, when you said you were ready to leave, I made a compromise, I did. We've done gone around the same bend now but three times, I'm afraid."

"Ohhh, Bert. But she *has* come, while you and the missus were asleep! I didn't want to tell you because I thought you'd feel bad for missing her."

"Well, ha! Isn't that a right kind of mess? No trouble, no trouble. Although, sets set you back a bit, fear. Come, follow me through here, it'll bring us right to the spot, it will! It's ehh, right by the entry to the Tarn… where we started off."

When he adds the last part, his green face colors a tad bit red. This news frustrates Mala, but not angers. *She* failed to tell him something too, so she guesses that makes them even. All that matters is getting to the Great Willow—whatever that is— before the day of nights. *The day of nights.*

She freezes and says, "Bert! No one has told me what happens during the day of night! What has everyone so frightened?"

"Oh, dear! Yes, ever so important, too! You mustn't be above ground when the night comes, not even for a minute! The air will rumble, the sky will go black, and then the wind will howl. On that terrible wind will come the beasts—snarling and growling and dripping fangs— looking for anyone and anything to devour. It's terrible, I tell you. Terrible!"

Poor Adalbert has worked himself into a frenzy, gesturing with his webbed hands as his throat threatens another croak. This is quite the traumatic event for the Greenwood. She also now understands the need for expediency.

"Calm *down*, Bert, I understand. Let's hurry to the veil, and I'll let you be on your way, back to the missus and your home."

Bert nods his pointed green head rapidly and grabs a hold of her hand. Despite everything, she can't help but smile at the sight of his flat little-but-big-for-a-bullfrog green hand in hers. *If this isn't right out of a fairytale, then I don't know what is.* They make way toward what she assumes is the place where the veil stands.

"All right, then. Here we are. Now, very important, you must remember, do not come out from hiding until the Seven sound their horn!"

Mala stares at the willow tree that they passed twice at least with a new appreciation. When she stands still and pays attention, she feels a vibration emanating from it, not at all unlike the vibration from the door that led her to into the clearing by the Greenwood. According to Bert, that was likely several days ago.

"Bert, tell me, how do you know the passage of days? You don't just wait for the… how did you say it? *Rumble in the air* to let you know when to take cover?"

"Oh, right, right! A little saying we have around here. *Whenever a cloud passes over the sun, a new day of rays has begun*! Isn't that nice, now?

Nice? No, not by Mala's way of thinking. She recalls the one cloud when she arrived, another at Ardie's nest by the bank of the Mere, and one when the Vague had come a-calling for her. That would be three days already. Just how close was this day of night?

"Bert, by my guess, I've been in the Greenwood for three days. Do you know when the day of nights will begin?"

Once again, Bert darts a sheepish look and lifts his sloped shoulders.

"I'm, ehh, sorry to say, but I've not been so good at keeping track these days... of the days. The rumble always lets us know, you see, and we stay close to home and so we don't... but that doesn't help you any, now does it?"

Mala sighs and shrugs as well. What else can go wrong? Just then a distant rumble pricks their ears. Mala looks to Bert for confirmation, Bert's expression of abject terror is answer enough.

"Bert? *Adalbert*. Look at me. Get home to the missus. I'll be fine, I'll just go through the veil and find someplace to hide out, it'll be fine."

She speaks more bravely than she feels, but there is no reason to endanger the bullfrog who so kindly helped her... even if he misled her a bit. Bless his heart, he hesitates in leaving her, so Mala kisses him on the top of his froggy head and all but orders him to march straight home to the missus, who undoubtedly is worried as could be by then. At the mention of his better half, he snaps to and retreats to the Tarn, but not before calling out several warnings and reminders, sounding like a nervous father sending his daughter off to college for the first time.

"Now, mind the rumble, the closer it gets, the closer are the beasts!"

Softer, further away, "*Underground*. You must go *under*ground to be safe. And no peeking. Absolutely none."

His voice now fainter, "Wait for the horn to sound, and not a moment befo…"

Bert's voice and *fwap fwap fwap* of his flat feet drops off as he rounds the bend that leads him back to the Tarn. The rumble is still distant but moving closer. Yet, Mala hesitates. This will be her third time passing through a veil, but this time it is with intent. What is on the other side? *Who*, for that matter? Dragonflies, talking birds and frogs, the Vague, and let's not forget a bona fide… wait. What exactly is Endelyn? A fairy, a queen, a princess, a ruler… a witch? All those things? She wonders if it would be rude to ask, assuming she makes it to this mystifying Great Willow.

The rumble is growing. All around her is the scurrying sounds of forest creatures. Caws and squeaks, rustling of leaves as birds take flight, the snapping and tapping of twigs and branches as they hurry along to wherever they shelter. Until then, figured they mostly stayed hidden from her for fear of a stranger but now, with a legitimate and concrete fear looming, they care not at all for the human interloper in their midst, and chipmunks, squirrels, porcupine and various unrecognizable animals pass her by on all sides. Some speak in passing, a quick *hello* an anxious *step aside* even a *beg pardon* and a *how d'ya do* but others skirt her with skittish glances. Several jump through the veil, causing Mala to cringe each time, fearing a painful thud as they smack against the bark, but they all go right through as if it is nothing more than air.

As she watches in amazement heavy, earth trembling footfalls shake the ground. They're coming from behind her. Though sick with dread at what she might face, she spins around as an enormous shadow falls over her.

Fur the color of milk chocolate. Claws as long as her pinkie. A tan snout. Four dagger-like canines parenthesize two rows of sharp teeth. It is a...

"Bearis Bear at your service. Not much time to waste little cub, through the veil now, with you."

"I-I'm not a cub," is all she can stammer in response.

To the bear. Sanding on his hind legs. *Just like Adalbert*. That just spoke to her. She needs to stop being surprised by every minor thing in this strange land. She lets the vocal bear shuffle her along toward the magic willow tree with no resistance.

She can't stop staring at the massive mammal. Particularly its teeth. He has a gruff but jovial sounding voice, which is at direct odds with the severity of those sharp teeth. But as he wraps one massive paw around her shoulders, protecting her from the whipping wind, the sweet smell of honey and flowers envelope her and she lets herself relax into the warm furry embrace.

Between the wind whipping up leaves and dirt, and the growing number of animals running amuck—now including larger ones like deer and coyotes—she quickly surmises the time of safety is growing short. The rumble is now a rolling bowling ball amplifying all around them.

Above the din the bear shouts, "My den is on the other side of the veil, we'll be safe there. Ready… now jump!"

Though Mala considers it more of a carry through than a jump, she and the bear are on the other side before she can blink. If she thought it would be quieter and calmer once through, she'd have been very mistaken. The only difference is the surroundings. Instead of sparse vegetation and clustered trees, overgrowth and towering trees of various evergreen crowd this part of the Greenwood.

There are many scattered areas of fallen trees and thick limbs. The creaking of the tall trees as they bend and sway in the heavy winds indicates that more will fall before the day of nights end. At first glance, the piles of debris and branches appeared haphazard. Now Mala notices that several have bear sized openings, so Mala is unsurprised when the great shaggy bear drops to all fours and heads toward the nearest one.

His thick sturdy paws, well-practiced at navigating the terrain, move easily through and over. However, for Mala it is more of a challenge. With so little time to spare, he encourages Mala to climb atop his back.

"Hold tight, little one," growls the bear as he crouches low for her.

He jumps with surprising grace over fallen and tangled logs, and Mala buries her hands in his fur. His flanks shudder with each heavy thump of his paws, and she hangs on to his thick coat.

Despite the chaos and fear, Mala is giddy with excitement. It should terrify and confuse her—and it does—but she is ecstatic. In fact, if someone saw her face as she rides on the back of a talking bear, through a forest of ready-to-fall-on-her-head trees, while a vicious wind rips and an angry thunder rolls, and while the threat of beasts looms on the horizon... they'd see a wide and wild smile beaming across her face. For the first time in her life, she feels *alive*.

Another, more primal emotion courses through her. She doesn't want to run. She wants to *fight*. Why are they running and hiding when they could face these monsters that terrorize the poor weaker creatures of the Greenwood, a land she's fallen in love with without even realizing it? She tries to get the lumbering bear to stop, but the wind howls so, and the thunder grows still more, and her small hands—even as buried in his fur as they are—cannot tug with any effectiveness.

She ducks as Bearis runs full speed at the just-right-for-a-bear opening at the nestle of fallen trees, and in an instant, they are in the cave's darkness. He doesn't stop once inside but continues further into the cave which Mala now sees as a long tunnel.

Ahead, a faint glow pulses. It's a light of some sort dimly illuminating their way. The sounds of the oncoming night fades, then ceases when the bear pushes a thatched screen made from branches, leaves and hardened mud with his powerful mitts in front of the opening. It would take at least four grown human men to move it, but the bear does so with relative ease.

As he turns back toward the soft light, Mala swings her leg over and slides down his flank in such a fluid motion, like she'd been riding on the backs of bears her entire life. She keeps one hand on the bears' back, and together they walk through the cave that is indeed a tunnel. She is just a head taller than the mammal on all fours by her side, so she doesn't need to duck at all in the smallish space. The sides of the tunnel, dug with claws and paws going by the long scrapes and scratches that marked it, is plenty wide for both.

They follow the curve of the tunnel and the soft glow brightens. An echo of hushed talking bounces off the walls. She cannot make out words but discerns the voices of several overlapping. When around the bend, the sight that greets her is awe striking.

The tunnel opens into an enormous cavern, as wide as it is high. Opposite the opening they'd entered through, stands another. She asks, "Where does that lead?"

"It takes us to the Great Willow," says Bearis.

She nods without looking at him; her gaze travels every inch of her surroundings. Mala cranes her head. Even if she stood on Jaime's broad shoulders, she would just about touch to ceiling. Tan mud, red clay, and stones of various sizes comprise the wide circular space. Set all around the room on shallow ledges are beeswax candles. This is what gives off the warm, flickering glow. Flattened logs and heaps of straw-like dried grasses are strewn about like sofas and cushions.

And in the center of the cave, a small cozy fire crackles. Around it are six bears of various sizes and shades of brown, sitting like men. But the most interesting creature of all at the fire is *not* a bear, it is — at first glance—another human girl. However, the more Mala stares at her, the more she realizes this is not a human at all.

For one, her size belies her age—tiny but with a face of someone of Mala's own age—and her skin, while flawless and smooth, shows hints of moss green, even in the fire light. Even her eyes are unusual, copper that matches her hair almost exactly. In a word, she is exotic.

Caught staring, Mala stammers an apology to the solemn-faced, unusual looking girl, and nods hello to the rest of the bears, who are staring at *her*. All conversation stops, and an awkward silence befalls them.

Bearis steps into it, claps his paws together, and announces in his booming, friendly voice, "All right, everyone, jaws shut, manners up, introductions all around. First up, my cousins, Baylor and Bab, their cub Banon of Mere. Aedina, Leader of the Guardians. My other cousins, Bodi, his cub Bryn of Tarn. And last, we have Brenna, my sister. Everyone, say hello to Mala of… ah, where's it you come from, again?"

"Ah, hello all. I'm, um, from a place called Rocky Knoll? It's— well—I came though the Everwood. It's a forest like yours… well, not exactly like yours, it's more like… ah, yeah, just… hi, everyone."

A flicker of a smile crosses the face of the green girl. As for the bears, they look puzzled. The two cubs giggle, and then they all follow suit. Mala, at the sight of the silly cubs falling over backwards in laughter, can't help but laugh, too. Their laughter echoes throughout the cave. But then a thud from above—one hard enough to shake loose some dirt from the high ceiling and send powdery dust down on their heads like tiny snowflakes—abruptly cuts off their hoots.

"Another tree down, no doubt. We'll have some work ahead of us tomorrow. Rest well tonight, friends."

Aedina catches Mala's eye and motions for her to sit beside her. At first, the two girls say nothing, and instead take turns studying the others profile as they stare into the fire. Both want to speak, but unsure what to say. So as is wont to happen in such moments, they speak simultaneously.

"I think we should fight the beasts," says Mala,

"I have met your Jaime," says Aedina.

Both look incredulously at each other, deferring back and forth as the bears watch with curious amusement. Bipeds are strange, they all concur not so quietly.

"You've seen Jaime? But where is he? Is he okay?"

"Yes, yes, he was well when I last saw him. I sent him along with my second in command, Mateo, to our home—the Havenheart. Is he—ah, is he what all of your males look like in your land?"

Mala laughs and tries to not roll her eyes. Even here, a strange land, girls swoon over him. Being only human, a flicker of possessiveness flashes inside her like a lit match, but she just as quickly extinguishes it. Instead, she responds with good humor.

"Oh, Jaime is a specimen all his own." What she keeps to herself is that, while there are other handsome men in her world, Jaime is the best.

An unspoken acknowledgement passes between the two young women; Jaime is Mala's and Aedina respects that it's so. Mala suspects Aedina lives by a similar code of ethics as her own. She dislikes the catty games girls her age play. She *does* fall prey to the trappings of vanity and competition sometimes. At least for Jaime, she does.

The wariness fades and the two diverse girls strike up a tentative friendship. Their conversation moves from polite questions to Aedina regaling Mala with the story of their meeting with Jaime, to which Mala admits that it sounds *exactly* like how he'd behave under such circumstances. She swears in his defense that he is much more graceful on his own turf.

Aedina becomes serious and asks Mala, "Did you mean it when you said you wanted to fight the beasts? I have asked this of our Elders many times in the past, to always be told it is too dangerous, as the beasts are too fierce. They say it means committing ourselves to certain death. But I say, if it is our job to guard the land, then we are failing. Perhaps you can convince the Seven where I could not?"

Mala grips Aedina's arm and says, "Once this day of night thing has passed, I'm going there. Endelyn came to me at the Tarn and…"

"*Endelyn.* That is good to hear. I have just come from the Great Willow; the Elders do not seem to know her whereabouts. However, they have sent me to track the Vague instead. Was she well? Do you know where she was going?"

Mala tells her all she knows, including her confrontation with the Vague. "I'm afraid I don't know where Endelyn went, though."

Aedina thumps her chin with a knuckle. "I'm certain she, too, is searching for the Vague." She is silent for a long moment, staring into the fire. At last she turns her copper gaze on Mala and says, "I believe I must escort you to the Great Willow, and together we will tell them what you have witnessed and endured, and ask permission to gather our guardians and prepare to fight on the next day of night."

At that, the great rotund bear claps his huge paws together and announces, "Well, now that that's all settled, what do you say for a spell of sleep. I'm mighty tired myself."

To emphasis his point, he adds a great, tonsil baring yawn, meanders to the nearest pile of dried grasses, and drops onto his side. Within seconds he is snoring. But the two girls, behaving like long lost sisters, cannot rest. They each have so much to tell and show one another. Mala tells her as much of her world and the events that brought her to this spot in the Greenwood as she could in short order, and Aedina does much the same.

Upon discovering one another's fighting skills, both so foreign to the other, they teach each other everything they can. Within hours Mala handles a spear and a dagger with efficiency, and Aedina flips, throat chops, and breaks restraints as fast and as well as Mala.

After two more hours, the girls grow tired and slump by the fire alongside the two sleeping cubs.

"Do you realize how amazing this is for me? In my world, we call them wild animals, and over there you never get this close to them, and they don't speak."

"Don't speak?! How strange. And sad. Bearis has been a dear friend for as long as I can remember, my only friend when I was still a wildling. If not for him I'd likely not have survived the days of night."

As if on cue, Bearis wakes and mumbles, "Silly brave girls. Ya don't go looking for trouble, not if you're wise."

Both girls smile at the enormous sleepy bear. From one another, each has learned everything that transpired before their fortuitous meeting—from Aedina's conference with the Elders, to Bearis deciding to go look for this human girl and bring her to safety along with them, and the dramatic and disturbing changes that have come over the Vague.

Despite their shared urgency to do something, they know they are unprepared to venture out before the day of night ends, so they resign themselves to rest, both sleeping fitfully with the tangled dreams of anxious minds.

32 JAIME AND MALA

Just as the warning rumble of thunder began, Jaime and Mateo reach the Great Willow. Even though Mateo has seen it many times before, he's as awestruck as Jaime. The description did no justice to the magnificence of the grandiosity of the aptly named haven. It nestles central of a meadow and worn dirt paths wind toward it, disappearing under a canopy of long, thick-leafed branches.

A familiar rose gold light emanates from within, seeping through the spaces between the sheltering branches. It is the same light Jaime saw shoot out from the strange door in the Everwood, instantly recognizable in its unusualness, but this time more welcoming.

Milling about all around them are various woodland creatures—many recognizable to Jaime, like opossum and squirrels—but just as many are not. Rabbits with the bodies of beavers, donkey-like creatures the size of cats, and furry lizards mixed and mingled with each other with ease and friendliness. Some glance at Jaime, a few '*hello*'s' and '*good day*'s' are called out, but all seem rather calm and content despite the growing rumble in the air.

The only one who seems to take notice or show concern is a small white fox trembling at the edge of the tree; so close to it, that he might as well be under the branches rather than outside them. It is Reve, of course. Elderly but just as anxious as ever, he remains the timid 'guard' of the Great Willow, alerting the Seven of any unusual activity.

"This place is incredible. I think that's the biggest tree I've ever seen in my life. But why aren't the animals taking cover? I thought you said that when the day of night came, all the Greenwood creatures hid below ground until it passed?"

"The day of night is almost over. However, that is true. Great Willow is enchanted, as are its grounds. Anything within its circle is protected, therefore anyone invited to stay in the perimeter is safe from the day of night. You will hear it, but it will not grow dark here, nor will the winds or beasts penetrate its barriers. It is what you have called *magic*."

Well, if *they* don't call that magic, then he doesn't know what is. He begins to say as much to Mateo, then notices the greenish boy looks a little pale-ish. When he catches Jaime's curious eye, he admits with a stammer he has never actually been *inside* the enchanted tree, as it is Aedina who meets with the Elders.

"Ah, I see. Well, no reason to be nervous. Wait. Is there? Anyhow, Aedina and Mala may already be in there, so let's go find out."

Mateo gives a curt nod and squares his sharp shoulders. Together, the oddly paired boys stride toward the bowed, ground sweeping branches, each parting a section and ducking under and through. Likewise, the simple opulence of the glowing, immense cavern-like space awes and amazes them. Though there are no sparkling gems or jewels, no material displays of wealth and riches, this is the residence of greatness. Ahead, upon a dais sculpted within the widest part of the massive trunk sits six figures, draped in simple cream-colored clothes, trimmed in delicate rose gold detailing. Each is as beautiful as the next, with eyes of teal set in strong but kindly looking faces.

Jaime does what seems appropriate, and bows low, if not awkwardly. He shoots a side eye at Mateo, only to find he is upright still, and tips a deferential nod to those before them. Turning to Jaime, a puzzled expression on his face, he asks, "Have you dropped something? Why are you bent so?"

"No, I have not dropped something. Where I come from, people bow before royalty."

"Well, we Viriscent do not *bow* as you say. We tip our head in reverence. Stand up, you look odd."

"Well, how would I know? You could've prep…"

The Elder named Gabrien—amused but impatient to hear of their journey and what brings them to the Great Willow—hushes their bickering. Mateo enlightens them of the events that preceded their visit, giving special detail to the encounter with the Vague and subsequent appearance of Endelyn.

The Elders astonishment surprises him. Gabrien silences him with a raised hand as they telepathically converse, and Mateo ignores Jaime's questioning stare.

Jaime is impatient to discover Mala's whereabouts, he'd expected to see her here, and cannot contain his disappointment at her absence. One of the mysterious angels—that's what they looked like, to Jaime—speaks to him.

"Human. Welcome to the Greenwood, I am Caryss. Your presence here is as a surprise to us, we must say. Aedina preceded your visit with her own and told us of your existence here in the Greenwood. You see, Endelyn had foretold of your companion—the human girl—but you... *you* are unexpected, but not unwelcome. I suspect we will need your help very soon. Can we rely on you, young human, should we need your service?"

"Ahh, well... yeah, sure. But what do you mean *service*? And, if you don't mind my asking, where is Mala? Endelyn said that she would be here..."

From behind Jaime and Mateo, a familiar voice calls out, "And she was right."

Jaime spins, and though there stands three figures, his eyes only see one. *Mala*. As the others watch on, they walk toward each other, both grinning. The hint of a blush blooms on Mala's cheeks; she is staring at his bared chest. He'd long forgotten Mateo had torn apart and reassembled his clothes, so now he resembles Tarzan more than anything.

She, too, has gone through a transformation. No longer in the clothing she had on before crossing into the Greenwood, but now attired much like Aedina, her hair wild and free and with several feathers worked into the small braids that fall over her bare shoulders. Jaime's appraising eyes deepen her blush, and he smiles wider.

Finally, Jaime speaks. "Hey Little. Still mad?"

Instead of the playful punch he expected, Mala closes the distance between them and wraps her small but strong arms around Jaime's waist and squeezes. He envelopes her in an equally tight embrace, feeling all the tension, the worry and fear subside. His relief at seeing her and holding her is almost more than he can take. Without even thinking about it, he tips her face to his, overwhelmed with the urge to kiss her. That she doesn't pull away, but looks questioningly up into his eyes, is all the encouragement he needs. Bending his head down as she raises herself on her tip toes, Jaime…

"Excuse me, humans?"

Maxis, with as much bad timing as any human, requests their attention. It is then, after pressing his forehead against Mala's for a moment, that he looks up and notices her companions. It is Aedina and the most enormous bear he's ever seen. He's only seen bears in the zoo, and once at a circus. Both experiences appalled and depressed him. The sight of such majestic animals being treated as objects of entertainment and amusement filled him with a contempt for humans. This bear, however, wore no costume and bore no chains around its neck.

After giving both Mala's companions a hello, he joins them in facing the six sitting members of the Seven. They look upon each expectant face—Jaime and Mala at the forefront, flanked by Aedina, the bear, and Mateo— with solemn consideration, perhaps appraisal even.

It is Mala who speaks first, boldly and without hesitation. "We want to fight the Beasts at the next day of night."

Hushed murmurs ripple like a wave from the various creatures who'd snuck into the haven to observe this monumental visit by humans. The surprised expressions of the Elders compare not at all with the shocked dismay Jaime feels. Once again, Mala is leading him into one of her grand adventures but this time, one with potentially deathly results.

Before he can speak, Gabrien raises a hand to silence any further comments. A weighted silence fills the air. Only the sound of the bear's heavy breathing behind Jaime disrupts the quiet.

"Welcome Mala of… Everwood. You are as Endelyn foresaw you. Brave and headstrong, *and* tenacious and precocious, too, I see. We admire your courage and willingness to fight for a land that is not yours, and for creatures you do not know. However, there is another battle we'll need your help for."

A sick dread sinks like a rock in Jaime's stomach. The Vague. That is the battle he wants them for. This is going from bad to worse. What if they, *or he*, refuses? Or asks to be sent home and forget this place ever existed? Can they? *Would* they? Jaime sighs. They will fight for the Greenwood. This is what every moment prior has led to, it is obvious.

The irony is that he here by accident, as some sort of by-product of Mala's gravitational pull, sucked into this strange land because he is a planet in her orbit.

As if she can hear his thoughts, she whispers, "There are no accidents, Jaime. You are meant to be here, as surely as I am."

Kaylen smiles down at the pair, and says, "And so, you are correct, young human. Just because my sister did not foresee it as so, we too, believe that there are no accidents. You, human boy, belong here just as your companion."

Mala beams at him with her *I told you so* smile, looking so self-satisfied Jaime laughs and shakes his head in defeat. "I suppose the veil wouldn't have opened to me if I'm not meant to be here, right? Still… fights? *Battles*? I mean, come on. This is, like, not in my wheelhouse, *or* my comfort zone, guys."

One look at Mala's flushed cheeks and blazoned eyes tells him she is in *her* glory, within *her* wheelhouse and comfort zone. He watches her with his usual mix of admiration and consternation as her eyes scan each Elder. Because *his* eyes are on her, he sees the change in her expression and the small gasp of surprise when her eyes lock on one of the Seven.

Jaime follows her line of sight to where it stopped. The Elder Maxis. He returns her stare, a smile tugging at the corners of his mouth. After a moment he tips his head, confirming something to Mala.

"I *dreamed* you. Many times, throughout my childhood. The dreams… they were so real. I thought… I always thought one day I would find you for real, but then you stopped… and now, here you are and…"

She trails off at the end, shaken. Jaime remembers those dreams, too. Even though she never spoke of them, he'd known of them. Mala only wrote about them in her journal… which he read. He never confessed it to her, and now, after so much time had passed, still could not.

In that journal, she'd written every detail she could recall, from the color of the sky to the cracks in the ground, with exceptional clarity. From it, he learned there seemed to be no pattern, no regularity to the recurring dreams, but what *was* constant was the sense of being protected, watched over, guarded even, by the larger-than-life man.

This figure—this man—remained at a distance, a glow of fiery red light surrounding him as his long blonde hair blew back from his chiseled face. She often awoke with a sense of peaceful protection around her like it was a force field, yet sad to realize it was just a dream.

Mala's onetime description of the dreams had struck even Jaime. They stirred something in him, too. Jealousy. To be jealous of a dream is a ridiculousness even he could acknowledge. Still… there was something so private, so deep about those dreams for her she couldn't share them even with Jaime, and it made him feel displaced and unneeded. He never tried to read the journal entries again.

As he looks at the six figures on the dais, he wonders once again who *are* these people, and where did they come from? As troubling as these thoughts are, it bothers him more that these super natural beings *should* have all the answers, and all the powers, yet they don't know where their seventh member is—their *future telling* seventh—nor can they get rid of the beasts *or* the Vague, and need a bunch of kids to do the job for them.

He is ready to ask these very questions, but he is pre-empted by Aedina, who is also irked… but for separate reasons.

33 AEDINA

She *is* irked. *Not fight the beasts?* Surely, they take precedence over the Vague, who is but a passive menace? True, it is gaining power, intelligence even, but it still is no match for the Guardians.

Unlike Jaime, she does not question why the Elders will not—or cannot—fight the Vague or the beasts. They are peace bringers and do not practice violence. With each of their respective talents, they are powerful. However, their unwavering tenet is that of non-violence. From this they cannot be moved.

She is so incensed by the resistance to the plan that she and Mala had worked on together in the cave, that she barely takes notice of Mateo and Jaime, aside from first observing the electric connection between the two humans, and noting the relieved and even pleased expression on Mateo's face as he caught her eye. This, she will ponder later.

Her goal is to persuade the Elders to allow them to return to the Havenheart and train all the Virescent in the new fighting technique learned from the human girl, who she now considers her friend and equal. Six days and nights of Rays will go by fast, and tmustt to train without relent if they are to be ready for the next day of night.

"Elders, please, you don't understand, we…"

Surprising sternness from the usually quiet Tobias halts her. "No, Guardian, it is you that does not understand. Endelyn is missing, we cannot sense her. If the Vague has her…"

He pauses, looking to his teal-eyed companions, most pointedly at Gabrien, who continues for Tobias, "Children, if the Vague has Endelyn—and we believe that it does—the Greenwood will never be the same. Without all Seven of us, working together, we are… diminished."

Jaime blurts, "Diminished? What the hell does that—"

"It means our powers are weakened, as the chain is broken. As it is now, we believe she is alive, but unable to communicate."

Maxis finishes Jaime's sentence, then Mala continues for *him*, with her eyes still locked on the blond God-like man.

"And this will affect more than just the Greenwood, won't it? It will influence my world—*our* world, too."

Almost imperceptivity Maxis, Gabrien and Caryss nod their assent. Tobias and Kaylen stare ahead. But it is Elsabet alone who looks outright emotional. Aedina and the others watch as she rises and makes her way toward them, first to Mateo, whom she places a delicate hand upon his tousled head and bows hers. Though she says nothing, she wins him over. She next moves to Aedina and repeats the gesture, this time raising Aedina's small pixie-like face, so their eyes meet. A single tear escapes from the corner of Elsabet's teal-colored eye, slips like a bead of glass down the curve of her flawless cheek and falls to the ground below. A delicate pink flower blooms it the spot where the tear landed.

Elsabet approaches the bear, this time smiling juslittle bit, as it is almost impossible not to smile at such a wondrous and shaggy fellow, and she takes his massive face into her pale hands and presses her small smooth forehead against his broad furry pate. The gentle giant closes his ameyesyes, and chuffs as they commune. After a moment, she steps back from the bear, but keeps her hands on either side of his enormous face for a few moments longer.

Upon releasing him, she glides toward Mala and Jaime, and stands between them. She reaches out her hands, expecting them to place their own into hers, which they oblige. Then Elsabet brings their hands together.

They are experiencing the same sensation as Aedina and the others had before them—a strange vibration prickling their skin and seeping into their bones. With wordless mental images, she conveys the urgency in which they need to find the Vague. As Jaime will later say, it is like telepathy supercharged.

After she lays hands on each of them, transferring her thoughts and feelings to all, she slips back to the dais, still never speaking a word, and reclaims her seat. A hush, like a pause between thoughts, falls.

At last, and without conferring with the others, Aedina speaks for them, "Very well. We shall seek the Vague, and Endelyn. But we must go first to the Havenheart. Is there anything more you can tell us, any direction you may sense is best?"

The others—Mala, Jaime, Mateo and Bearis—all agree, as she knew they would. No one could have felt the impact of Elsabet's projected feelings, and not done what they are bid.

"We thank you. Elsabet was most connected with Endelyn, and she believes they can be found in the north Edges…" Gabrien pauses, glancing at his companions on the dais before he continues. "…the home of the beasts. It was the last time she communicated. She has, of course, often been to the west Edges…"

Here, Gabrien looks to Mala and Jaime, and continues "…where you both came into the Greenwood from. However, much of the Edges are unsafe, as their veils are unstable, and we believe the Vague found its way through one of these points."

This is new to Mala and Jaime, and even Mateo. Aedina, however knew much of this, with thanks to Soji. But, a new question forms in her mind as she listens, one she had to ask.

"Gabrien, if anything can come through the Edges into the Greenwood, then does that mean anyone from the Greenwood can get *out* through the Edges?"

Of all the things she has never seen the Elders do, squirm is highest on the list. Yet all six shift and give one another looks. It is Maxis who responds.

"That is not a simple question to answer, Aedina. It is not so simple."

"But if there are veils that outsiders come through, then we could go out, correct?"

"Yes, but only with guidance from an Elder. Aedina... all of you, we forbid use of the veils at the Edges. Is that understood?"

All understand, but Aedina does not accept it in her heart. She wants to ask, *but why?* Before she can, Gabrien raises a hand, silencing the ready words at her lips as if he knows what they are.

"No more." Then, as almost an afterthought, "Please. There will be time for questions after. Once the day of night has passed, you must ready yourselves, and make way to the north Edges. It should take two days' time to arrive there."

"We shall do as you ask. But, how do we even fight a thing we cannot even touch? Can you at least tell me this much?"

Though her tone is insolent, her question is legitimate. How *can* they fight this thing and free Endelyn? But then, just as the thought enters her mind, another follows. She abruptly turns to Mala, who looks at her, and speaks her very thoughts aloud, "We don't fight it, we trick it. We send it back through the veil it snuck through."

Mala again locks her eyes on Maxis, and finished with, "Don't we?"

34 Unexpected Encounters

Mala's mind whirls. Between the incomparable Great Willow and its unshakable familiarity, the magnificence of the Elders, seeing Jaime at last, and then… *Maxis*. To see the face and learn the name of who she's come to think of as her guardian angel; she has no words. Tears and wild laughter well inside her, yet she bottles them.

Not even Jaime can understand the depth and magnitude of Maxis effect on her as a child. His presence in her dreams were the most profound gifts she'd ever know, making her believe she was safe, protected, cherished even. He made her believe she was special, and was perhaps her first love, if one could love a figure from a dream, that is.

The way he looks at her there from up on the dais, with his eyes boring through her soul; what does it mean? Why had he come to her for all those years, without rhyme or reason? And then why had he disappeared, leaving her bereft and longing for those familiar reassurances that only his presence could provide.

The joy at seeing him—really *him*, and not just a figment of her overactive child's imagination born from a need to believe she more than just an average girl—clashes with a wave of anger and hurt.

Despite feeling overwhelmed by all the conflicting emotions waging a battle inside her head, she compartmentalizes. This too, will be a mental drawer she closes for now, and will reopen later for further examination.

She must instead focus on the present moment. Here, underneath the vast canopy of branches and leaves, in a rose-gold lighted enclosure, standing before six ethereal figures with three unusual companions and her wonderful, sweet and steadfast Jaime, they must set down their plan for ridding the Greenwood of the Vague forever.

Everyone's eyes are on her, waiting for her to explain. Her intuition tells her she is right, but the weight of their collective stares makes her doubt and hesitate. The sudden warmth of Jaime's hand as it wraps around hers reassures and fortifies her, just as he knew it would, and gives her courage to continue.

"So, from what I understand, these veils at all the Edges—they lead to other lands. That's why you try to keep everyone away from them, isn't it?"

Mala doesn't wait for a response. "The Vague is something we can't kill, it's not even alive, at least not so we can relate to, so we have to send it back. The question will be, *how?*"

At this, Mala looks to each of her companions and the seated Elders, lingering longest on Maxis, but the question is rhetorical. She finishes by saying, "One of us must pass through and try to get it to follow. Once it is through to the other side, we must destroy the veil."

Everyone, save Mateo, agrees. His face is draw in consternation as he asks the most obvious question, "But who will be the one to lead the Vague through the veil?"

35 JAIME'S DOUBTS

Jaime listened to both Mala and Aedina with open admiration. However, the question of who will lead the Vague through the veil troubles him... assuming it was even possible to do so. But that is not all that concerns him. Not only does he agree with Mateo, he has his own doubts.

"Let's just say that someone manages to lead the Vague out of the Greenwood and back into whatever strange place the veil leads to. What happens to that person, once through? And how do we get them back before we destroy veil?"

Just as he expects, no one has the answers to those queries, and deafening silence meets them. But then, as predictable as the sunrise and sunset—at least in his world—both Aedina and Mala announce, "I'll do it!"

Mateo and Jaime drop their heads in exasperated defeat, releasing the breath they'd been holding.

Of course, of course, of course.

Those two *would* volunteer, before everything had been thought out, every detail taken into consideration. There were many times over the years when Jaime felt certain Mala's escapades and ideas would get her or both killed… figuratively and literally. This is one of those literal times. He tells her so, and Aedina.

Like two doe-eyed cartoon characters, they blink at him, as if *he* is the one saying reckless and ridiculous things. Instead, and behaving as twins, the girls turn away from him, pretending not to have heard a word he said, and implore the Elders to choose one of them to sacrifice their safety, perhaps even their lives for a mission that might not even work.

He gapes at Mateo. He must be a companion in rationality. However, he instead sees the unmistakable look of a man ready to throw himself upon the sword for the woman he loves, even if he doesn't know he loves her. Well, he will not be the coward in the crowd, so he throws his own rationality out the window along with the rest of them, and blurts, "No, I'll be the one."

Mateo echoes the offer, then Bearis. Gabrien spoke before the arguing could begin, "Were Endelyn here to lend us her vision, we could advise you. I'm afraid that we can give you no guidance, and you must decide amongst yourselves how best to proceed." He pauses, his distress written on his face, then adds, "We are most sorry."

Kaylen is quick to follow Gabrien's solemn words with an invitation they cannot refuse, perhaps because it is more of a command.

"Please shelter here, in the Great Willow until the day of night has passed. You shall dine first, as we are sure you must be famished. Elsabet can escort you, Aedina and Mala to sleeping quarters. Tobias will bring you, Mateo and Jaime. Bearis, I believe we have just enough space for you," she adds with a teasing smile.

They discover there is room for several Bearis-sized bears and more inside the trunk of the majestic willow. The Elders stand, and in single file walk around the dais, disappearing one by one behind it. The last of the Elders, Maxis, waves a come along gesture, which they comply. Aedina leads the quintet, with Bearis lumbering a heavy-footed last. No one speaks, they are awestruck. Not even Aedina has ever been within the great trunk, as it is the inner sanctuary of the Seven.

As they near the waiting Elder, Jaime studies him. *So, this is the mysterious figure of Mala's dreams.* The man-God has an imposing presence. *If* you're impressed by chiseled muscles, stature, and perfection. He looks like something out of Norse mythology. *Thor. That's who he resembles. Great.* All that's missing is the hammer. The only thing that irritates him more than the flawlessness of the guy that seems to own a piece of Mala's heart, is that from the moment she walked into the haven tree's asylum, his teal eyes have been on her. Even now, as each of the five walk past him, he only looks at her. If he notices Jaime giving him the evil eye, he doesn't much care. But then, why would he? He is a God of sorts, and Jaime's just some seventeen-year-old kid.

Jaime walks by Maxis and notes with male pride that he is nearly as tall as the Thor wannabe. But his smug satisfaction dissolves when he hears him say, "Wait."

He is speaking to Mala, and Mala only. She is behind Jaime, but he knows, without turning around, that Maxis put his hand on her forearm to stop her. He hears her small gasp, can imagine her heart stutter, and cannot help his own hands from clenching into fists. He stops as well but doesn't turn to see what his mind already envisions.

"It's okay, Jaime. I'll be fine."

Mala's voice, as familiar as his own, but with a tremor. Not of unease, but of excitement. What can he do? Say? Nothing. Turning his head only slightly, he nods once. He straightens his spine and walks away from the two figures at his back.

Had Mala been looking, had she seen him as only she could, perhaps she'd have run after him, forgoing the thrill of meeting a dream in the light of… day…but, no. She's locked within a teal gaze like a magnet to steel. And so, Jaime walks on, feeling like… like a guy who's lost his best friend.

36 DREAMS ARE SOMETIMES REAL

Feelings are a funny thing. If they were a person, Mala would call them a jerk. How can they change and flip, and betray *without warning*? Until the moment before she saw Maxis, her thoughts were all of Jaime. Telling him everything that had happened to her, hearing of his adventure, hugging him, and just looking at him.

Then, when she looked up at the dais, her heart turned inside out. She'd wondered if she'd ever get a chance to speak to him—*Maxis*—alone. Until the moment she noticed Maxis was last at the massive tree's opening, that is. It was then that she knew he wanted to speak to her, too.

Just as Jaime had observed, Mala felt his eyes on her the entire time they stood before the Elders. But why? Who or what is she to *him*? He leads her away from the tree, one hand at her elbow. The heat from his hand travels up her arm and straight into her chest.

When she stumbles, his grip tightens and steadies her, but he says not a word. She, too, walks in silence, letting him lead her towards the furthest edges of the tree's fortress of branches, as far from the base as possible without leaving the sanctuary of the haven itself. The myriad of animals that mill about disperse as they approach, and Mala smiles at them as they bob their heads and wave with their furry paws.

At last they are alone, standing side by side facing the curtain of silvery green leaves that separate them from the retreating night beyond. She reaches up and presses one cool leaf between her fingertips, caressing the smooth surface with her thumb. This is a moment she's been hoping for her whole life. Now, here it is, and she is tongue tied and shy.

She sneaks a glance at him, and her heart catches in her throat. He is as beautiful—no, more so—as in her dreams, but now close and in minute detail. High cheekbones, firm jaw line, straight Grecian looking nose, and faint lines at the corner of his eye that deepen when he smiles. His long, dark blonde hair had the highlights of one who's spent a lifetime in the sun, his skin, a golden hue. The garment he wears mostly hides his physique, but she can still recall how muscular he appeared in her dreams.

"This must be a shock for you. I am sorry."

His voice is deep and quiet, his words slow and careful, like warm honey. Maxis sighs and looks down at her. Mala stares hard at the leaf in her hand, tracing the jagged veins on its narrow face with her eyes and willing herself not to cry.

It was the *I'm sorry.* She was never a fan of those words; sometimes they hurt as much as the offense that pre-empted them. *Sorry* makes her *feel,* and she works so damn hard to *not.* So, she clenches her jaw, wraps her arm—the one not fidgeting with the leaf—across her body and digs her nails into the back of her upper arm.

Don't cry. Don't cry. Don't cry.

But the telltale prickling sensation is there behind her eyes and the leaf becomes a watery blur, and though she tries not to blink out a drop, one fat tear slides down the curve of her cheek, hot and betraying.

Maxis' heart is pained, more than even he can believe. This girl, this *human,* has captivated him for time beyond measure. Lifetimes. Yet he is only an observer of her life, not a participant. What cruel rules they live by, both Gods and men.

He steps between her and the leaves she so adamantly studies, and takes her narrow shoulders between his powerful hands, and as he kneels before her, he pulls her close, convincing her to look into his spellbinding eyes.

"There are things out of our control—*all* of ours. I had no choice in how I came to you, no choice in leaving you. I— what you feel? It is not unfounded… and it is not unreciprocated. All I can tell you is I have been with you for more than this lifetime. More than many. In this, as in those before, we will not be. We cannot."

Why.

That is the word in her head, the word she cannot let pass her lips. Nothing of this makes sense, and somehow it all does. She *feels* it, the correctness of it. But not the *why*. Her Guardian Angel—as she's come to think of him—he is a perfection and an ideal for which she's always needed to believe existed. It insures she will never, ever settle for anything less than amazing.

Everything in her life has led her to now, to *here*. She knows, in her heart of hearts, that this is her only moment to cherish and accept her fleeting gift before it is again gone from her life. The moment calls to mind a quote she heard but not fully understood at Jaime's grandfather's funeral, spoken in eulogy: "The price we pay for love, is grief." And though this is not a death, nor is this a love of any traditional sort, it feels like the same.

She looks down at the larger than life God-like man kneeling before her, asking for understanding and forgiveness for things he professes to have no control over. In this moment, Mala sees merely a man.

Her hand hovers, then rests atop his head. The echo of ten thousand years or more in which two figures remain within arm's length of one another flashes before her closed eyes. Next, she sees herself as a child inside his eyes; a lost, lonely girl who felt too much, hurt too deeply, and she saw *him* standing near, watching from afar, placing a hand upon her sleeping head and instantly smoothing her worried brow. Even when she couldn't feel him, he had been there.

He has never left her. He has *never* left her. He…

"You never left me. You never will, will you?"

Mala smiles, a genuine smile through standing tears that obediently refuse to fall. He lifts his head to smile back; a smile that is exactly like the moment a cloud filled sky parts and reveals the sunshine.

"So, you *do* see? I so hoped you would. If I could give you more, I would."

"I was inside your mind, I could see… It was like I could see forever. I see, but I don't know if I understand. But it's okay. For the first time in forever, I feel like everything is okay. Or at least it will be. Because of you."

Maxis closes his eyes, then grasps both of her hands, kissing one palm, and then the other, and pressing them against his cheeks. Mala bows her forehead to his, and like this they remain for some time.

She will keep this moment locked away in her heart and mind, hers alone. Perhaps one day she may write about it, give it air to breathe again; *life*. But that will be a long, far way down the road, when the loss feels less bitter, more sweet.

She pulls away first, drawing in a shaky breath. He squeezes her hands once more before standing, and together they return to join the others. There is no more to be said, and though the air between them is still electric, there is a peaceful calm between them.

Later—much later—she will understand that moment with Maxis, has changed her forever, and for the better. Not so much tamed but tempered her. Through his eyes she sees that she is infinitely loved, she is a gift to him as much as he to her. There is no greater gift than that; to know you are forever loved, cherished and held high. It emboldens *and* humbles her.

At the entry to the inner chamber of the tree, they pause. Mala gazes at him, knowing this is where they say goodbye. Maxis places his big gentle hands upon her head, bends low, and presses a lingering kiss at her crown before resting his cheek against the top of her head. She grabs hold of his wrists, willing him to stay a moment or few longer. He looks up and behind her, and she knows instantly Jaime is standing there, undoubtedly pained by the sight before him.

She nods a wordless goodbye to Maxis, which he reciprocates, before turning on his heel and striding out. Mala faces Jaime and takes a deep breath.

"Everything is fine, Jaime. But can we—can we just not talk about this? Not now, at least?"

Poor sweet Jaime—with his deep black coffee eyes staring at her with such an array of visible emotions playing across his handsome face—struggles with what to say, what not to say, and at last pulls from deep within regular Jaime's semblance.

"Come on, Little. Let's get some meat on those chicken bones of yours."

He smiles, and though she knows the smile is hollow, she returns it slips an arm around his waist and tucks her head against his chest. After a moment, he drapes one lean arm around her. As they walk through the unusual foyer, he tightens his hold, pulling her tighter against him. Everything is *not* fine. But it will be. The second he drew her close, she knew it to be so.

"So, this is the inside of a tree, huh?"

"Ha. Not like any tree we've ever seen, that's for sure. Look at the walls. They're incredible. Where does that light even come from, you think? Oh, and look up. You haven't even looked up yet."

The entire tree is hollow, the trunk alone wide enough for all five to stand in a row, and still not touch the intricately patterned illuminated walls with an outstretched arm. Craning her head, walking a slow circle Mala spies a staircase etched into the thick inner trunk and winding up and into a network of huge branches large enough for even Jaime to stand upright. It is to the lowest of these that Jaime leads her, and together they climb up and into the opening to see the others, less Bearis, are already seated and dining.

"It's about time. Sorry, we couldn't wait. We were famished. Come, sit beside me, we have much to discuss," announces Aedina with surprising good cheer.

"Yes, Aedina, Jaime and I have some ideas; we'll fill you in," adds Mateo, also in cheerful spirits.

Mala can't help but chuckle as she takes her seat on the floor at the low table. Mateo has picked up some human verbiage it would seem. As much as she wishes to plan and strategize, the sight of the food before them overwhelms her. Exotic fruits, meats and cheeses, thick bread with golden crusts, and more. Hollowed gourds— some filled with what appear to be wine, and some with water—sit in the middle of the full table.

After a quick debate—and a glance at Jaime, who raises one eyebrow in mock Mala fashion—she reaches for the wine. She returns his look with her own, daring him to comment.

"Careful there, Birdie. That's some potent stuff."

She rolls her eyes at him, but after one sip, understands why they are all in giddy spirits. It is strong. For a while, the four sit, eat, and drink like old friends, sharing stories and anecdotes from their very different lives. She is most amused by the story of how they had come across Jaime, the fabulous sounding Murphius, and the hysterical mental images of him flat on his back.

"Wait, whatever happened to that crazy looking— what'd you call it? Tortanine! We lost track of him when we got steamrolled by that hippo-elephant thing," wonders Jaime.

"Steamrolled? What is steamrolled?" Aedina angles her head at them.

"Um, hippo-elephant? Did I miss something else?" asks Mala.

This leads to another story, and another explanation, resulting in *another* new phrase for Mateo to teach the other Virescent, which Aedina teases him on. Then Aedina grows somber. She says she is thinking of those still at the Havenheart. What will become of them, should they fail? What if they cannot return? Or worse, fail in their mission? What will happen to all who live in the Greenwood?

They all become solemn at this thought, taking in the weight of their collective burden. As if on cue, Elsabet and Tobias appear in the curved opening, ready to lead them to sleeping quarters. They say their farewells, with plans to reconvene in the morning, when they can together depart from the great meadow and pay visit to the Havenheart before starting their journey to the north Edges… and to the Vague.

37 THE VAGUE

It wants more of *everything*; thoughts, sensations, ideas, knowledge, pain, joy, love, hate... everything there is to have, it wants. Because the Vague is not *so* evolved, it confuses want with need, believing they are the same. It has yet to absorb sympathy or empathy; apathy is its parent, and from that it bases all else.

Its newly acquired feeling, *desire*, causes yet another novel emotion. Anger. It shocks and delights the Vague with its sharpness, it *likes* angry almost as much as it likes *want*. It *wants* the girl's angry for itself. Better still, she had more feels that the Vague could sense but had yet the vocabulary for. The Vague forms lips just to smack them together. The sound is like mud sucking a shoe.

There is one feel it does not like at all. Confusion. The girl made it feel confused, she is something other than those in the Greenwood, other than those in its previous world. Now that it can think, it can remember, and what it remembers is this feeling now named confusion when it left the other world for this one. Was it pushed out? Yes. But how? The Vague does something new once more. It ponders.

The Vague is also doing something all living creatures must do to survive. It is *adapting*. However, and because of that parent attribute of apathy, it discards the emotions it finds distasteful— compassion, kindness, selflessness are of no appeal, no use. No, the skills that interest the Vague are only those that insure its survival, its idea of growth. It is hungry for more than what the boring creatures of the Greenwood offer.

The one they call Endelyn is a start. Soon the Vague will get beyond the exterior wall she put up. She is strong, this one, but the Vague is getting stronger. And it is getting smarter.

38 The Path To Havenheart

To their collective surprise, they all slept soundly, dreamlessly. The magic of the Willow was at work with its tranquil aura and calming beauty, they can't help but feel peaceful and joyous. Or maybe it was the sweet wine from the night before. Whatever the reason, they awake refreshed and ready.

The five meet in the grand foyer, stretching and rubbing the sleep from their eyes as they make way toward to opening of the tree. Five of the seven Elders sit at the dais in wait for them. It was Maxis who had vacated his seat, which sits as empty as Endelyn's. Mala is unsurprised but saddened. Jaime's curious stare is on her, but she ignores it.

Jaime accepts something important happened between her and the annoyingly attractive Elder. But now she seems different—*older* is the word that comes to mind—and this change tilts his world. For now, he will honor her wishes to not speak of the encounter, but to himself he vows to ask her. Whether he wants to hear the answer or not.

Both Aedina and Mateo are eager to be on their way to the Havenheart, it has been so long since they've been home and they miss their people. Aedina is most anxious and excited to see Raven and Towe, and to introduce them to their new friends.

Bearis is first to make his departure, he too is in a hurry to return to his family and clan. He plans to gather his strongest companions and meet the others at cross path between the Mere and the Havenheart; a sort of halfway between the two, and from there they begin the journey to the north Edges.

The remaining Elders step down from their throne and walk them to the leafy entrance. Each places a hand on the four friend's heads, offering wishes for safe journey and success. And with a final farewell, they were off.

At first, they travel quietly and with haste. They have little time to spare, and the Havenheart is still half a day's journey, longer if they stop to rest. The two humans slow them despite moving as fast as they can, and are still no match for the stealth like agility of the Guardians.

Mala lets her mind wander wherever it wishes, apart from allowing thoughts of Maxis to linger. Thinking of him makes her feel hollow and even guilty with Jaime so close and so astute to her feelings. Instead, she focuses on the scenery, the sound of the wildlife in the trees and the ground below their feet. Branches and larger limbs are strewn about, remnants from whatever wild things had gone bump in the night.

There is also an unmistakable lightness to the Greenwood this morning, as if the entire wood rejoices at the end of night and the long respite from it that is now at hand.

Aedina, too, relishes the calm spirits of the first day of Rays and confirms Mala's intuition by explaining that a celebration always follows the day of night. It is a display of gratitude to have survived once again. They do no work on the first day of Rays and communities spend their time together rejoicing. It is more reason for Aedina to encourage the others to hurry. She wants to be home.

Home. That is perhaps the first time since joining the Virescent people and becoming their Guardian leader, that she thought of the Havenheart as such. She smiles to herself, and as she looks up, she catches Mateo watching her. He returns her smile. A beam of sunlight spills over his face, and Aedina *sees* Mateo for the first time since... ever.

Mateo, surprised by Aedina's eye contact and the smile that accompanies it, almost doesn't recognize the strange pulling at the corners of his mouth. When was the last time he had smiled, laughed—not sarcastically— or joked? He spends so much of his time angry and resentful, and only now realizes the time he wastes with such pettiness. It isn't Aedina's fault she is faster and more skilled than he; it is just the way of things.

He can also admit Aedina mastered a skill that he has been failing at: selflessness. His thoughts often revolved around *his* wants and needs, *his* hurts and disappointments. Thinking back, Mateo realizes the sacrifices she makes for the community. He knows she longs for the freedom of wildling life, where no one depends upon her, and she answers to no one. Yet, she chooses duty and responsibility over freedom.

Would he have been so giving, were it him? He thinks not. Even his new human friend, as tall and ludicrous as he seems to Mateo, is more selfless than he. Even now, as he walks behind his human girl—who he is upset with, despite trying his best to hide it—he keeps a watchful eye on her, mindful of every raised root or low branch that might trip or gouge her, heedless of those that trip or scratch *him*. This is what it is to put another's wellbeing before your own.

Jaime, who *is* ignorant of how many times he is tripped up or gouged, watches Mala skip along, wanting and *not* wanting to know what is in her head as she moves through the forest. Has he lost her? Was she ever even his to begin with? He feels... possessive. He shudders at the word. That was his father's mindset. He had wanted to own and control Peggy and let no one else near her. He will not repeat that pattern.

With a hardened resolve, he wills himself to let it go, let *her* go if he must. He has no real idea of what is between Mala and... *him*, but he can't and won't compete against Maxis for her love. It is his, or not. And he plans to find out.

With his mind set, he allows himself to take in the sun's beauty dappling the Greenwood. The air holds the new day's freshness, reminding him of both the moments after a summer sun shower and a crisp spring morning all in one. He loves it here. The realization hits him with a suddenness. Mala loves it here and would likely stay if given the option. But would he?

Several hours pass in this companionable, if not contemplative silence. It is Aedina who breaks their respective reveries, announcing that they will stop at the boulder ahead, and rest for a while before continuing. Ever the perceptive leader, she sees the others are slowing, and though they did not ask or complain, a break is due.

"Aedina, I don't think that's a boulder… I think it's Murphius," exclaims Jaime. He jogs to the Tortanine, calling, "Murph! Hey Murph, old boy, is that you? It is you! Buddy? Aren't you glad to…" Jaime trails off, looking down at the Tortanine, then back at the others. All three, as they look at Jaime's sad and confused expression, feel a sinking in their chests. Aedina drops her spear and shrugs off her leather satchel and runs to Jaime and Murphius.

Mateo and Mala lag, exchanging a pensive look as they gather her discards. They reach the trio as Aedina kneels before the unusual animal, it's dog like face cupped between her small hands, and Jaime hovering above, his hand on the knobby hump that was Murphius' back.

"Is he…" Mala begins.

"No. At least, I don't think so. He's still warm, his eyes are open—he even blinked—but it's like… like he's not here," answers Aedina.

Says Jaime, "It's like he's in a coma. That's what we'd call this where we come from, at least. What can we do?"

"I fear this is the work of the Vague." Aedina's expression is grim.

"There must be something we can do to help him! Bring him to your Havenheart with us, at least. We can't just leave him here."

Jaime is insistent, the rest are dubious. The Tortanine must weigh as much as all of them together, and then some. Even if they can get it to walk on its own, it will slow them, but they cannot sway Jaime. He tells the others to go ahead without him, he will stay behind with Murphius and help him along.

"We are in this together, Jaime. I won't leave you behind," says Mala.

Sighing heavily, Aedina agrees. "Yes, Mala is correct. We are stronger and better together. We will help Murphius as best we can. I just don't know how..."

Until now, Mateo has been silent, but not from indifference. He is contemplating ways to move the Tortanine. An idea dawns on him. No one will like his choice in help, but it is necessary.

"Rest here with Murphius. I may have someone who can help. I will return soon."

Before anyone stops him, Mateo is off like a flash. There is nothing to do but wait, and hope. Aedina, looking at Mala and Jaime, senses the two humans could use some time alone. Poor Murphius, in his trancelike state, is of no intrusion, so she busies herself gathering berries alongside the path.

Mala sits by the heartsick Jaime, who now sits beside the large creature, petting his silky soft head and murmuring tender words to it. She covers his hand with hers, curls her fingers around his palm and squeezes. It gratifies her when he squeezes back. He gives her a small, sad smile.

"Jaime, there's something I want to tell you."

Jaime, though he doesn't turn to look at her, feels his heart stutter and dip. He is not prepared to hear what she'll say, but is rendered mute as the Tortanine, powerless to stop her. In his head, he shouts, *I don't want to know* repeatedly.

So, when she announces, "Nothing happened. Nothing will ever happen between Maxis and I..."

He almost didn't hear it. In fact, his brain at first heard, *Maxis and I are together, I don't love you,* and when he unscrambles fact from fear, there is a loosening in his chest. The ringing in his ears stops, his heart rate slows.

"Jaime, did you hear me? I said—"

"I heard you, Little. I'm just taking it in. What… no, never mind. You don't have to say anything more about it. About him if you don't want to."

Maybe Jaime will never understand who or what this Maxis is to her, to her life. He heard the truth in her voice, but more importantly, he heard a calmness, a contentment there. Whatever she feels about the Elder, even if it is love, she is not *in love* with him.

Mala is quiet for a moment, but then says, "It's okay. I just… I just haven't figured it out myself. I guess he is—or was—my Guardian Angel? I have questions, ones that I don't know if I'll ever get the answers to, but somehow, I'm okay with that. For now, at least."

From behind them, Aedina speaks up, "I, too, have many unanswered questions about my life. The Guardian leader before me, Soji—she was wise. What she said to me has always remained in my thoughts. *We do not always get the answers to our questions, nor should we expect they are owed to us. Some things must be accepted, on their own, and something we call finae.*"

"I believe you—or Soji—are right. I think the equivalent to your *finae* in our world is what we call 'faith'. It is similar—believing in something you cannot see or touch—and trusting that all will be well in the end."

After Jaime listens to the two girls, he nods. "Well, ladies, I guess from here on out, we'll just have to have faith, won't we?"

As both Mala and Aedina smile and agree, a sudden tremble in the air shakes the leaves and the earth rumbles. Mala is the first to see what sent Jaime scurrying for shelter not so long ago: rings of rippling air like circles in a pond after a stone toss.

"Oh, not again," says Jaime.

"Jaime? Aedina? Wha-what's happening?"

Through the central ring, an unmistakable crown of wavy hair, tip of a spear, fingertips, hand, arm and foot… it is Mateo bursting through the warped hole with a flourish as he tucks and rolls toward them, giving a hearty laugh as he springs up and bows before them.

"That's how you human's do it, isn't it Jaime?" Mateo smirks, referring to Jaime's embarrassing bow before the Seven back at the Great Willow.

"Yes, something like tha—"

"Oh, hold your spears, I've a surprise for you all."

On cue, a succession of fat, pinkish Rhinello's squeeze and pop through the wavering rings of air, led by shrill Milly.

"Well, *hello*, again, tall dark and—huh, not so stinky anymore, are you?"

Milly's stout snout tests the air just shy of Jaime's face, who recoils and nearly falls. Her three companions laugh and trill as loudly as her, exclaiming and fawning around both Mala and Jaime while Mateo pretends to study the trees, and Aedina glares at him.

Pulling Mateo aside, she hisses, "What were you thinking? Bringing Rhinellos of all things? You *know* what the rest of the trip will be like, don't you?"

"My apologies, Leader. But this was the only way to get Murphius to the Havenheart. We cannot carry him, correct?"

His false humility makes her want to strangle him. Instead, she grits her teeth and agrees. "But once we are home, it will be *your* problem to get rid of them, and yours alone."

Before he protests, she pivots to face the group— Milly, Tilly, Tula, and Bela, a stunned looking Mala, and Jaime—and whistles. Everyone, save poor Murphius, stops speaking and turns to the Guardian leader.

"All right listen up. As Mateo has likely told you, we need your help. We believe the Vague has struck

Murphius mute, and we need to bring him to the Havenheart to keep him safe. As you may already know, these two humans are here to help us."

At hearing the word *humans*, the four pachyderm stare anew. Jaime and Mala now understand what zoo animals must feel like. The four snort, sniff, and chatter as they circle them, touching their hair and arms with prickly trunks until Aedina reclaims their attention.

"What say you, Rhinellos?"

"Right, then. Help we shall," trills Milly.

"Not every day we get to see a human, let alone two. Aedina, you cheeky wildling, you. You tried to trick me before, but I was on to you, I was." To the other Rhinellos, "I was, you know. Said to myself, *now that there, that is no Edges dweller, there. That there, it's a hu-man.*"

She splits the word apart for emphasis, and the three *tut-tut* as if they, too, had known it all along. Aedina motions for Jaime and Mala to stand—and darts sheepish Mateo a look that says *I'm not done with you, mister*—she offers the Rhinellos the praise and apology they are waiting for.

"No fooling you, Milly. You're too wise for me. You are all not only, uh, beautiful to gaze upon, but smart, and… strong. So much stronger than us."

The massive creatures take her praise and her hint and set to lifting the stony Tortanine with their sturdy trunks. Between the four, and with considerable grunts and groans—along with a few loud blasts of gas from the said fours rotund backsides—they raise Murphius between them, bracing his lifeless body against their ample flanks. They can do nothing about his furry pate and feet that dangle, but at least they can transport him to safety.

"Now, now, don't you worry about a thing, dears. Milly and her girls will get this heavy fellow where he needs to be in no time. We'll just take him through a circlet and get a jump start. And you, Guardian, *you*, stay out."

Rhinellos are notoriously picky about letting anyone use their circlets for travel, and Mateo had snuck through uninvited.

"Yes, Milly, my apologies again," calls Mateo, not looking sorry in the least.

The air before them ripples and expands, then the four Rhinellos and lone Tortanine squish through like a marching band through a black hole. When the loud pop signals the closing of the circlet, Aedina heaves a sigh and slumps.

"It is your great fortune, Mateo, that they chose *not* to walk the rest of the way with us," chastises Aedina.

"Yes, Aedina, I know this to be true," says Mateo with mock contriteness.

They all laugh, even Jaime, who is feeling better at knowing Murphius will be kept safe from harm until they figure out a way to undo whatever the Vague has done to him. Their moods lightened, the four continue their journey to the Havenheart, listening to Aedina and Mateo tell them all about their home and those who live there.

The rest of their travel is uneventful, and at last they spy the straight line of tall trees marking the boundary of the beloved home ground. They are the tallest Mala or Jaime have ever seen, reaching so high to the sky that their tops look like pinpoints. A single willow tree is all that breaks the line, an unmistakable veil to both humans' now trained eyes.

Aedina leads Mala and Jaime through, making good on her threat of leaving Mateo to manage the Rhinellos when they arrive. Affecting another one of his newly learned bows, Mateo steps aside and ushers the others through the veil.

39 HAVENHEART

The Havenheart surpasses Mala's expectations. She knew, by the name alone, it would be a peaceful place, yes. Her imagination took her as far as a cozy community and happy villagers, but the actual sight of that and more is enough to bring a tear to her eye.

"It's beautiful," she sighs.

The charm of this almost primitive camp-like abode affects Jaime, too. He drapes an arm around Mala, understanding why she is so struck by the sight before them.

The veil has set them on a hilltop which looks down on the valley below. The Havenheart, from this vantage point, is indeed heart shaped. Two curving arcs meet at two points, one concave, the other convex. The edges slope down into the valley where elflike children work and play.

All along the base of the valley walls are cave-like holes with thatched doors propped open. Through the center, running like a jagged break dividing the two sides, is a narrow stream with clear sparkling water traveling over smooth rocks. It enters and exits through two narrow tunnels at both ends of the village. Before and below them is a curving staircase etched into the earth, leading to the floor of the valley. Aedina has already reached the bottom and is being met by two boisterous small children.

"Shall we?" Jaime grins.

"We shall," answers Mala.

He motions for her to lead and follows her down to the stares and whispers of the gathering crowd. Despite feeling self-conscious and like awkward giants, they smile and wave to everyone. The smallest of the already little Virescents are the least wary and approach them the moment they reach the bottom, circling them and giggling.

"Now, now, back away little Viries. My apologies, you are not only their first humans, you are the first non-Virescents invited into the Havenheart. Ever."

Turning to the gathered crowd, she raises her arms to silence their murmurs and giggles.

"Everyone, please give welcome to our new friends. Jaime and Mala of Everwood. Let us help them feel at home here, for they have come to help us."

Oohs and *ohhs* and repeating of their names and that of Everwood ripple across the crowd. They are trying the words on for size, tasting what is exotic on their tongues.

One of the smallest ones asks, "What's wrong with their skin?" An older one hushes him as the rest giggle.

The tiny wildling—now a Virescent—named Towe approaches Mala. He tugs at the hem of the skirt Aedina made for her when they were in the cave, and gestures for her to bend down to his level. Mala complies, and once eye to eye, the beautiful once-wildling child places a small dirty hand on each cheek and draws their foreheads together.

Feeling Mala's wide smile against her palms makes the boy smile, too. Raven follows suit, repeating the same gesture, but her solemn little face remains serious, so Mala mimics her expression. This causes her to smirk, knowing she is not at all serious.

Both children move on to Jaime, craning their skinny necks up to look at him until he obliges them by squatting down. Mala notices the twitters of the females in the crowd; this place does not differ from home in that regard. She stifles a chuckle.

"Hey" calls Mateo from the top of the stairway, using another word learned from Jaime, "I could use some help up here."

He has one arm outstretched through the other side of the veil and struggles with whatever is over there trying to push its way through.

"Now would be good…" he calls to Aedina and company.

"I said stay over there ple…" he says to whoever is over there.

Something shoves him hard enough to make him to stumble, and an unmistakable pink trunk sniffs its way around the opening.

Milly's mottled pink face peeks through, "Tu-*luuuuu*. Just thought we'd help bring…"

Mateo's hands shoving her head back through the veil cuts her off, and he throws an *okay, you've made your point* glare in Aedina's direction. Having made her point, Aedina obliges and dashes up the stairs to help Mateo with their unwanted guests. She calls over her shoulder for more help, explaining as she climbs.

Somehow, they will have to bring the helpless and very heavy Tortanine through the veil, preferably without the help of the nosy Rhinellos. It takes their combined efforts, but somehow, they manage to not only politely dissuade the oversized beasts from crossing through the veil into their sanctuary, but also carry Murphius down the earthen staircase.

While most of the Virescents *ooh*-ed and *ahh*-ed around the dormant animal, the foursome walk together to a quiet spot away from the rest. Aedina brings them to a shade tree by the stream where they can at last discuss their plans to defeat the Vague and rescue Endelyn.

"*If* it's even possible. You said before that no one has ever been rescued from the Vague's grasp," says the ever-pragmatic Jaime.

"This is true. However, no one has before attempted to do so, either. We do not know what power the Vague has, not since it evolved," concedes Aedina.

"Forgive me for saying so, Aedina, but the Guardianship has ignored this problem of the Vague for too long. We have no choice, we must go swiftly and fiercely, right away."

"We agree… mostly, Mateo. But we mustn't rush headlong into something we do not understand. Despite what little time we have, we must make certain to study this adversary before we attack."

Both Mala and Jaime sit silent as the two Guardians volley back and forth, both feeling as though it isn't their place to put forth opinions and ideas about a land that is not their own. However, the two are deadlocked, and turn to the humans.

"Well," says Jaime, "From what we *do* know of the Vague, it is no longer is apathetic. It has feelings—like, um, wants and desires—now, and that makes it more dangerous. So, what does it want?"

After a pause, Jaime, Aedina, and Mateo shift their sights on Mala. She blinks back at them.

"Me? You think it wants *me*? But why? If it has Endelyn, wouldn't she be way more valuable to it than me? I don't have any special powers, no magic, nothing. I'm just a human girl from another world… right?"

They all contemplate for a few moments, no one having an answer that will shed any light. Jaime, however, senses the niggling of something in the corner of his mind that he can't quite place his finger.

"So, when the Vague found you at by the Tarn, what did it say to you? Why do you think it backed away?"

Mala thinks back to the strange encounter. She recalls how angry it made her when it tried to threaten her, and how it appeared confused and uncertain when she projected her anger at it. Even though she had felt fear, her dominant emotion had been the anger.

"Interesting. Aedina, Mateo? Do you know of anyone else ever resisting the Vague in such a way?"

Both shake their heads, puzzled.

"For as long as we've known of it, the Vague has always been passive and indifferent; if a woodland creature was unfortunate enough to walk into its waiting blackness, it was lost to it. We don't know when or how that changed."

"Hmm. I have a theory. I think it's actually simple. I think the Vague—each time it traps something inside it—absorbs the creature's thoughts and feelings. Maybe even its hopes and fears, as well as its wants and needs," says Jaime.

"So, it's gaining intelligence. Maybe we can just reason with it, and tell it to back off?"

Mala is half serious, half joking. Nothing can be that easy.

"Ha. Well, we could try, but I wouldn't bank on it. No, I suspect we will have to outsmart it. I also think, assuming it has Endelyn, its intelligence is that much greater, and our mission will be that much more a challenge."

This revelation disappoints Mateo and even Mala. They want something to fight physically, not mentally. Aedina, however, is prepared for both scenarios, and say as much to the others.

"Very well. Let us celebrate with the others for now, and after daybreak, we will meet with Bearis and his companions and make way to the northern Edges to find this Vague. We will go with just us four, and no others. Is everyone in agreement?"

They are. All see the wisdom in her plan. As Raven and Towe run toward Aedina, impatient to have her attentions, they join the rest of the Virescents at their equivalent to a town center. Fires are lit, over which Viriscents prepare food: exotic looking vegetables, broths, and stews, planks with fruit, cheeses, seeds, and nuts.

"No hot dogs or mac-n-cheese here, huh?" Jaime chuckles.

Mala elbows him. "Well, I've been thinking of becoming a vegetarian, so I guess now's a decent time as any to start."

They let themselves get lost in the party-like atmosphere, accepting the food and drink offered them from shy green hued children, acknowledging the curious stares with smiles, and answering questions when asked. They clap along to the rhythmic drumbeats and strange songs, but Jaime draws the line at dancing despite the performer's persistence—and Mala as well— who's gotten up and follows along as best she can.

Jaime watches her with a smile that doesn't quite make it to his eyes. Though they've all promised to set aside their worries until after the celebration, Jaime can't help but wonder at what is next. His gut tells him something will go wrong. And it seems there is no changing course, as they are all—Jaime included— committed to protecting the Greenwood and its people.

"A feather for your thoughts."

Aedina had snuck up and sat down beside him. She stares up at him with curious copper eyes.

"A feather, hmm? Where we come from, we say *penny for your thoughts*. Funny, right?"

"Well, Jaime from Everwood, I do not know this penny you speak of, but I know that the thoughts in your head are not all together happy ones, are they?"

"You've got me there, Aedina. They are not. Do you think I'm wrong to have concerns for this mission we about to go on?"

"No, Jaime, I do not. I share your worries. By the looks of our happy warriors over there, they are quite the opposite, it would seem."

Jaime looks across the circle at Mala and Mateo dancing ridiculously, laughing and falling about, and even singing. Both out of tune, and Mala only repeating the choruses.

"I see Mateo has lightened up. Who knew?"

Aedina laughs. "Ah, this is the Mateo I used to know. I believe he has come around again."

Jaime notices her gaze soften as she watches him, her smile not quite reaching her eyes, either.

"Aedina, something has puzzled me since we arrived in the Havenheart. Where are all the adults? You and Mateo look to be the oldest, and I believe you're the same age as Mala and me. So, where are the grownups?"

"Jaime, we are not like your kind. There are no *parents*, no mother or father you spoke of. We are from the willow trees—the veils. I suppose I would say that the trees are our parents, and we are born from them. If you recall Mateo's reaction when you explained your *door*? That is why. Willow trees are sacred in the Greenwood, they give us life, they shelter us, they are a part of us as much as we are a part of them."

Jaime finds it impossible to comprehend. Sure, they all are kind of greenish, but this means these human-like people were *trees*.

"Wait. I don't understand. You start off as babies— um, tiny versions of yourself—and you grow up. Right?"

"No Jaime, I am as I have always been. Mateo is as he has always been. The same for everyone you see here. We are as you see us, no smaller, no bigger. Raven and Towe will always be as small as they are now. Their minds will grow, and they will mature to independence, perhaps even become Guardians if one day they are worthy."

"Wow. Mind blown. So, you get older in your mind, but not your body? Everyone came from the willow trees—the veils—as they are? That's the idea, right?"

Aedina laughs at his odd expression, but nods. There *is* more to it than that, and perhaps one day she will have time to explain it all to him, but for now, this is enough for the human to grasp.

"Yes, Jaime. That is the idea, as you say. Virescent are *born* of the Havenheart veils, but wildlings like me come from elsewhere in the Greenwood. It is the Guardian leader who must bring wildlings to the Havenheart and give them a home with their fellow— what did you call us, greenies?"

Jaime ducks his head and gives her a side glance, hoping she didn't take offense at the term he'd used early in their meeting, but Aedina chuckles and he relaxes. She looks up at the sky through the trees, her brow furrowing.

"Soon we will be leaving. Enjoy this time with Mala, here in our home. We know not what lies ahead."

"I will. May I suggest you do the same as well? With Mateo, that is."

As she stands to walk away, she opens her mouth to give a sharp retort, but then stops. They both looks again at Mala and Mateo still partaking in the festivities, but now with Raven and Towe at their heels mimicking and following along. Barely looking back down at him, she nods once and walks away.

Jaime is glad to see her head in his direction, even more so to see Mateo smile at her approach. Mala disengages herself from them and searches the crowd. Jaime waits for her eyes to find his, wondering what *her* expression will be when their eyes meet.

When at last they do, his heart catches in his throat. She stands alone in the crowd with her hair wild and long, dressed as a native. A beam of sunlight shines on her. She looks angelic. Like a wild angel. But more than that, she looks like she belongs here in this strange land. Though it isn't the first time he's wondered at that possibility, it is the first time he believes it.

Jaime's eyes have been so focused on Mala that at first, he doesn't notice the crowd has grown quiet. Their gazes have also turned to Mala, and they've cleared a space around her, so she stands alone. As he observes their awestruck and reverent faces, all turned to Mala, he realizes it's not just him being love struck. Something is happening to her in that beam of light that touches nothing and no one else.

The glow has mellowed into the familiar rose gold hue, and is not only *on* her, but seems to be *in* her, emanating out from her hair, fingertips, and toes, even her skin, through her pores. She looks down at her hands, touches her hair. Surprise and confusion is written on her face, but she is smiling and unafraid.

While this happens, a cloud passes over the sun. *Day break.* Yet the light she exudes only grows stronger as the Havenheart dims. She reaches out a beckoning hand to Jaime, and beams of light reach out ahead of her and land at his feet.

Jaime rises, hesitant to step into that streak of light, fearing the change to come. But her smile is so easy and calm, reassuring him that all will be well, and as ever before, Jaime is powerless to resist her. So, he walks into her light, step by slow step until he is before her, looking down into her peaceful face with an immeasurable love.

With cautious fingertips, he traces the frame of her face, feeling the pulse of the vibrating light as he follows the contour of her forehead, temple, cheek and last, chin which he holds between thumb and forefinger. He is going to kiss her. Now, here, in this strange light before these strange people, he is going to kiss her.

He lowers his head to hers, and for the first time, their lips meet and linger. Her light flows from her mouth to his, filling him with that strange vibration, and though he cannot see it, the light travels through them both, so that together they form a sphere of light.

Only they could hear the words whispered like a chant inside the sphere that says, "Guide them, protect them, surround them with light, keep them safe from harm. Guide them, protect them, surround them with light, keep them safe from harm. Guide them, protect them, surround them with light, keep them safe from harm."

The light diminishes, fading from the edges and inward until it is a ball of rose gold light hovering above their heads, and like a switch being flicked, the light goes out and the dim sphere drops into Jaime's hand. He recognizes it as the knob from the door in the Everwood.

The spell, now broken, sends a ripple of surprise and awe throughout the Havenheart. The Virescent surround them with murmurs and blessings of good wishes and even gratitude. Neither quite know how to react, nor understand what happened. They search for Aedina in the crowd, and find her high upon the staircase with Mateo, looking down on the scene below. She waves them up. It is time.

40 To The North Edges

When Jaime and Mala reach the top of the stairs, Aedina grasps Mala's hand. With a firm squeeze and a radiant smile, she says, "That was extraordinary, you must know. The Seven have placed their power within you—within you *both*—leaving them most vulnerable. We must hurry and waste no time."

Neither fully understands what this means, but they understand the urgency they now operate under. Aedina calls out a farewell to her people.

"My family. We have witnessed something never seen in all the Greenwood and will likely never witness again. Let us give thanks to our friends, now family to us."

Cheers and shouts meet her words, and Jaime and Mala accept with tentative waves and smiles.

"I ask that all of you remain within the safety of the Havenheart until our return. No one should leave through the veils, allow no one in. Be well."

Well wishes follow them through the veil, and with that, the unlikely foursome are on their way. Hurrying, Aedina explains the power of the spheres, or as much as she knows of them. Each Elder possesses one, it is called their Life Source. Together, they created the light that the Great Willow emanates. She believes that without it, the enchanted tree and therefore the Elders, may be left vulnerable to the beasts and even the Vague as anyone else. This is the cause for the renewed urgency, for without the Seven the Greenwood may revert to the days of darkness.

What Aedina does not tell them is that while Jaime and Mala stood within the fabulous light, the Elders spoke to her, too. It was they who told her the significance of their gift to the humans, and the consequence of their failure should they not remove the threat of the Vague.

Jaime, recalling the sphere in the door, asks Aedina if it is possible there are more than these seven magical balls of light floating around in the universe.

"I-I don't know…." It is something Aedina has never considered. But the question piques her curiosity in much the same way it has Jaime's.

Though she says nothing, Mala harbors much the same suspicions as Jaime. Is the sphere meant to be hers? Is it possible? How? Why? Wouldn't Maxis have told her? Surely, he knows? She sighs. Only shrewd Jaime hears it, and she smiles reassuringly at him.

Hours pass. They speak in fits and bursts, but there is a wariness with their urgency. The forest seems different, but perhaps it is their collective imaginations—the force of their own foreboding that makes it feel so—for the same bright sun still shines through the same leafy branches, the same birds still sing as gaily as before.

The forest animals, now aware of and intrigued by their new human visitors—thanks to Milly and her shrill companions—meet them with pleasant and curious greetings. They are cheerful and oblivious of the more serious goings on, as the four kept the news away from the Rhinellos. They know only of the plight of poor Murphius and the existence of the two humans. As expected, gossip of both has spread through the land like wildfire.

It isn't long before they have quite a following. Creatures of all sizes and species trail after them as if they are the Pied Piper leading them. They contemplate how to dissuade them but realize it will be a fruitless endeavor. They can only hope the animals will lose interest and return to their homes.

However, and much to their chagrin, by the time they reach the veil to the Mere, they've amassed a following not unlike a parade. Instead of dispersing as they travel further, *more* join, feeding off the excitement. They perceive something big is happening, and no one wishes to miss it. When Bearis and his two companions appear through the veil, it is all but confirmed that an escapade will begin.

"This is Barron and Baxton. They are as strong as they are trustworthy."

Bearis speaks with an urgency that underscores his impatience to begin the adventure. For Mala and Jaime, every moment since they stepped into the Everwood on that moonlit night has *already* been an adventure like no other, filled with mysteries and wonders, sights they'd never seen and creatures they'd never imagined existing outside of Mala's fairy tales and fantasies.

The question is: what will be this adventure's conclusion? If every story ever told had an element of loss or grief, then why will theirs be any different? This plays on each of their minds. Will the price they pay for grand adventure and a tale less ordinary cost them something they love? If the laws of universal balance apply, then the answer can only be yes.

Still, this is the path they are willingly on. Whether conscious or subconscious, they each chose their journey, so they each plan to take it to its end, however it may turn out. The sphere will protect them. Hopefully. That none know how it works is of concern, but its presence in Mala's pouch offers them some sense of security and optimism.

And despite their respective concerns, they are all pleased to see Bearis. His smooth baritone voice falls over them like a welcome blanket, and both Aedina and Mala hug him in tight embraces that made them practically disappear in his thick fur. He chuckles low and is pleased by their obvious joy in seeing him.

Jaime and Mateo high five the bear's great padded paws with jocular friendliness, another gesture Jaime taught the Virescent boy, who adopted it with ease and just a bit of overuse. He's high-fived everyone they've come across, causing a small amount if ill will from a few unprepared fellows. The exasperated Aedina smoothed it over. She thanked Jaime for the alternative form of greeting with a tone more sarcastic than grateful.

Bearis, Aedina and Mateo discuss the travel plans as Jaime and Mala listen on, unable to contribute since they don't know their way around the Greenwood and wouldn't even know which direction to begin in.

"We should travel alongside the Mere until we reach the Archeia Waters veil. It is there that the paths split, one leading to the Tarn, the other to the Fierce Wood veil. It is more dangerous that way, however, it is the fastest."

Bearis's idea sounds fine until he says *Fierce Wood* veil. Jaime shudders at the thought; anything by such a name cannot be good. Just passing the Archeia Waters veil gives him the creeps, he is not soon to forget the ghostly pale hands and lavender hair rising from the swirling waters. His relief is obvious when Mateo counters Bearis's suggestion with another, less nerve-wracking route.

Then Aedina squashes it. "I agree, Mateo, that would be an easier route, especially for the humans—no offense to you both. However, our time is limited, and that path will intersect the Rhinello territory. After Mateo's not-so-courteous dismissal of Milly and friends, I fear they will not receive us well."

"Ah, yes, this is true. Very well, the Fierce Wood it is, then. Jaime, Mala, we will explain as we go."

With that, they walk again, heading, toward the unpleasant sounding Fierce Wood veil. At least they'll be going along the Mere for a time, a prospect that pleases them all, for its beauty is unmatched.

From the others, Mala and Jaime learn that the Fierce Wood is literal. The woods itself—the very trees—are combative. Though they cannot un-root themselves, their long sharp branches have an impressive and whip-like reach and speed. The feisty apple tree in the movie Wizard of Oz comes to Mala's mind, and she mimics the tree's gravelly raspy voice.

"Are you hinting my apples aren't what they ought to be?"

Without missing a beat, Jaime replies, "Oh, no. It's just that she doesn't like little green worms!"

They both laugh at the shared recollection as the others stare at them with tilted heads.

"Apples? No, these are barb-berry trees. No worms, just spikes. I wouldn't recommend trying to eat one either."

Mateo is serious, and Mala and Jaime opt to not explain their reference. Instead, they reassemble themselves in a more somber state and listen on. The barb-berry trees are more like an R rated version of Dorothy's G rated apple trees.

"Okayyyy, so how do we get past these nasty buggers?" Asks Jaime.

"Carefully," states Bearis with a toothy smile.

"Yes, Bearis is right. Carefully. The barb-berry trees rarely, if ever, get visitors. We must ask their permission to pass though, however, they are more inclined to attack first and ask questions later."

Mala asks, "So, who's the lucky winner that gets to go first?"

They take turns looking at one another. No one *wants* to be the one to test their skill and luck with angry barbed fruited trees that can attack. But just as with any unpleasant task that must get done, *someone* has to do it.

"No takers, huh? Well, I guess it should be me," states Mala.

She is no more inclined to meet these trees as anyone else, but perhaps the sphere will protect her. Even if she Doesn't know how to use it.

"I'll go with you," announces Jaime in that familiar *I can't believe you've roped me in again* voice he is notorious for using.

"As much as this goes against my instincts as a leader, I think our best chances are with you humans. They, like the rest of us, have never encountered humans before. Perhaps your unusualness will give pause for thought."

"Then it's settled. Let's get this over and done with before I lose my nerve. How much further before we reach this Fierce Woods veil?"

Stone-faced Aedina and Mateo each raise one outstretched hand, a finger pointing dead ahead. Jaime, Mala, and all the still present forest animals turn their heads in the direction they point. The two humans sigh. The animals gasp.

Even the veil leading into the Fierce Wood appears ragged and displeased. Its spindly branches are sparse of greenery, its bark more gray than brown. If it could speak, surely it would say, '*stay out*'. But Mala and

Jaime will go in, heedless of the warning, for it is the fastest route to the north Edges.

"Alrighty, then. I guess the plan will be we go in, convince these guys to let us through, and if they do, we'll call you through," says Mala.

"And if not…" wonders Jaime.

"Well, I guess we'll worry about that if the moment comes."

She has no plan for *if not* because she never does. Yet, he rationalizes, things *do* always seem to work out when she is around.

He slaps his hands against his thighs and says, "Alrighty indeed. Let's go."

The surrounding forest, which had until this moment been abuzz with chatter, hushes as the pair readies themselves to cross through the droopy veil. Mala will lead with Jaime close behind, ready to grab her and pull her back to the safety of the Mere side of the veil, with Aedina, Bearis, and Mateo right there waiting as well. Surrounding them are two rings of animals; Bearis's companions waiting to help, followed by the wildlife watching with mixed awe and excitement.

Mala, once committed to something, is never one to hesitate long, so before Jaime says another word, she is through the veil and face to face—well, bark—with a packed and swampy forest. The light filters through the gray mottled trees in a sleepy haze, struggling against the vast mist that rises from the damp forest floor. Not only does the light struggle to fill the air, so does the warmth. The chill is enough to raise goosebumps on her arms, making her wish for her long-gone thermal shirt.

Pale moss climbs up the thin trunks and limp fern droop at their bases, of which there are perhaps over one hundred in haphazard rows. No birds call from their branches or pick at the prickly berries that resemble oversized blackberries with silvery porcupine spikes.

So quiet and still is the wood, that she doubts the tale she was told. Jaime steps through behind her just as she hears an odd sound. She raises a silencing hand back at him, which he immediately obliges by freezing in place.

She can't at first place the sound, or its location, for it seems to be coming from everywhere and nowhere. It reminds her of a thousand ice cubes cracking in rapid succession, *chink-plink-plink-chink-plink,* and when she looks up into all those thorn-fruited branches, she places the sound with widened eyes and dread.

The whole lot is bending and turning down toward the duo, now frozen in place. Their vicious looking spike tap against each other. This is the ice cracking sound's source.

Those closest to Mala and Jaime draw down the lowest, and though there are no discernible faces to the animated trees, they *are* looking at them. One, towering before her, reminds Mala somewhat of a snake in its movement, almost slithering toward her, its multitude of barb-berried branches now almost eye level. Just like a snake, the too-close tree jerks its backward, just as a snake does before launching forward. But instead of a venomous bite, this thing will shoot spiked fruit in their direction like guided missiles.

"Wait!" shouts Mala.

The barbed assailant freezes. It draws back and stretches out its chinking-plinking branches in a hold back motion. Mala could never explain *how* she knows this is what the tree is doing, yet she knows it to be true.

"Please, we need you to let us pass through your wood. I—"

She is losing its interest. It again moves snakelike toward her, followed likewise by the others.

Mala shouts the first words that come to her head. "If you don't let us through, the Greenwood will die. And—and so will you."

With shock, she realizes the truth in her words in a way she had not before. A door opens in her mind. She had fallen in love with this unique world, connecting with it in a way that defied explanation, ignoring the odd flickering of something that felt like recognition, and crediting her love of fairy tales and fantasy for the serene acceptance of the bizarre.

She's been dismissing those feelings of familiarity from the moment she arrived, chalking it up to her vivid imagination. Her oft recurring dreams of unfamiliar worlds? Simple. They are just the dream-state jumbles and mix of places and characters in those beloved stories that she's read and watched religiously. Right?

But now, here in this frightening forest, she permits herself to *see*. Yes, even this Fierce Wood is familiar. She has been here before, in a dream. A flash and a flicker, just images that left her feeling odd and a little sick even when she awoke. Were she to retrieve her old journals from childhood, she'd likely even find mention.

These thoughts pass in seconds, all while she watches the tree pause yet again, hovering and contemplating.

"Please."

Mala holds her breath, staying as still as possible as her heart thuds against her chest. Jaime, too, has been so silent and still that she's forgotten he is here. They watch as the trees right themselves to their full stature, beginning with the one closest to them and working backward through their jagged lines into the distance. This is when Mala notices the second veil in the distance, almost a pinprick it is so far, yet still unmistakable by its contrast to the rest of the drab forest it lives in.

She motions Jaime to signal the others but keeps her eyes on the tree. It appears they are now ignoring their intruders; looking like an angry old man, arms crossed his chest, nose in the air, but eyes slanted down at the offending party. This is how Mala perceives the trees. Ready to let them pass, but begrudgingly.

As much as it tempts her to express her gratitude, something tells her that her silence is more welcome than her words. So, when the others follow Jaime through the veil, she communicates to them with a finger to her lips to be quiet. At the sight of the towering trees and their dangerous offspring, they oblige without question.

Seven silently walking beings—two humans, two Guardians, and three lumbering bears—trek though the mist and muck filled forest, alert to the discarded barb-berries strewn about the forest floor. Though the fruit itself is dried out or mushy from over-ripeness, the spikes are well intact and pointing every which way with painful looking sharpness, waiting to impale a careless foot.

The only sound from the trees that betray their illusion of disinterest is the telltale *'clink-plink-plink'* of the jostled barb-berries behind them as they pass below. No one dares to look up or behind them, no matter how tempting the urge is. Instead, they keep their eyes trained on the ground and the willow as it draws nearer.

They carry on this way for what seems an hour, if not longer, keeping sight of the willow in the distance and mindful of the watchful trees around them. Mala's instinct to be quiet is merited; any time one of them makes a sound—a throat clearing, a sniffle or a cough—the surrounding trees respond with an agitated wave of rustling branches that sets off a chorus of barb-berry cracks and taps.

At last, the bright-leafed willow is only a few yards away, and the relief is palpable. It appears they will make it through the Fierce Wood safely.

And then chaos ensues in rapid succession. Just as Mala, who leads the pack, sets foot to the base of the veil, a piercing howl tears through the hush. Thunderous roars follow. The howl came from Baxton Bear, last in line, and as he cups a hind paw with his two huge forepaws, he rocks in agony. From between the mass of fur and claws, the telltale spikes of a barb-berry pokes out.

In his haste, he'd overlooked the fallen fruit and stepped on a needle point. Blood seeps through his mitts and onto the dirt. His companions, alarmed by his cry of pain, posture and growl at an unseen enemy.

The others try in vain to hush them, but it is too late. Their noise and movement agitates the trees. They twist and bend toward the group. Their branches retract like hundreds of baseball pitchers ready to throw the first pitch. There is no batter waiting to receive, but seven comparatively defenseless individuals trying to escape.

"Go!" Aedina hisses, trying to shuttle Mala, Jaime, Mateo and the bears ahead and intending to assist the injured bear.

"Please," says Bearis, "all of you go ahead through the veil. I will help Baxton, he is my responsibility."

There is no arguing with a twelve-hundred-pound bear. Even Aedina accepts this… with reluctance. As barb-berries whizz and fly all around them, Aedina pushes the others through, and with a last glance back at the two bears, she jumps through the veil.

Mala is consoling the inconsolable remaining bear while Jaime and Mateo check everyone for cuts and scratches, of which there are few. Aedina gains a future scar along her thigh, a gift from a passing barb-berry's spike, but otherwise she is as unharmed as the others.

They pace as they await Bearis and Baxton, fearing the worst as the moments pass. At last, and just as Mateo is ready to go back for them, both bears tumble through the veil in a tangle of bloodied and barb-spoked fur.

The all rush to the sides of the two injured bears, remove the spikes, and assess the injuries. Mateo reaches inside his satchel, extracts strips of Jaime's former clothing, and tosses a handful to him. Jaime needs no further instruction, and they began wrapping the worst of the wounds as Mala and Aedina comfort the pained but stoic grizzlies.

Baxton suffers the most injuries, with the worst of all being his hind paw. The spike has gone straight through the thick pad, he cannot walk far in such condition. Though willing to carry on, it is Bearis who decides his friend is unfit for such travel and task, and orders him to remain behind and seek shelter with a nearby bear community. Mateo runs ahead to find the bear den, and when he returns, two cheerfully plump sows and a clumsy cub in tow trail behind him.

"Now, cousin. What've you gotten yourself into? Come along with us now, we'll take good care of you," chides one motherly female.

The other chimes in, each kind and motherly, "Yes, now come along and the rest of you don't worry a thing about old Baxton here. You stop back again after your little adventure and we'll put on a pot of honey tea to go with those Anhael flowers you find."

Mateo knew to not disclose their mission, so, to not alarm anyone else in the Greenwood, told them they were en route to gather the illusive Anhael flowers near the north edges. Once upon a time, the unusual flowers had grown in abundance throughout all the Greenwood, but because of their sweet and intoxicating flavor, they had all but become extinct and grew only in the most sparsely inhabited regions of the land.

Mala wonders about the drinks they'd had at the Great Willow, which Aedina confirms is the nectar from the Anhael flower they'd enjoyed. She sees why they are so popular; the taste doesn't compare to anything she's ever known before.

With sad goodbyes and heartfelt well wishes, they part ways with the pained and disappointed bear and continue on their way. As the others walk ahead, Mala studies Bearis for unseen injury. Written in her drawn brow and down turned mouth is her worry for the great mammal. He chuckles and ruffles her hair with a giant but gentle paw, telling her it will take more than a few pointy barb-berries to take down old Bearis Bear, worry not. Still, she sticks close by her furry friend for much of their journey.

"At the next day break, we will rest," announces Aedina.

"How much further do we have to go before we reach the north Edges," asks Mala.

"Yeah, and what should we expect when we get there," adds Jaime.

Aedina hesitates, looking north with a troubled expression, then answers. "I believe we will arrive before the next day break, if we have no more obstacles. However, I cannot say with certainty what we will find in the north Edges. You, see, no Guardian has ever entered the Edges before now, the territory is unknown to all but the Seven."

Mateo continues. "They say it is where the beasts live, bound by the laws of the Seven to never cross the boundary that separates the Edges from the Greenwood, until the day of night, that is."

Jaime's voice is grim as he asks, "So, basically, no one goes there unless they have a death wish, right? That's kind of what you're saying. Isn't it?"

Aedina does not temper her response. "I am afraid it is not *kind of* what he is saying, it *is* what he is saying."

So, there it is, out in the open, no longer a hint or a question. Once said, Jaime feels foolish, misled by his own denial of what they are up against. *Of course*, the beasts have to go *somewhere*. And obviously, it is the north Edges; the place they are destined to go into.

The Seven wants them to leave the beasts for another time and go straight for the Vague. Fine, but *how* did they expect them to do so in the beast's territory?

Mala, too, is dubious. However, unlike Jaime, she is not surprised. In fact, she has already figured out what it is the Seven intend for them to do.

"We are to enter the north Edges at the next day of night when the beasts leave to ravage the Greenwood. There is little to do now but to wait and plan our entry."

Aedina and Bearis nod in solemn agreement, Mateo meets Jaime's gaze and shrugs, and the four looks to Jaime for his consent. With one of his infamous world-weary sighs, Jaime caves and says,

"Well, what are we standing around here for? Let's go find a place to chill until it's go time." Without missing a beat, he calls over his shoulder, "I'll explain it later, Mateo."

They all laugh, even though only Mala and Jaime understand the terminology, the rest can surmise it is yet another one of his polysemous words that Mateo will now adopt into his own vocabulary with relish.

A short time later they come upon a small, shallow, and clear body of water. With the sun beaming through the trees and the earth around it level and dry, it makes for the perfect resting place.

"Now, we have chill," announces Mateo.

"Ah, close, buddy. Now we *will* chill," corrects Jaime.

Everyone stretches and mills about. Jaime and Mala take Aedina's cue of refilling their water bottles, which are hollow gourds dried in the sun, not much unlike the birdhouse gourds Mala's mother had grown years before in their sizable community garden. Except these have heavy leather covers tied with rawhide strings to keep the water from spilling out.

Bearis and Barron wade into the shallow pool and wash away the caked blood from his fur, and Mateo stretches out on his back in the warm grass and falls asleep. To the casual observer, it is if the oddly paired friends are on a carefree hike, rather than a dangerous mission to defeat the Vague and save the Greenwood. The irony is lost on no one... except perhaps sleeping Mateo.

"Pay no mind to him. He can rise ready to fight as quickly as he can fall asleep. He is the bravest warrior I've ever known."

At Aedina's words, Mala swears a slight smile touches Mateo's lips, even though his eyes remained closed and his body at rest. She smiles at the couple, who like Jaime and herself, haven't quite realized that they *are* a couple.

At least, Mala hadn't until the kiss in the Havenheart. There'd been scant time to think about that kiss, as they've been on the move from almost the moment after it happened. But now, here in the unexpected peaceful clearing, she can reflect without distraction.

The shallow pond is small enough that they are all visible from every side, so she takes this time to take a solitary and slow walk around the water's edge. Jaime looks up at her from his perch on a flat rock, wondering if she wants company, but her slight smile and gentle head shake is enough to let him know she needs time to herself. He takes no offense and watches her for a moment as she wanders away.

He too, wants a moment to think about the kiss, the moment they shared, and all that it meant. For the rest of his days, every time he thinks of that electrifying moment, Jaime's heart will skip a beat and a shock wave will shoot through him like the clichéd bolt of lightning. He suspects it is something more than that classic cliché of love-struck passion, though. After all, how many people can say that their first *real* kiss involved magical gold light emanating from their partner and into you, while in a village in a magic forest, where small greenish people watched on? Definitely not the norm, he is sure. But, setting all the magic and strangeness aside: it is pretty amazing on its own.

But now what? It's selfish, he supposes, to be thinking about his own wants while the very lives of those in the Greenwood are in danger, and yet watching her walk away made it hard not to wonder at what is in her head. Is what she wants the same as what he wants? And as much as she assures him that Maxis is not a threat, he can't put him out of his mind. Sure, *she* knows there is nothing between them, but did Maxis?

Mala senses Jaime's fears and worries as much as her own. It is more than the effects of growing up together and being in tune with one another's feelings, she senses his thoughts, if not the actual words.

Maxis still worries him, his feelings about their kiss, his guilt for thinking selfishly… all of it.

Curious, she gazes at the others. Can she sense their thoughts as well? She turns her gaze first to Bearis—still splashing in the cool water—and concentrates. Stinging pain. Sadness. Calmness, too. Those are his thoughts, which come through only slightly more abstractly than Jaime's. Concentrating harder, she picks up more; he is sad to have parted with Baxton. His injuries hurt more than he lets on. His calm is of a deep inner well of faith that all will be well in the end. She smiles at his conviction, and vows to incorporate that mindset into her own thoughts.

The other bear is easy to read, his thoughts are in the present. The water is refreshing, he is hungry and excited for their adventure. Next, she turns her attention to Mateo still dozing—or pretending to—in the velvety green grass.

His thoughts are more complex, more than she'd have given him credit for. He worries for all of them, the humans included. But ideas, plans and strategies for defeating the Vague and even the beasts also fill his thoughts.

Aedina's thoughts are of the same mixture as Mateo's. Ever the leader, she frets about keeping them safe, worries about making the best choices. Mala also senses that she hopes that the humans stay in the Greenwood. This thought, and the kiss, have loomed in her thoughts.

She wants to stay. If only it were that simple, though. There is so much more to consider than just her own wants and wishes. Her family, for one. Even now, their worry and fear for her safety must be terrible. She can't even guess the differences in time from home and the Greenwood.

By Greenwood time, they've been here at least a week. Is it the same back home? Longer? Shorter? There is no way of knowing until they return. Assuming they *can*. Because that is also a consideration they've yet to acknowledge.

And then, there is Jaime. What does *he* want, if given a choice? He's always followed her lead until now. But leaving everything they've ever known for a strange land filled with strange creatures, not to mention magic and monsters to boot? She fears that she would be asking too much. So much to think about.

Knowing other people's thoughts is less appealing than she imagined. In fact, it is downright exhausting. A tiredness sinks into her bones so intense her legs buckle. Tiny black spots in her peripheral connect and her vision darkens. If not for observant Bearis, who is closest to her, she'd have fallen hard, but instead lands in a blanket of honey brown fur.

Bearis cradles the passed-out girl, carrying her across the water toward her worried companions. Jaime, almost frantic with concern meets him halfway, but Bearis shoos him away.

He says, "I have her just fine, thank you."

"What happened? Is she hurt?"

"Now, there, settle yourself, boy. The girl has exhausted herself, is all. Saw her start to sway, knew right away she was going down. You go make a comfy spot for her. She needs rest. You all do."

Bearis is so calm and commanding—easy at eight feet tall on his hind quarters and pushing over one thousand pounds—that Jaime can only obey. Perhaps the bear is right, she's been going nonstop. They all have. Rest is what they require before this next chapter in their adventure. Once convinced that she is all right, Jaime and the others consent to resting. There will be time enough to determine their next step, and for now, they can do nothing but wait.

The two grizzlies form a loose but protective semi-circle around the foursome, Mala being already ensconced within the cozy crook of Bearis' paws as he lay beside her. Were Jaime not so concerned for Mala's health, he'd tease the great bear that he'd make a great mama bear, but as it is, he settles himself close by and wills his mind and body to relax.

His last image before giving into much needed sleep is that of Mateo, across from him, who upon making eye contact with Jaime raises his hands in a thumbs-up gesture and displays his cautious pride in using the very human symbol for *all is good*. Jaime returns the gesture one-handedly and drops his head. Like the others, he is fast asleep within minutes.

41 Strange Dreams

They all sleep and dream strange dreams. However, none of them will recall them except Mala. Hers is not exactly a dream, but a visitation of sorts. She is hovering in an ethereal-like state in the Great Willow, just above the dais. Standing before it in a semi-circle are the Elders. She sees and hears them, but they seem unaware of her presence.

Maxis: "This trickery is more than distressing, it is wrong."

Gabrien: "It is necessary. You see that, yes?"

Caryss: "He is right, Maxis. It is the only way."

Gabrien: "You should not have spoken alone with her, Maxis. I am surprised at your impulsiveness."

Tobias: "Can you blame him, in fairness? Let us be mindful of the cost of his silence."

Elsabet: "Tobias is right. Take pity on Maxis, his heart is torn."

Maxis: "Thank you both, but it is not pity I need, but truth. She should have been told. She should be told."

Elsabet:

"If she is meant to know, she will figure it out for herself. That is the way it must be. It is written."

Kaylen: "Still, if only we could give her at least some guidance."

Maxis: "I do not believe that will be necessary…"

Gabrien: "Have you been watching her? I thought we agreed you would stay away."

Before Mala hears his next words, she is pulled away, as if through thick clouds, and back to consciousness. Jaime's and Bearis's voices replace those of the Elders.

Her eyes flutter open to the sight of everyone peering at her, Jaime so close that his breath fans a wisp of hair from her face.

"Geez, what is wrong with you people? Can't a girl catch some z's around here?"

She smiles to soften her words, and the crease in Jaime's forehead smooths. He touches her face and says, "You, uh, you were kind of, um, glowing there for a few minutes. The light woke us all up and well… it was coming from you."

Sweet Bearis breaks the strange enchantment and Mala's discomfort, "Well, if we're all rested and ready, now's a good a time as any to discuss this plan you seem to have, little one."

Mala pats the flat furry forehead of the wise bear as he nudges her to standing. Then, speaking with more calm and confidence than she feels, she lays out her idea.

"Like said earlier, I think—no, I *know* that we need to wait until the day of night begins. When the beasts have left the north Edges, we will be free to sneak in and find the Vague. If it *has* gained intelligence, then we can only hope it is limited. We all agree it wants *me*. So, let's give it what it wants."

As expected, they meet her idea with a vehement '*no*' from Jaime, and Aedina poking at the holes in her plan. This, too, she is prepared for.

"Mala, your plan is sound... I am sorry Jaime, but it is. However, the beasts are as keen as they are hungry. They will sense and smell us the moment they are free to do so. How do you propose we get past them?"

"I have been thinking about that. You all are skilled at climbing trees, yes?"

Jaime groans. The others nod. Mala takes a surreptitious glance down at her hands, her body, expecting to see the strange light, but it has already disappeared and she appears as she always has, perhaps with more of a tan than she'd have this time of year. Well, the time of year it is back home.

There is something akin to reverence in the eyes of the two Guardians and the bears. In Jaime's... worry. She tries to stay out of his thoughts—of all of theirs—but they come. Jaime believes something was happening to Mala, changing her into someone or something else.

The others' faces match their thoughts and even mirror Jaime's, but with more welcome.

Mala drops her hands on her hips. "Well, it's been a while since Jaime and I have, but I think we will be fine. We'll be fine, Jaime. We can wait them out, once they have dispersed, we are free to return to the forest floor."

It is as sound a plan as they have, even Jaime concedes… at least on the first half of the arrangement.

"Fine. I don't like it, but fine. But if you think I'll let you put yourself out there as bait for a- a lunatic to grab you, you're crazy," sputtered Jaime.

Mala grabs his hand and squeezes, attempting to calm him.

Mateo, who's been mostly listening, says, "I understand your concern, Jaime. But we will all be there to protect her. I'm afraid we need to draw the Vague out from wherever it hides, lest we walk into its trap unawares."

"And my friend, should that happen, we are all good to no one," adds Aedina.

"Human, my cousin and I will let no harm come to her, I promise you," says Bearis.

Jaime's wide-eyed gaze lands on each of them. He crosses his arms, uncrosses them, and throws his hands in the air. "This is crazy, you know. All of you, you realize how crazy this is?" No one answers. "Damn it. Fine. Great. I guess we're all climbing a tree and luring a monster out of hiding with human bait. Awesome."

Jaime stalks away from the quiet group. They understand his frustration and anger; there is nothing to be said to ease his mind. Mala moves to follow, but Mateo stops her.

"Sometimes, you just needs to be angry for a while. Give him time to think, he will come around," says the Virescent boy with a sidelong glance in Aedina's direction, speaking as much to her as he is Mala. This might be his version of an apology for his past belligerence and hostility toward the wildling leader.

Judging by Aedina's returned glance, and accompanying grin, all is forgiven at last. The two strolls off together, nudging and bumping against one another.

Despite Mala's personal turmoil, she grins at the pair. They are good for each other, *with* each other. As are she and Jaime.

She takes Mateo's advice and lets Jaime blow off steam. One look at him, plucking rocks from the water's edge and skimming them across the glassy surface, is enough to make her think Mateo is right. He needs time to cool off.

She sits down on the cool grass, stretches out on her back, and stares up at the blue sky through the swaying branches high above. It is a good time to think about the strange dream, having no one around her as even the bears have wandered off to the far side of the pond.

Mentally, she lists what she knows, or at least believes she knows. The dream was more than a dream. It felt like the odd dreams of her childhood where she'd hover just above the scenes below her, always so vivid and other worldly that she'd swear they were real and not fantasy. Is she finally allowing herself permission to accept the impossible? Yes. They *were* real, and they were trips to the Greenwood. She kicks the mental door all the way open at last. She *has* been visiting this place for some time, and never realized it until just now.

Jaime is right. Something *is* happening to her, changing her. Mala is learning who she is. But if she isn't just a small-town girl, as she's always considered herself to be, then what exactly is she? Or who?

The Seven know. They were talking about her, in that dream-like visit, and somehow Maxis discerned she is awakening to some mystery about herself. Yet, for whatever reason or rules that apply in their world, no one can help her figure it out.

The only person she ever talked to about her problems is now squatting down by the water, his back still to her. He hunches his broad shoulders, tips his head down, almost as if in prayer. Does Jaime ever pray? Funny, of all the things they've ever spoken of, this was never one of them. She stills her mind, willing it to focus on Jaime's.

Perhaps he feels her prying in his head, or maybe senses her stare. Whichever the reason, his profile swings her way, and though he doesn't turn enough for them to make eye contact, he still jerks his head; a signal he is ready to talk.

Mala goes to him without hesitation. For a while, they sit staring out over the water. She slips her hand into his, and when he doesn't pull away, leans her head against his arm. After a moment, his tips his head to meet hers, so his temple rests on her crown.

"Everything will be okay, Jaime."

"Nothing will ever be the same, Little."

"No. I don't think it will be."
"I love you."
"I love you, too. Always."

42 The North Edges

They spend the rest of the time in the clearing by the water practicing fighting maneuvers. They will avoid the beasts at all costs. However, Aedina insists they can never over-prepare.

At last the first rumble of thunder rolls in the far-off distance. Mala has a sudden sense of ill-preparedness; what if they are not ready? What if her plan is poor, and she puts everyone at risk? Aedina senses her fears and settles a firm hand on her shoulder.

"We are all in this together. It will work. A warrior must always believe she will defeat her enemy. Remember."

Mala exhales. Her lips form a grim line meant to be a smile at the encouraging words. She is right of course. If she does not believe in herself, she is doomed. They *all* are. She pats her pouch for the sphere—Jaime insisted it remain with her. It's reassuring warmth seeps into her hand with a gentle hum. She still doesn't know how to use it, yet it lends her a perception of security.

They gather their belongings, spears, spikes, and pouches, and leave the food and drink behind. There will be no time or interest in such things once under way, and no matter the result, it will come soon enough.

A jagged line of pines marks the border of the north Edges, reminding Mala—and Jaime as well—of the line of evergreens along their apartments, although these are much taller. Here, the sunlight struggles to push through the dense and deep green trees. It's as if they purposely block the light to keep this part of the forest in perpetual darkness. At once, the coldness oozes out from within, making them shudder.

They climb as high as they can, and in pairs. Bearis, the larger of the two bears, climbs first, with Barron close behind. Their vantage point keeps the others and the forest floor in sight.

"What I wouldn't give for those flashlights we left in the Everwood!" swears Jaime.

Instead, they have to adjust as much as their eyes allow to the darker woods. They also must blend in with the trees, an easy feat for all but Mala. Her blonde hair is like a beacon, so they cover it as much as possible using a wide strip of her old black shirt. Once tied around her head like a bandana, Jaime jokes that she looks something like a ninja, pirate, and a Virescent rolled into one.

"Still cute, though. Don't worry," he winks at her.

It is good to see him joke around, even in such tense circumstances, perhaps *especially* in such circumstances. This is the Jaime she knows and loves. Something changed back at the pond, she is unsure of what, but something settled in his mind and calmed him. Acceptance comes to mind. Acceptance for everything that is, everything that will be. Whatever the case, he seems to be ready for what is coming, or at least as ready as any of them can be.

The thunder rolls closer, and therefore louder. Everyone chooses a tree, staying close enough to hear one another if called. They intend to remain silent until the threat passes, but if a call for help is necessary, they need to be within earshot.

The first to climb are the bears. Mala and Jaime climb next. Aedina and Mateo keep a watchful eye on the pair as they ascend. They are adept and reach an impressive height with little difficulty thanks to the multitude of foot friendly branches, much to everyone's relief.

Lastly, and with the most speed and agility, are Aedina and Mateo. Once they are all in their respective perches, there is little to do but wait. They struggle to see each other through the branches, and the dirt below seems miles away, but this is still their best option considering the choices. Assuming the beasts bypass them, the worst thing they must battle are the winds that accompany the night. They'll need all their might to hold on as the narrow treetops bend and sway with every gust and gale.

As if on cue, the first rustle of wind starts like a distant wave across the forest and rushes toward them as they grip the sappy bark in anticipation. It is a mild gust. It does not lull them into believing it won't get worse.

As the thunder changes from a long rumble to more a series of cracks, the winds pick up, as expected. Each wind-wave comes with a quicker and more intense one on its heels. The tree tops totter with almost impossible to believe flexibility.

The wind—as it tears and whips through the branches—sneaks into hollows and holes through which it screams and howls, making Mala wish she could cover her ears… an impossibility if she is to remain lodged in her spot. She tries in vain to squint through the blizzard of pine needles to spot the others. Jaime, who is below and opposite her with his face set, nods to her. He is safe. She is safe. So far.

Despite the dizzying height, Mala peers down again. This time, slinking across the earth, are a pack of oily looking black creatures. That she can see them with clarity only means their size is frighteningly impressive. Their movements, slow and slinky, remind her of wolves stalking prey, though not even the largest wolf known to man compares with these beasts. Running past the tree trunks like flashes are gray and white-streaked animals, smaller and sleeker looking, as well as confused looking, rotund, and hairy bipeds.

For one heart stopping second, one of those upright walking Neanderthal things stop right below their tree and look up. Even from where she is, Mala sees that its eyes were huge, bulging repulsively from wet sockets. Horrified, she watches as it opens its gash of a mouth as if to speak, but a fat, forked tongue slips out from between jagged yellow teeth and tests the air like a snake.

Her revulsion is so intense she jerks backward, forgetting where she is, and loses her balance. She'd have fallen to the ground, but for Jaime, who saw her every reaction. When she pulled back in horror, he was ready to steady her, needing only one steady hand at her elbow to do so. Her heart races as she meets his eyes again, this time with a silent thank you. He grim expression has not changed since the clearing.

Something in Jaime *had* changed back there, and it would shock her to know what caused it. When Jaime had walked away at the pond, he *was* furious beyond speech. So intense was his rage that he feared what his hands would do. He wanted to shake Mala, punch Mateo, scream in Aedina's face. He was so enraged he'd have fought the imposing bears. His helplessness, his lack of influence, his fear… it all together formed a toxic anvil in his head; it consumed him.

He mustered every ounce of control, and made the choice to walk away. He was stronger than the rage. He was not his father's son. The blood pounding in his ears subsided, the rock he didn't realize he'd been clenching with white knuckles loosened and fell to the ground with a tap. He exhaled and crouched down by the water's edge intending to splash his face with the cool water.

That was when he saw it. *Him.* Or his reflection, at least, in the rippling water. *Maxis.* He sneered, feeling the anger boil again. But then a voice inside his head spoke.

"The feeling is mutual I can assure you. Or, at least, it would be, were I permitted. As it is, I am not," said Maxis' vision.

Jaime thought back at him, "Great, isn't getting into her head enough for you? Now you've got to bother me, too?"

"I don't believe I am a bother to Mala." Jaime made to stand. "Stop. Wait. I apologize. It is most unlike me to speak so... rudely. Please, listen to what I must tell you. The only assurance that should matter to you, is the one she gave you. There is... nothing between us. Her heart is yours alone."

Though the face in the water was expressionless, Jaime heard subtle insinuations suggesting not all his words were sincere. Still, Jaime let him continue.

"As I have been sent to watch over her, it is you who must protect her. She has been a challenge, I am aware. You have..." A grudging pause. "you have done well, Jaime of Everwood. We are grateful to you."

Everything that had eluded him came to him in that instant. Jaime understood who Mala is. *What* she is. The air left his body in a rush; it knocks the wind out of him as if Maxis had punched in the gut. She is...

"...behind you. I am out of time, Jaime. Do not leave her side. She will need you more than ever. Protect her Jaime... for all of us."

Just as Mala approached, the mirage disappeared, leaving him staring at the smooth magnified stones below the shallow water's surface in consternation. Man, he hated that guy. Jaime didn't need some mystery magic dude to tell him to protect Mala, he already intended to. It was what he'd always done, always *would* do, simple as that.

When she slipped her small warm hand into his, he forgot his anger, replacing it with a tender love for the special soul beside him. Like the Elders, Jaime resigned himself to letting Mala discover her truth in her own time, if she hadn't already.

As they sway and hang on for dear life, Jaime wonders how much Mala knows, how much she understands. *He* is acting differently; she sees it in him as much as he sees the changes in her. Even the way she talks has changed; she sounds more like the Elders than the Mala of Rocky Knoll. She is *still* Mala. He is *still* Jaime. This much will never change. He hopes.

What *has* changed is the intensity of the night. The howls and shrieks of the wind mix and mingle with those of the beasts below, and while the sky blackens and darkens and blankets the earth below, the beasts are now luminous. Their green and white lantern eyes are like lasers in the dark. It is impossible to know how many there are from their narrow and dim perspective, but the shapes keep passing by, and the laser lights of their eyes come from all directions. They head out in the same direction, though... toward the Greenwood, away from the Edges, in search of prey.

Most will come back dissatisfied and hungry, and this will only make them angrier and more aggressive the next time night comes to the Greenwood. Unless, of course, their night reign ends.

Helplessness agitates and frustrates Mateo, He fumes in his perch with Aedina. Guardians guard, fight and protect, not hide. Their position is an affront to everything they stand for. Aedina feels the same emotions. But they are outnumbered and ill prepared for a battle of such magnitude. Even with all their Guardians beside them, they would still not be a match for these vile creatures. Seeing them for the first time makes Aedina acutely aware of this.

Bearis and Barron do not trouble themselves with such matters. They live by a series of simple wisdoms. Never worry about that which you cannot control., They can control neither the night nor the beasts that come with it. Therefore, they wait. And since there is nothing for them to do while they wait… they slept.

Meanwhile, the wind and the beasts continue to howl in the blackness. However, one thing had changed. The growls of the animals are now more distant. After no more beasts pass below, the humans and the Guardians stretch and flex their aching muscles and make their ways back down the trees, pausing often to survey the dim landscape for telltale pricks of light.

At last, their feet—and paws—touch land again and they reconvene. The four walks between the bears with Bearis in the lead, his burly companion staying watchful at their backs. Everyone's eyes scan the forest around them expecting something to jump out.

Yet, when it happens, they are all startled with heart bursting shock. It is a biped, almost identical to the one Mala saw from high in the tree's safety. Up close, it is worse. A foul smell precedes it, sickly sweet yet putrid at the same time. It is the smell of decay, filth, and of death. They all recoil, all except Bearis, whose hackles stand like spikes along his back as he crouches in readiness to attack. Without hesitation, Barron rushes to his side, replicating his stance.

The bears form an impressive barrier between the beast and the foursome, yet they too are poised to fight. As for the vile beast, its mangled face contorts with confused rage. All over its body, tufts of coarse long hair quivers as it hisses and growls through a mouth unable to close do to its countless pointy protruding teeth.

It knows not what to make of the sudden and unexpected group; never has prey walked into their lair, let alone challenged them. It makes a move, like a feign, and ferocious growls by the bears answer it. With huge lidless eyes it stares at them, undecided. Bearis helps it along by moving closer. Barron mirrors his every move, and both bare their sharp white fangs.

The beast takes a step back. It side-steps the group, who turns with it, stalking its every move. Jaime notes with disgust the rivulets of drool dripping from the corners of its vicious mouth. Mala watches as the hands—claws—flex spastically making its sharp black nails click and scrape together. The misshapen and mottled skull, the caked dirt—*or is it blood*—covering it in patches draws Mateo's sickened gaze, while Aedina locks in on the soulless black eyes. It is a sight none of them will soon forget.

Then, as suddenly as it appeared, it darts off into the dark with a grunt, perhaps realizing it is no match for such a group, preferring the helpless victims that await it in the Greenwood. They heave a sigh of relief, and all but Bearis relax their tense bodies. He remains in protective watchful posture, something they are all grateful for as they again walk forward, toward more of the unknown.

They continue for ten, fifteen, maybe twenty minutes more before Mala stops, putting a hand back against Jaime's chest.

"Do you hear that?"

Everyone stills, listening into the night, but all they hear is the now familiar sound of the wind, distant howls, and intermittent rumbles of thunder.

"It's Endelyn. She is calling us. This way."

"Mala, it may be a trap. Let us go with care," cautions Aedina.

"It *is* a trap. But we must continue ahead," she replies.

She leads the way, bypassing the bears, much to Bearis' consternation... and Jaime's. But since only she hears the voice, they follow her lead, leaving her vulnerable. They all peer hard into the darkness, watchful for any telltale pinpricks of glowing light to alert them to a straggling beast's presence, but they see none.

Mala is oblivious to it all—the wind, howls, the anxious worry that emanates off her friends—even the ground beneath her feet and the alarming creaks and cracks of the surrounding trees as the gusts push and shove them against each other. All she heeds is the sound of the not-really-Endelyn's voice guiding her toward its source.

By the time they stop, the day of night is halfway over. They are in the north Edge's heart and running out of time. If they do not find and defeat the Vague and leave the Edges, they will be trapped in there when the beasts return to their prison.

"Why have we stopped? Do you not hear the voice anymore?" asks Mateo.

"We are here. *It* is here."

They look around but see nothing but the same night dark forest they've been looking at for hours. But then, Mala points. In the gloom, an even darker shape is visible, even if just barely. A cave stands less than a yard away. It must have risen with great and sudden force, for uprooted trees and bushes hang and sag on top and along its sides, and one straggly pine dangles by a long root over the gaping entrance, twisting and waving in the wind like a rat being held by its tail. Something powerful uprooted and fractured every tree; all save one. Leaning against the cave is an ancient looking willow, an unmistakable veil.

From within the mouth of that black cavern appears a faintly glowing figure. It is Edelyn, smiling serenely and beckoning them to join her. When Mala moves to do so, Bearis blocks her and nudges her backward gently but firmly.

"Can't let you do that, little one. Sorry," says the bear, keeping his eyes on the figure.

"It is all right, my furry prince. All of you. *This* is what I am here to do. You must remain, while I go inside," states Mala.

"If you go," says Jaime, "Then I go."

"We *all* go." Adds Aedina.

With a sad expression, Mala goes to each of them—not unlike Elsabet had at the Great Willow—beginning with Bearis.

"Sweet, sweet Bear. In my world, I would've called you and Barron my knights in shining armor. Thank you for keeping me safe."

She turns to Mateo. "Mateo, you and I—in another life—must have been or *will be* brother and sister. We are so alike, aren't we? I would be proud to call you brother."

She smiles and hugs the embarrassed but honored Virescent. Mala takes Aedina's hands. "Ah, and *you*, brave and beautiful Aedina. I've never had a girlfriend until you. I am so fortunate to have met you, and to have learned so much from you. You are as great a leader as there ever will be."

The girls hug. Last is Jaime, who stands arms crossed in refusal to accept the obvious. She is not going in there, at least not alone. '*No,*' says his body language even before his words can. The closer she steps to him, the more he refuses her eye contact. But once she is before him, her upturned gaze boring into him, imploring him to look into her eyes, he is powerless.

She unfolds his crossed arms, removing any barrier between them, and steps into the embrace she created. He wraps his arms around her now frail feeling body, wanting to hold on forever. But as quickly as she pulled him in, she pushes him away, so she can once again see his face.

As he gazes back at her, he sees both the seventeen-year-old girl he's known most of his life, and the *other* Mala, the one he doesn't know, but wants the time to discover.

And now, it seems, he is denied the chance. He sees her plan now as if it is written in black and white. She will sacrifice herself, giving the others a sliver of opportunity to shove the distracted Vague back through the veil from which it came. Until that moment, only Aedina had known her plan's extent.

"Jaime, my Jaime," she sighs. "This is the way, the *only* way. You must see that."

"This *can't* be the only way. We didn't take enough time to think about it, I know we could find another way."

Mala shakes her head. "Jaime, everything will turn out the way it should. Trust me. Have I ever steered you wrong? Wait, don't answer that."

He tries to laugh, but a choked sob escapes instead. How did this happen? How did they go from a normal life to… this? It isn't possible, and yet, here they are. Saying… *goodbye*? She jerks her head at the figure meant to be Endelyn. She—no, *it*—smiles at her, waiting. Its eyes are not the familiar teal of the Seven, but black like drops of coal. He wants to rip those eyes from its head, but Mala senses his lunge before he follows through, and squeezes his arm.

"Jaime. I need you to trust me. Look at me Jaime. *I need you to trust me*. Okay? Can you do that?" He nods. "Good, now, promise me, you will not hesitate. Jaime, if you do, you will doom all the Greenwood, every innocent creature that lives here." In a whisper she hisses, "I can feel Endelyn, the real one. She is fighting to hang on, but she can't much longer. Our time is almost up."

With a force that Jaime hadn't anticipated, Mala pushes him back, forcing him off balance. Just as quickly, Aedina and Mateo flanked and hold him back, followed by the surprised but quick bears. Mala walks away from them and toward the mouth of the cave and the waiting Vague, giving him one last regretful look before she strides to her destiny.

43 Mala's Choice

She blocks the painful image of Jaime's devastated face from her mind and focuses on the thing before her. It *has* evolved since she last saw it. Its vocabulary is broader, less childlike and more that of a cunning teenager. The process is not unlike that of human growth patterns... newborn and infantile helplessness, toddler impulses and tantrums, and now the mind of a willful teenager. Except this is no human. This is a creature whose evolution never included the capacity for love, empathy and compassion. For whatever reasons, it can only absorb undesirable qualities and ideas. So, while it may have started out as something ill-defined or constructed, and therefore vague, it is that no longer.

She asks it, "What are you?"

"I am the Vague," it replies after a pause.

"But now you are more."

"Yesss. I am more. I want more."

"What do you want?"

"You. It is all in you. This one, she tries to hide it from me. But I see it."

She struggles to hear Endelyn, the true Endelyn, but she has gone silent.

"I don't understand. What is she trying to hide from you?

Mala is stalling for time. She is unsure what to do next and draw it closer to the veil.

"Come inside. I won't bite."

It chuckles; an odd disjointed sound, like it is trying it on for the first time.

"I see you are developing a sense of humor, Vague. You have mastered taking form. You look just like Endelyn."

It preens like a beauty contest contestant before the judges. It has also learned vanity and pride. Mala now knows how to manipulate it, but she will have to take great care in blocking her thoughts from the perceptive thing. The false Endelyn's eyes narrow. Mala fills her mind with thoughts of, *how perfectly the Vague changes shape. I wish I could be as skilled.* And *it is so much smarter than I am.* She must use its newfound vanity against it.

"You think I am easily fooled, human? I am not. Come inside where the wind won't get you."

It wants her to be out of sight from the others. It is wary of them. She cannot allow this to happen. Again, she states she'll be glad to come in, but a second voice in her head, purposely accessible to the Vague, thinks, *ah, so the Vague does have a weakness, it fears the children outside.*

The Endelyn shape trembles, bits of black smoke burst through her cheek and abdomen; the implication of its perceived weakness enrages the Vague.

"Come inside, or I will take them all. I can, you know. I don't have to wait like a passive fool and hope for new souls. I can take them whenever I wish."

Mala's guarded thoughts tell her the Vague is lying. If it is true, it would've done so already. *If it isn't scared of them, it would at least remain at the opening of the cave, but it is afraid.*

Aloud she says, "I apologize, I hadn't realized how powerful you have become."

She is confusing it, angering it, and making it doubt itself. The Vague moves toward the cave opening as if to prove her wrong.

"Join me, and I will set the Elder free. She is no use to me anymore."

Mala, for the first time in their exchange, wavers. She can set Endelyn free, and...

It lies!

Endelyn's voice inside Mala's head is weak with effort, but strong enough to shoot through both Mala's and the Vague's consciousness. One look at the shuddering blackness that now grotesquely bulges through the seams of false Endelyn, and Mala knows it is losing control, blinded by its rage. This is her chance.

She needs to grab a hold of that form before it is nothing but intangible smoke and pull it toward the veil.

Without warning, Mala runs at it sidelong. A series of things happen, almost in slow motion. She reaches the Endelyn-shaped Vague and wraps her arms around it like a defensive lineman going for the tackle. Coldness seeps into her bones and travels up her spine into her skull like the worst brain freeze she's ever known.

Jaime shouts, "No," from what seems like miles away, just as the real Endelyn shouts *NOW i*n her head.

The day of night is coming to its end, and the daylight returns. Mala pushes the startled Vague closer and closer to the willow tree. Her strength is giving out, not just in her body, but her mind. As her strength leaves, the Vague grows stronger, It pushes back against her. They are at the precipice of the veil. It locks her in an embrace.

From deep within her mind she hears Endelyn. *"The light is in you, Mala. You must use it!"*

Mala remembers the orb... but she had slipped it into Jaime's pouch when she'd hugged him.

"No, Mala, it is in you*. Use it. Now."*

Somehow, the Vague, for as much as it tries, cannot revert to its smoky form. It is Endelyn's doing, and it is taking everything she has to hold on. The time has come. She closes her eyes and imagines the rose gold light sitting in her chest. Warmth creeps back into her chilled bones and the fog lifts from her brain. Then she imagines - no, she *wills* the light to swell and fill her entire body and sends it out through her every pore.

The Vague tries to recoil from the heat and light, it shudders in revulsion, now off balance, confused, and weak. With a renewed sense of strength, Mala - whose back is now to the veil - drags the Vague backward toward the tree.

From where Aedina and the others watch, they see nothing but the sphere of light she's become, a blinding and pulsing ball of brightness. Then, the light blinks out.

No one moves. They hardly register the sound of the Seven's horn in the distance, or the fading darkness. But then, like a cannon's blast, Jaime shouts Mala's name and runs toward the willow tree. The others follow, straining to decipher the shapes on the ground in the pre-dawn light. Jaime falls to his knees in front of a pile of leaves. Aedina is first to realize it is no pile of leaves before them, but the crumpled body of Mala, unmoving.

From the cave's entrance Endelyn staggers out. Her effort has depleted much of her aura, her face wan and exhausted. Mateo, Aedina and the bears rush to help her, leaving the distraught Jaime alone with Mala's broken looking body.

He brushes back the tangle of blonde hair, revealing her still as porcelain face. "Hey. Hey. Wake up, Mala, wake up. Come on. You need to wake up."

He pulls her into his lap, willing her to awaken. Desperation in his eyes, he looks to the approaching group. Mateo and Aedina have draped Endelyn over the ample back of Bearis, they and the other two bears approach.

"You can help her. I know you can."

"Oh, dear Jaime. We can do nothing for her here, I'm afraid. We must get her back to the Great Willow. Quickly."

"Can't you use your magic to get us there?"

"I am too weak. Without the other Elders, I can do very little."

"Is she... is she dead?" Mateo gulps.

Endelyn lifts a pale hand and bows her head. A faint and flickering glow pulses from her palm. The others watch with bated breath. The light fades out and she meets Jaime's eyes.

"She is not dead, my children. Not as you know death. But she is... trapped."

"Trapped? What does that mean, she's *lost*?"

"She is… with the Vague. She didn't push it through the veil, so she did the next best thing. She... absorbed it. They are trapped together, inside of her. We need to get her to Elsabet. I believe she can help her find her way back. But they will need all of our strength."

As they stare down at Mala's lifeless form, Mateo speaks from the back of their semi-circle, "Uh, friends? We have another problem to deal with right now…"

Morning has fully arrived, and with it the return of the beasts. From every direction, the sounds of growls, grunts and howls. Their footfalls are heavy and careless; twigs and branches snap and crack as they amble through dead leaves with dragging feet and paws. From the sounds of it, they are no less hungry and therefore no more satisfied as when the departed the north Edge.

It is only a matter of moments before they crawl and slink through the clearing. They all look to one another, hoping someone has a plan or a route of escape.

There is only concern and helplessness. Endelyn speaks in a whisper. "Jaime. The sphere. You must use the sphere."

Jaime stares at her, confused. Then the proverbial light bulb pops in in his head. But, to his knowledge, it is Mala who had it last. He searches the folds of her clothing, but Endelyn stops him.

"It is on *you* Jaime. It belonged with you, and Mala knew it to be so."

Jaime recalls the tight hug Mala gave him just before she approached the cave. He reaches into the pouch around his waist, and sure as daylight, the orb is there. The moment it touches his hand, warmth and a steady, rhythmic pulsation emanate from within.

"What the hell is this thing, anyhow? How do I use it?"

Endelyn smiles down at him and explains as much as her weakened body allows.

"There is a sphere for each Elder. They are... our Life Source. Without them, we perish. We are not infallible, Jaime. The one you have... it belongs to Mala."

If she expected Jaime to be surprised, she would've been mistaken. It only confirms what he suspected, no matter how dubiously he did so. Mala is an Elder. An eighth to their Seven. She belongs here, in the Greenwood. His sense of loss doubles. Even if they revive her, she will still be lost to him.

"I still don't understand. What am I supposed to do with it?"

She motioned for him to stand. "You will lead us out, with the help of Mala's Life Sphere. Hold it in both of your hands before you, now concentrate Jaime. Find her in your mind and tell her we need her light."

"But you said she-"

"That doesn't matter, Jaime. She can —she *will* hear you. Call to her."

He is desperate to get them out of the north Edges, but he feels foolish and under pressure as they stare expectantly at him. To add to his stress, the beasts are now coming into the clearing. The only thing keeping them from attacking is their surprise at finding their prey has come to them. It won't be long before their hunger outweighs their trepidation.

He cradle-carries Mala to Bearis and places her alongside Endelyn. Then he exhales and closes his eyes. In his mind, he calls out to Mala. *Little, if you can hear me, we really kinda need your help right about now.* Nothing. He opens his eyes to see the same expectant eyes on him… and more beasts crowding the clearing. It won't be long before they try their luck.

He closes his eyes more tightly. *Come on Mala, I know you're out there. Endelyn says so. I need you—we all do.* There is a stronger pulsation from the sphere, more heat. He opens one eye to look, but no light emanates from the orb. *Mal, I know you're there. I can feel you. I can't do this without you.* Nothing. He again opens his eyes to see the same sights.

Jaime's panic rises and still nothing more than the faint pulsing. He thinks hard. Mala, in her infinite stubbornness and contrary nature, responds most animatedly to Jaime's antagonism and teasing. So, that's just what he will do.

It's okay, Little. I understand if you're too weak to help us. I always knew I was the tougher one. You just sit back and relax, while I do all the heavy lifting, ok...

Is he imagining it, or is the sphere grown hot in his hands? He dares to open his eyes. It's working. The rose gold light shoots out in every direction, even through his hands.

The beasts recoil, parting a path for Jaime and the others to cut through. As much as he tries to not look into those hideous faces, their fangs and claws and misshapen faces will forever haunt his dreams. Still, he presses on, maintaining a steady stream of mental teasing and poking to maintain the connection with Mala.

At last, the line of pine trees is in sight and they hurry toward it. Jaime stands watch, the glowing sphere in his outstretched palms, warding off the agitated monsters that follow their every move from a safe distance. As he ushers the others through, the orb loses strength and brightness. Mateo is second to last and beckons him to follow.

He is almost through the tree line when something hot and rough wraps around his ankle. Sharp teeth—or claws—pierce the thin flesh, and the fracturing of delicate ankle bones is audible. Jaime cries out in pain. The others jump into action. Mateo and Aedina grab his wrists and pull, Bearis and Barron run past him with roars and snarls to fight off whatever has gotten a hold of him.

With a sudden jerk and a yelp from behind the tree line, Jaime is free but far from undamaged. Aedina inspects and wraps his mangled appendage, confirming the break. Mateo retrieves a walking stick from the woods, and Jaime steels himself for a painful journey ahead.

At his insistence, they carry on; a solemn lot with a growing following of Greenwood creatures, all in awed reverence at the two lifeless bodies now on Bearis's great back. He bears their weight with great care, well aware of the treasures he holds, and mindful of their safety always.

When they approach the Fierce Wood veil, there is no question they will bypass it in favor of the longer route. No one has the strength or presence of mind to battle with irate and vicious trees this time around. So, they travel in somber silence, afraid to hope.

At last, after two breaks of day, they reach the Mere. They rest their exhausted bones and replenish their water supply. The woodland creatures who've steadfastly followed along also take respite along the embankment, some drinking the cool water, others even going in for a swim. From the sky came a familiar sight: a large yellow bird swooping in and landing just before them with a heavy thump and a racket of one-sided conversation.

"Well, 'ello there! Why, isn't this quite the crowd, I say! Now, now, why so glum, why so—ohh. Dear me. Is that—is that my funny little bird girl there? *Oh.* Is that— why I say, it's Endelyn, it is. Right, right."

Despite the pain shooting from his leg into his entire body, Jaime smiles. This is no doubt the infamous Ardie Mala had told him about. She is as described, and more. He watches as she approaches the lifeless girls, still on the back of the resolute bear, who declines all offers of aid.

Jaime even chuckles as she waddles and pushes aside the slower moving lookers-on and *tsked-tsked* them. But then his heart softens toward the boisterous bird as she brushes the hair back from Mala's brow with a motherly stroke of her feathered wing, then presses her head against her cheek.

"Now, like I said, why the glum faces? There's celebrating to be done here. I've just come from the Great Willow, they're expectin' you, you know. Seems you've gone and released all those poor creatures from that nasty Vague, you have."

This is the first they've heard of such wonderful news, and the first bright spot in their grim travels.

"Right, right, on with you. You've got to get these two back on their feet, now don't you?"

Ardie, with her great wings and pushy persona rouses everyone and gets them moving again, and with renewed energy at that. As the group — and their entourage — start back on the path to the Great Willow, Ardie calls out once more.

"Oh, and tell that ridiculous Tortanine of yours, he is not welcome at the Mere. Nearly knocked me over, he did. I'll have none of that rudeness here, I say. Right, right."

This lightens Jaime's heavy heart. Murpius is alive, and as underfoot as ever. Ignoring the pain in his leg, he pushes the others to move faster, and before long, the imposing sight of the massive meadow and even bigger tree is in view, preceded only by its heavenly scents drifting in the air.

If their entourage is at least one hundred, the courtyard of the Seven's haven has more than double waiting. They part the way for the group, calling out cheers and gratitude as they pass. Closest to the front is Baxton Bear, his paw bandaged, and Murphius, looking doleful as ever. At the dais, it is only Gabrien who stands before it, waiting for them.

"Welcome back, children. Please let us go quickly into the grand foyer. The others are waiting."

The five follow, leaving the menagerie to wait outside the entrance. The Elders have formed a semi-circle, motioning for Bearis to take the center with Mala and Endelyn still on his broad back. When Jaime, Mateo and Aedina close the circle, Elsabet speaks.

"We have little time to spare. Please, join hands, everyone. Jaime, place the sphere between them."

Jaime looks down at the dull orb in his hand. He'd held on to it so tightly the entire time, unaware of the cramping and oblivious that the intricate design on the orb's surface had etched a pattern into his hand that will remain there for all of Jaime's earthly days. He places the sphere between the two girls, who are curled toward each other in a heart shape—their heads bowed together and knees touching. He marveled at how much they resemble each other, looking almost like twins were it not for their hair being distinct shades of blonde. After a brief hesitation, he returns to his place between Aedina and Elsabet, and locks hands with them. The familiar pulsing from Elsabet's hand travel through his and up his arm, making the hairs stand up on end.

As she speaks, Jaime glances around the circle, noticing for the first time that the constant rose gold light is flickering, like a fluorescent bulb as it dies. His eyes meet Maxis's, who stands stone-like across from him, and his blood rises to his temples. It is Aedina who gives his hand a squeeze, bringing him back to task at hand, and he listens to Elsabet's instructions with greater concentration.

"Close your eyes, bow your heads, and clear your minds of everything but Endelyn and Mala. Join me in these words. We surround you with light, you are safe from harm, come back to us. Come back to us."

They repeat the verses over and over, and just when Jaime is about to give up hope, the room brightens. A shadow falls before his closed eyes, and though he is afraid, he opens them a little at a time.

The first sight he sees is small bare feet—feet he'd recognize anytime, anywhere. He allows his eyes to travel up, afraid they are deceiving him. At last, he looks at her face, as familiar and sweet as ever, save one difference. Her eyes—before a vibrant hazel—are now the same disconcerting teal as the Elders. The smile that dimples Jaime's cheek falters, then returns. She is still his Mala… just something more as well.

He touches her hair, her face, and then pulls her in to a tight embrace. The others laugh and cheer, feeling his joy along with their own. Endelyn, now restored to her full luminous beauty speaks.

"Come, we must greet everyone in the courtyard and share our joy."

She leads them to the dais, where now there is an eighth seat carved. Jaime is first to spot the change. The Elders take their places in their rightful order. Kaylen, Elsabet, Caryss and Endelyn, beside her Gabrien, the empty seat, then Maxis and Tobias. If Mala sees this, she makes no indication, but looks upon them with shining eyes and a bright smile.

Endelyn says, "Welcome, everyone. Before us we have some of the greatest heroes the Greenwood will ever know." She gazes at Aedina and Mateo. "Our brave Guardians, how do we repay you?"

"No repayment is necessary, Elders. I do have a request, though," Aedina boldly states. "I would like for Mateo to be named Guardian Leader. He has proven himself in every way. It would honor me to be led by him, as would the other Guardians, I am certain."

Mateo, as flattered as he is surprised, steps up and only slightly less boldly responds.

"Elders, A-Aedina, I thank you, but I must decline. Aedina has led us unfailingly. Her judgment and bravery is without compare."

The Seven chuckle and grin at them both. It is Gabrien who delivers their pronouncement, "It appears we have not one but two able leaders before us. Therefore, it only seems fitting that we have two Leaders of the Guardians. What say you, Virescent and Wildling? Can you lead together?"

Stunned, the two look at one another, and then nod a vehement yes to the Elders.

"Very well, it is done. Now, Bearis. You and your two companions have shown a bravery and loyalty that we cannot ignore. If not for you, we shudder to think of what may have happened. What can we do to show our gratitude?"

The bears, humble by nature, are stumped for a reply. They need little, want less. All they require is land to roam and food to eat, things of which they have in plentitude. Endelyn, knowing their humble ways, speaks for them.

"My sweet friends, I see you are struggling with your answer, which makes you all the more deserving. As we already have Guardians of the Greenwood at our service, perhaps you could be the Ambassadors to the Great Mere?"

Bearis ducks his head, paws the ground, and replies, "Well, I've never had a title before. That would be kind of nice, now wouldn't it, fellas?"

His companions bob their heads hard enough to make their jowls flap. Next, all eyes turn to Jaime. The excess attention makes him blush, but he straightens and juts his chin. Again, Endelyn speaks for the Seven.

"Brave Jaime. There are no words to do justice to your courage and steadfast loyalty. What is it you want most of all?"

Jaime knew the question would come, and he is ready for it. But now that they put it before him, he hesitates, knowing everything is about to change either for the better or the worse. Mala's eyes are on him, but he stares ahead at the dais.

"I would like—what I would like more than anything—is to return home. To the Everwood, and Rocky Knoll... with Mala, of course."

"This does not surprise me, human boy. I can imagine how you would with to return to your home, and everything you know. However, I must warn you, once you leave the Greenwood, you may never return. Is this a risk you are willing to take?"

"I am. But what... what about Mala?"

"We cannot answer for her, you must ask her yourself."

For a moment Jaime freezes, afraid to turn to her. When he does, her lips smile, but her eyes are sad. He will not hear what he'd hoped for.

"Oh, Jaime. I..."

"Before you answer, Mala, I would like to speak."

It was Maxis voice from the dais. Jaime grits his teeth and turns to the Elder with a glare, which Maxis ignores.

"It is true. Your... companion may not return once he has left the Greenwood. However, once *you* have mastered your powers, you may come and go as you please."

Mala turns to Endelyn for confirmation, afraid to believe.

"Yes, my dear, it is true. Your particular gifts are unique and most valuable to us. We will very much need you, but you needn't despair of your former life. You may, in many ways, have them both."

It is too good to be true... yet it *is* true. There will be many complications, many obstacles to maneuver, but they are willing to try. They have much to discover about themselves, Mala's powers, and what their new life will look and feel like, as well as understanding their place and purpose in the world.

The Elders declare it time to celebrate. It's as if the entire Greenwood has converged the Great Willow's courtyard. Dancing, dining, and laughter fill the air and spread out as far as the borders of the Edges.

But not all the Greenwood celebrates on this day. Far off, deep in the North Edges, foul beasts scowl and sneer and wait for their time to come once again. But that is a story for another day…

EPILOGUE

After the great celebration, the forest animals, led by the Elders and Guardians, brought the humans back to the clearing from which they came. This was the West Edges, and its predominant characteristic was its invisible veils, explaining why they could not see where they'd come from.

Endelyn, who'd done most of the exploring and therefore knew most about the Edges, believed that Mala's skills were now developed enough to find their veil, and return to the Everwood. Nervously, and with shaky confidence—especially with all eyes expectantly on her—Mala agreed to try.

The Elders agreed that Mala could and *should* return with Jaime and relieve their worried families before she returned to the Greenwood for a longer stay. Jaime agreed to worry about that day when it came. With hugs and tears, they said their goodbyes, Jaime feeling the most saddened. He would miss this place, its inhabitants, and his new friends, and especially clunky, slow, and ever affable Murphius who'd greeted him with predictable exuberance at the celebration.

Once they'd bid adieu to each and all, Mala turned to the expansive field. She stood stock still for a few moments, her hands at her sides. Then, slowly she stretched her arms out before her, her eyes still shut, and felt the air before her, stepping sideways as she did. To Jaime, it looked like how a blind person felt features on a face, which was in fact similar to what she was doing. Except, instead of human faces, she was feeling the faces of the invisible veils, searching for the familiar one, using touch as much as intuition.

At last, she stopped, and turning to Jaime with those hard to get used to eyes, announced, "This is the one. I'm certain."

Jaime, needlessly fearful she would change her mind if he went through first, made a gallant motion of chivalry, at which she rolled her eyes and reprimanded him for worrying too much. Still, she humored him, and with a final wave, went through the veil to the other side. Jaime, always a worrier, had a moment of anxiety, afraid she'd chosen the wrong veil and was in danger, gave a hurried, wave and quickly followed her through.

He followed her so quickly that he knocked her to the ground and fell on top of her. When she shoved him off her, he noticed her eyes had returned to their hazel hue.

"Geez, I think I'm going to start calling you Murphius. Nah, maybe just Murph, for short. Now get off me, ya big oaf."

They both laughed, and Jaime, though hobbled by his injury, still helped her up, immediately noticing with relief that her eyes had returned to their normal color. Looking around, they realized it was daylight in the Everwood. The air was still cool and crisp, and the leaves were much as they'd left them, scattered dry and brown on the ground. Also, their backpacks slumped right where they'd been dropped, outside the door that was no longer a door, but just an old oddly placed willow tree. As quickly as Jaime's still injured ankle would allow, they made their way out of the woods, anxious and concerned at how long they'd been gone.

As it turned out, they'd been missing for nine days. The town was in an uproar, their parents distraught. When they came out from the woods, unharmed, save Jaime's broken ankle, and seemingly no worse for the wear, they were met by a local police officer who been stationed at the woods for his shift. He greeted them warmly, as if they were his own children, and ushered them into his cruiser, while he radioed into the station the good news.

To their embarrassment, they were the town celebrities, and spent a few weeks making the news. They kept their story simple, and stuck to it: They'd had the stupid idea to go into the woods on a moonlit night to try research barred owls in their natural habitat. Their Ecology teacher unwittingly backed up their story by confirming it was indeed the subject they'd paired up on for a research paper, luckily for them. They guessed they had gone further into the woods than they'd intended, and when Jaime fell, badly twisting his ankle, Mala refused to leave his side. They lived off the snacks and water they'd packed, and when Jaime at last felt strong enough, they made their way out.

After a while, and as big things do, the story faded away, and life went back to the appearance of normal. Jaime and Mala only spoke of the Greenwood when they were alone, and it was only then that they decided a plan.

After graduation, a long—for Mala—seven months away, Mala would accept an internship abroad for a small literary company, and thereby excusing her long absences. The internship would be a ruse. As for Jaime, he was unsure as to what was next. All he knew for certain, was that he needed time to adjust to this strange and unexpected plot change. He thought his life would go in one direction and found that everything he knew was all wrong. He remembered a line from and old poem they'd been forced to read and dissect line by excruciating line in Mr. McCann's poetry class.

> *"But little Mouse, you are not alone,*
> *in proving foresight may be in vain:*
> *The best laid schemes of mice and men*
> *Go often askew,*
> *And leave us nothing*
> *but grief and pain for promised joy!"*

The poem was "To A Mouse" by Robert Burns, and at the time, Jaime remembered most how much the poem bothered him. He thought perhaps it had been the imagery that bothered him so and made him sad. But now, considering everything, he realized it was a foretelling of sorts, a warning to him.

One thing he did know for certain: he needed to write it all down. He suddenly felt the compulsion that Mala had always felt, a need to put words to paper, in black and white, and give the jumbled thoughts in his mind an order and purpose. He needed to make them tangible, for if he could see the words with his eyes, his mind could believe it were real, and not all a dream. At least, that was what he'd hoped. For the time being, he had seven months with Mala, and he wouldn't be wasting a single moment of them worrying about the months that were inevitably to come without her.

As for Mala, she felt a constant pull in both directions, half of her heart belonged in a world with Jaime, the other in a far-off land. She, too, needed time to adjust to their new normal, and was grateful to her oddball status for keeping the questions at bay. She worried mostly for Jaime, who at times became more contemplative and distant than usual, staring far off into space, lost in thought. But she supposed she was much the same, really. They both needed some time to think, and to process what everything meant.

More than a month after their infamous disappearance, Rocky Knoll experienced a warmer than usual December. Jaime was finally able to ride his motorcycle; his ankle had healed. He purposely revved it several times, hoping Mala would hear it from her bedroom. He couldn't stop the smile from forming at the sight of her bursting through the door, and putting her hands on her hips in mock anger. He turned off the ignition and removed his helmet, nodding his chin in her direction.

"Jaime Cromwell, don't even tell me you were going to take off on that old relic without me."

Jaime, with that stupid smile plastered to his face, said nothing and silently held up her helmet. In a flash, she bound down the stairs and leapt onto the bike, snatching and then fastening the helmet over her mop of hair as she did. A few moments later, they were out on the open road, a strangely warm December sun beating on their backs, and going nowhere, without a care.

About the Author

Elsa Kurt is a multi-genre published author, speaker, and Path to Authorship coach for new and aspiring authors of all ages. She has published over twenty books, ranging from children's, YA, contemporary fiction, romance, and guidebooks for aspiring authors. To learn more about Elsa, visit her website at elsakurt.com, or on social media @authorelsakurt. Elsa loves to hear from her readers at authorelsakurt@gmail.com.

If you enjoyed this book, please leave a review on Amazon!

Want to check out Elsa's other books? Find them here: https://www.amazon.com/Elsa-Kurt/e/B01E1VFRFQ

www.ingramcontent.com/pod-product-compliance
Lightning Source LLC
Chambersburg PA
CBHW071158100726
47908CB00002B/418